Owl Be Home
for Christmas

Owl Be Home for Christmas

A Meg Langslow Mystery

Donna Andrews

St. Martin's Paperbacks

This is a work of fiction. All of the characters, organizations, and events portrayed in this novel are either products of the author's imagination or are used fictitiously.

Published in the United States by St. Martin's Paperbacks, an imprint of St. Martin's Publishing Group.

OWL BE HOME FOR CHRISTMAS

Copyright © 2019 by Donna Andrews.
Excerpt from *The Falcon Always Wings Twice* copyright © 2020 by Donna Andrews.

All rights reserved.

For information, address St. Martin's Publishing Group, 120 Broadway, New York, NY 10271.

www.stmartins.com

Library of Congress Catalog Card Number: 2019029130

ISBN: 978-1-250-30532-9

Our books may be purchased in bulk for promotional, educational, or business use. Please contact your local bookseller or the Macmillan Corporate and Premium Sales Department at 1-800-221-7945, ext. 5442, or by email at MacmillanSpecialMarkets@macmillan.com.

Printed in the United States of America

10 9 8 7 6 5 4 3 2 1

Acknowledgments

Thanks, once again, to the wonderful team at St. Martin's/Minotaur, including (but not limited to) Joe Brosnan, Hector DeJean, Melissa Hastings, Paul Hoch, Andrew Martin, Sarah Melnyk, Hannah O'Grady, and especially my editor, Pete Wolverton. And thanks to David Rotstein and the art department for another beautiful cover.

More thanks to my agent, Ellen Geiger, and also to Matt McGowan and the staff at the Frances Goldin Literary Agency for handling the business side of writing so brilliantly and letting me concentrate on the fun part.

Many thanks to the friends—writers and readers alike—who brainstorm and critique with me, give me good ideas, or help keep me sane while I'm writing: Stuart, Aidan, and Liam Andrews, Chris Cowan, Ellen Crosby, Kathy Deligianis, Suzanne Frisbee, John Gilstrap, Barb Goffman, Joni Langevoort, David Niemi, Alan Orloff, Art Taylor, Robin Templeton, and Dina Willner. Thanks for all kinds of moral support and practical help to my blog sisters and brother at the Femmes Fatales: Alexia Gordon, Aimee Hix, Dean James, Toni L. P. Kelner, Catriona McPherson, Kris Neri, Joanna Campbell Slan, Marcia Talley, Elaine Viets, and LynDee Walker. And thanks to all the TeaBuds for two decades of friendship.

Special thanks to Margery Flax for finding me someone who could answer my questions about the inner workings of a fine hotel, and to the expert she found, Charlie Decker of the Grand Hyatt New York. Anything strange about the way the Caerphilly Inn operates is obviously something I forgot to ask him about.

It's not a book until it has just the right title—and *Owl Be Home for Christmas* came from the talented Dash Taylor—son of my writer friends Tara Laskowski and Art Taylor. Thank you, Dash!

And above all, thanks to the readers who continue to enjoy Meg's adventures!

Owl Be Home
for Christmas

Chapter 1

"HOO! Woo-hoo HOO! . . . HOO! Woo-hoo HOO!"

The gray-haired couple standing at the tinsel-decked front desk of the Caerphilly Inn started slightly, and glanced over their shoulders in the direction of the hooting.

"That's just the ornithologists again, Mr. Ackley." Sami, the desk clerk, had probably been hired for his soothing voice. "Having their conference here, you know. Owl Fest."

"They haven't brought in live owls, have they?" Mrs. Ackley's face was anxious. "Surely the hotel wouldn't allow them to do that."

"Jane's terrified of birds." The man put a protective arm around his wife's shoulder.

"Of course not!" Sami managed to look shocked at the mere suggestion. "That would be completely against the Caerphilly Inn's policies."

Which was why we'd been confiscating all the live owls various ornithologists kept bringing into the conference, and taking them a few miles down the road to temporary quarters at the Caerphilly Zoo. The owls, that is, not the ornithologists—although I'd been tempted. Two screech owls, a barn owl, and a northern saw-whet owl so far.

Sami batted absently at the poinsettia partially blocking his view of the couple and glanced at me with a slight frown, as if to suggest that perhaps I should go and deal with the latest owl infestation. This might be my grandfather's conference, but the hotel staff knew perfectly well who to ask if they wanted to get something done. They'd probably be coming to me even if I wasn't Grandfather's official conference organizer. My mind strayed to the three—or was it four?—pages of conference-related tasks in my notebook-that-tells-me-when-to-breathe, as I called the three-ring binder in which I kept my monumental to-do list.

"They're practicing their owl calls," I said. "Maybe I should go remind them to keep the door to their conference room closed, since—"

"HOO! Woo-hoo HOO! . . . HOO! Woo-hoo HOO!" rang out again.

"No, no, no! That's completely wrong. It's HOO! Woo-hoo HOO! . . . HOO! Woo-hoo HOO!!"

If there was a difference between the two calls I couldn't hear it. And the couple at the desk didn't seem reassured to learn that the hooting came from ornithologists rather than owls. I could understand how they felt. I wasn't thrilled either at being snowbound this close to Christmas in a hotel with a flock of hooting ornithologists. Although if they'd just stick to the hooting, I could live with it. Unfortunately, I suspected before long they'd be back to shouting, arguing, pounding their fists on tables, and maybe even throwing more drinks at each other and getting into more fistfights. Just like yesterday. Only yesterday—at least in the morning—they could all stomp out of the hotel when they lost their tempers, and maybe even drive into town to get away from it all. It would take a brave soul to venture out into today's subfreezing temperatures and blizzard conditions. And until the snow let up, no one was going anywhere.

Which was what Sami was explaining to the couple—who were apparently under the delusion that he could summon them a taxi. He was having a hard time making himself heard above the Christmas carols playing over the speakers strategically placed throughout the lobby. Obviously someone had just jacked up the volume. To drown out the hooting? Or did someone hope hearing a choir singing "peace on earth, goodwill to men" would have a calming effect on Mr. Ackley?

"I'm sorry, but there simply isn't anything we can do until the storm lets up," Sami was saying. "All the power and telephone lines are down, and it's not even safe for snowplows to be out. But the hotel has a generator, and plenty of supplies, and we'll be doing everything we can to keep our guests safe and comfortable until the snowstorm is over."

"How long will that be?" Mr. Ackley asked.

"At least another twenty-four hours." Sami visibly braced himself as he delivered the bad news.

"Twenty-four hours!" Mrs. Ackley wailed. "How is that possible?"

"Now that's a fascinating thing." Sami's ordinarily calm, mellow voice took on a note of excitement. "Normally we don't have that much snow in Virginia, but right now the polar vortex has dipped unusually far south. And there's a low pressure system over the Atlantic . . ."

I suppose there was no way I could have warned the Ackleys that Sami, the calm and ever-helpful desk clerk, was one semester away from getting a bachelor's degree in meteorology from nearby Caerphilly College. Most of the time, he remembered that guests who asked about the weather only wanted to know whether to don sunscreen or carry an umbrella. But he was having a hard time keeping in check his fascination with the freakishly huge winter storm now stalled over most of the Eastern Seaboard.

I should probably interrupt him before he started explaining isobars and isallobaric pressure gradients again, and drawing more maps of the polar vortex.

As it turned it, I didn't have to.

"I'm sure this is all very fascinating." Mr. Ackley's voice clearly communicated that he didn't think any such thing. "But what we really want to know is whether we'll be able to make our plane this evening."

"I'm afraid it doesn't look very likely," Sami said.

"It's been twelve hours since the snow started, and word is both of the county snowplows are now stuck in drifts." I decided Sami had spent enough time in the hot seat.

"Chief Burke just sent out a bulletin that police and emergency services are suspended until further notice," Sami added.

"And even if Sami could magically transport you to the airport, your plane won't be flying," I went on. "You'd have to go west of the Mississippi or south of Atlanta to find an airport still open."

"And when the Chicago and Atlanta hubs shut down . . ." Sami let his words trail off ominously.

"Amtrak's called it quits, too," I said. "This storm's already one for the history books."

"But we need to get home for Christmas." Mrs. Ackley's voice held a note of rising panic. "All three kids are coming home!"

"If we miss our flight today . . ." Her husband frowned at Sami, and then visibly checked his irritation and forced his face into what he probably intended as a friendly, apologetic look. "I know it's not your fault."

"I do understand," Sami said. "With so many planes canceled at what's already one of the busiest times of the year, it's going to be very difficult for the airlines to reschedule everyone."

Difficult was a tactful way of putting it. I'd have said well-nigh impossible.

"But still—this is unacceptable." Mr. Ackley seemed to be regretting his brief apologetic moment. Did he think good weather was an amenity he could demand from the hotel along with clean towels and room service? "I expect you to do whatever you can to deal with this. You have my cell phone number—"

Sami managed to maintain his smile as he held up a slip of paper. I refrained from reminding Mr. Ackley that cell phone service had also fallen victim to the storm.

"Call me as soon as you have news for us."

"Yes, sir. M—" Sami stopped himself in mid "Merry Christmas," wisely sensing that under the circumstances it wouldn't be well received.

Over the lobby speakers a choral rendition of "I Heard the Bells on Christmas Day" gave way to an instrumental version of "We Three Kings" as the couple threaded their way through the various Christmas trees and masses of poinsettias festooning the lobby. They reached the elevators, pushed the UP button, and stood glaring back at Sami while they waited. Either they hadn't noticed they were standing directly under a ball of mistletoe or they were in no mood to make use of it. Sami picked up the desk phone and held the receiver to his ear. The body of the phone was below the level of the counter, so unlike me they couldn't see he wasn't dialing.

"I thought you just said all the phones were out," I said.

"I could be making an internal call. Last time I checked, that still worked. And besides, logic clearly isn't his strong point. And maybe I should cut them some slack. They're from Florida. They might never have seen weather like this before."

"That might be true if they've always lived in Florida," I said. "But at their age, they could also have retired to Florida. Possibly from someplace like Michigan or upstate New York that gets a lot of snow and has the resources to handle it better than we can. They may have inflated expectations."

"Even Michigan and upstate New York aren't handling

this one all that well," he said. "A pity the cable's out and I can't show them what's happening all over."

"And for that matter, a pity they didn't believe the weather reports and get out yesterday morning while the getting was good."

"Yeah." He wasn't looking at me—in fact, it probably appeared to the frowning couple as if he were talking into the phone. "Believe me, if there were any way for the Ackleys to leave the hotel right now, I'd move heaven and earth to arrange it. And even if they're able to get home, who knows if their kids will be able to travel. You shut down half the airports in the country and it screws up so many schedules that all the others are bound to have some problems, too." He breathed a sigh of relief when the Ackleys stepped aboard an elevator.

"I'm sure Grandfather's ornithologists will be just as annoying when it's their turn to leave," I said. "And that will be even closer to Christmas, and there will be so many more of them."

"But that won't start up until tomorrow," he said. "I'll worry about them tomorrow. Maybe a miracle will happen, and this storm will speed up and only dump a foot of snow on us instead of more than two."

I'd heard closer to three, but if Sami hadn't, I wasn't going to depress him.

"Cheer up," I said. "At least there's no doubt we'll have a white Christmas."

"Well, that's something." He sighed. "Meanwhile, if you're going back to the conference rooms—"

"I'll close the door to the lobby on my way there."

I turned and took a couple of the deep yoga-style breaths my cousin Rose Noire was always recommending for times of stress. And I tried to let the sight of the Inn's lobby, beautifully and extravagantly decorated for the holidays, rekindle my Christmas spirit. Elegant wreaths and garlands graced all the walls and their evergreen scent mixed with that of the spicy potpourri bowls to perfume the air. Across the room, where a fire burned briskly in the huge fireplace, a dozen red velvet stockings trimmed with gold and sparkling faux gems hung from the mantel. To the right of the fireplace was the main Christmas tree, almost brushing the twenty-foot-high ceiling. It held so many ornaments you only saw the occasional glimpse of green, and its lower branches were invisible behind the hundred or so intricately wrapped empty present boxes arranged in a semicircle around it.

Yes, the lobby decorations were fabulous. I made a mental note to say so to my mother, who'd been in charge of them. But no matter how fabulous they were, I'd still rather have been snowbound at home.

My eyes veered from the Christmas cheer inside the lobby to the floor-to-ceiling glass wall that normally gave a view of the Inn's elegant outdoor dining terrace and the perfectly manicured garden beyond. All I could see today was snow. The flakes were tiny, but they were falling so heavily I couldn't even make out the shape of the enormous oak tree at the far end of the terrace.

At least if I was snowbound at the Inn over Christmas I'd have most of my family here to celebrate with me. Grandfather and Dad were here to attend the conference. Rose Noire was helping out part-time with logistics in return for attending any panels she found interesting. Mother was here with Dad, keeping her distance from the conference itself, but finding plenty to occupy her time. She had elegant teas with Rose Noire and with some of the women who were attending the conference or accompanying their spouses. She chivvied the hotel staff into fixing any decorations that had strayed from perfection. She went around doing sketches of ideas she might want to use in planning next year's decorations. And she had brought along industrial quantities of ribbon and wrapping paper and set up a highly useful present-wrapping nook in the Washington Cottage, where she and Dad were staying. Most of our family, knowing we'd be tied up with the conference until the evening of Sunday, the twenty-second, had finished our shopping early—and once we'd seen the weather reports, we'd brought all the presents along, in case the storm was even worse than predicted and we were still snowbound on Christmas Eve. We'd miss the family members who were traveling—my brother, Rob; his fiancée, Delaney; my grandmother Cordelia; and Caroline Willner, a friend of such long standing she might as well be family. They'd taken a Caribbean cruise together. I wasn't sure whether to feel envy or astonishment. Astonishment that they were willing to set foot on a cruise ship so soon after the epic disasters we'd all gone through on one a few months ago. And envy, because they were probably all lounging in swimsuits sipping drinks with paper parasols in them, very far away from any thought of snow. For a moment I allowed myself a pang of envy. And a brief flash of resentment at Grandfather's assistant, who was spending the holidays with family in Bermuda, instead of being here to run the conference. Then I stifled both feelings. After all, palm trees and temperatures in the eighties didn't exactly feel like Christmas, did they?

And most important of all, my husband, Michael, and our twin sons, Josh and Jamie, had moved into the hotel with me. If only—

My cell phone buzzed to announce an arriving text. What now?

Chapter 2

I pulled my phone out of my pocket and looked around to make sure no one was watching—texting only worked for those of us to whom Ekaterina Vorobyaninova, the hotel manager, had entrusted some kind of special app that worked with the hotel's Wi-Fi system—and only within the hotel. She didn't want the system overloaded. I also had a hotel-issued walkie-talkie for communicating with Ekaterina and the rest of the hotel staff, and Grandfather's satellite phone, which wouldn't let me talk to anyone east of the Mississippi unless they had one, too.

When I was sure no one was watching, I pulled out the phone and felt relief wash over me when I saw the picture Michael had just sent. It showed him, Josh, and Jamie seated in front of a wood fire, which meant they were back at the hotel, in the Madison Cottage where we were staying. They'd gone out at first light to practice their cross-country skiing before the storm got bad, and even though Michael promised they wouldn't leave the Inn's grounds—wouldn't even stray all that far from the hotel itself—I'd been fretting for the last hour, ever since the snow had escalated from picturesque to heavy and menacing, accompanied by temperatures in the twenties.

"Settling in for board games and pizza," he texted me. "You're welcome to join us if you can sneak away."

I texted back "thanks" and put my phone away. I wasn't optimistic about sneaking away from the conference for more than a few minutes. With one last glance at the whirling white snowscape visible through the glass wall and then another more longing glance at the nearest bit of evergreen, I marched over to the door leading to the hotel's conference space and reentered what I'd started thinking of as Owl World.

The central part of the Inn's conference space was what the Inn called the Gathering Area. To my left was another glass wall, not quite as large as the one in the lobby. I'd had the hotel staff draw the draperies so the conference attendees wouldn't be reminded of the blizzard quite as often. Straight ahead was a wall lined with tables for the exhibits and handouts and containing two sets of double doors leading to the Hamilton Room, the larger of our two conference rooms. On the wall above it, a huge banner with a picture of Grandfather proclaimed "J. Montgomery Blake and the Blake Foundation welcome you to Owl Fest 2019!" Across the Gathering Area on the right were more tables along another wall, the doors to the Lafayette Room, and the entrance to the wide hallway leading to the Dolley Madison Ballroom. Immediately to my right were the coffee, tea, and water service and the registration/information desk—now staffed by Rose Noire. She looked up, waved to me, then closed her eyes and went back to what I assumed was some kind of meditation. If she was still trying to beam harmonious and cordial vibes into the conference attendees, I hoped it was working.

The middle of the Gathering Area contained half a dozen white tablecloth-covered tables, each seating five or six people. A man and a woman sat at one, engaged in an intense discussion of a large collection of papers spread out between them. Both of their badges were decorated with the blue ribbon that designated a speaker. I deduced they were probably ironing out the logistics for a presentation they were about to make.

Evergreen and tinsel festooned the walls, poinsettias and Christmas cactuses sat on every table, and the speakers played Christmas carols at an almost subliminal level. But in spite of all that, the mood was light-years from the seasonal cheer of the lobby.

I eased open the door to the Hamilton Room, where a relatively young professor with a charming Australian accent was talking about owl courtship and reproductive behavior.

"Here's an excellent example of courtship feeding," the speaker was saying. "Note that the male powerful owl is offering his mate a rainbow lorikeet." The screen at the front of the room showed a rather dramatic picture of two gray-brown and white owls—the powerful owl, I'd already figured out, was the name of an actual Australian owl species. The owl on the left—presumably the male since he was the smaller—had what looked like a tuft of blue, green, yellow, and orange feathers dangling from his beak; fortunately that was all you could see of the lorikeet. The other, slightly larger owl was staring at the lorikeet with rapt attention. "Copulation usually follows the acceptance of the food offering," the professor went on, with almost perky enthusiasm. I decided I'd seen enough.

I eased the door closed and went over to see what was happening in the Lafayette Room. It was supposed to contain a roundtable discussion on something or other. I'd grown wary of the roundtable sessions, which were intended to be free-form—though moderated—discussions of topics of interest. From what I'd seen on Friday, the lion's share of the arguments seemed to arise in the roundtables. Especially if my least favorite attendee, Dr. Oliver Frogmore, was in attendance.

But for the moment, the Lafayette Room contained only two morose scientists wearing blue speaker ribbons on their badges. They looked up so hopefully when I opened the door that I felt a brief pang of guilt that I wasn't actually planning to join them. I waved and gave them an encouraging thumbs-up, and they slumped back into dejection. Obviously the owl porn in the other room was the bigger attraction in this time slot.

At least for the time being, things were quiet. Maybe Rose Noire's efforts to beam calm and harmony were working after all. Maybe I had time to do some of the things I ought to have done already, like making the changes Grandfather wanted to the program for tonight's banquet, and—

"Ms. Langslow!"

Or maybe not. I turned to find one of the scientists bearing down on me. Dr. Edward Czerny, who currently held second place in the running for the Most Annoying Conference Participant Award I was going to give out, if only in my own imagination, when Owl Fest was finally over.

"What can I do for you, Dr. Czerny?"

"Dr. Frogmore's next panel begins at eleven and we have no copies of his handouts!"

Deep breath.

"That's because Dr. Frogmore never sent us any handouts to be copied," I said. "I finally gave up and assumed he wasn't using any handouts."

"This is incredible," Czerny moaned. "Why didn't you ask for them?"

"I did," I said. "I emailed him at least three times about handouts. Possibly more."

"Why didn't you email *me*! I always take care of his conference logistics."

"Because neither you nor Dr. Frogmore told me that." I could only just refrain from adding that I wasn't a mind reader. "I don't suppose he bothered to forward you any of the multiple emails I sent." Dr. Frogmore was the uncontested leader in the Most Annoying Conference Participant competition. Czerny was a very distant second, and no one else was even close—not even, for a wonder, Grandfather. And I had the feeling at least half of Czerny's annoyingness arose out of his frantic attempts to keep Dr. Frogmore happy.

"We need copies of these made ASAP!" Czerny whined, thrusting a manila folder at me. "If Dr. Frogmore doesn't have his handouts—"

"No problem." I ignored the proffered folder. "I'll show you the way to the business center."

I turned on my heel and began striding briskly toward the business center. After a few seconds Czerny followed.

"This is ridiculous," he said when he caught up with me. "Who has time to stand over a copier in the middle of a conference?"

"Not me." I kept my tone cheerful. "Right in there." I held open the door to the business center. "You can use your room key card to run the copier and submit a copy of your bill with the charges for reimbursement. Any other questions?"

I smiled rather insincerely at him. He was blinking back at me with an anxious expression on his face. There was nothing wrong with his features. Or his teeth, as far as I could see. If he ever managed a smile, he might be reasonably attractive. But every time I'd seen him here at the conference, he was either whining or blustering. Someone needed to take him aside and tell him to smile more. If I were doing a makeover on him, I'd also work on his terrible buzzard-like posture, which took at least three inches off his height—standing straight he might almost be eye-to-eye with me at five ten.

He sighed heavily. For any other scientist at the conference, I might have relented and run the copies. Not for a man I'd overheard agreeing so enthusiastically when, right in the middle of a presentation by one of the female scientists, Dr. Frogmore had said, very audibly, "But what can you expect? Women have no head for statistics."

Still, I did feel a little sorry for Czerny. I glanced at the time on my phone, and then at my much-used conference program.

"Dr. Frogmore's presentation isn't for nearly an hour," I said. "You have plenty of time."

As I walked back down the hall toward the conference area, I had the prickly feeling you get when someone is watching you. I didn't turn around. If Czerny wanted to waste two or three minutes of his photocopying time glaring at me, that was his problem. At least while he was in the business center he wouldn't be interrupting panels, complaining noisily about the food and the accommodations, or dragging me aside to explain the many ways in which they did things so much better at the conferences Dr. Frogmore organized at Buckthorn College, the small but reasonably prestigious private Oregon college where they both taught.

We still had years before Josh and Jamie, our twins, were ready for college, but I'd already made a mental note to veto Buckthorn if either of them showed an interest in it.

Back in the conference area I answered several attendees' questions about the weather, put in a request to the hotel staff for more coffee, and apologized, for the third or fourth time, for the program book's unfortunate misspelling of Dr. Chwalibog Fijalkowski-Bartosiewicz's name. I was just beginning to relax a little when—

"Where's Blake?" I winced at the loud, grating voice that had become all too familiar over the last two days. Then I braced myself and made sure my face wore a polite, helpful expression before turning around.

"Sorry, Dr. Frogmore," I said. "He went off to prepare for his next talk. Is there anything I can do to help you?"

Oliver Frogmore scowled at me. Maybe it wasn't meant to be a scowl. Several of my aunts were fond of telling children "If you keep making a face like that it might get stuck." Perhaps that had happened to him—his face had gotten stuck just at the moment when he'd noticed a really bad smell and was about to explode with complaints about it. Could you call it "resting bitch face" when a man was wearing it? The phenomenon needed a gender-neutral term.

"I prefer to talk to Blake." Dr. Frogmore spoke without bothering to look at me—his eyes were scanning our surroundings. "Where is he? In his room?"

I stifled a sigh and took a seat on the edge of a nearby table. I'd noticed conversations with Dr. Frogmore went better when he didn't have to look up at the person he was talking to, and at five foot ten I was a good four inches taller than he was, in spite of the height added by his well-polished shoes. Though I had to admit, as lifts went, his were subtle. He cut a dapper figure—his well-tailored tweed suit emphasized the vertical and managed to downplay his no-longer-flat stomach, his monogrammed shirts probably impressed people who cared enough to notice that sort of thing, and his red silk bow tie finished off the erudite professorial look. I wondered, not for the first time, if the gleaming silver-white of his wavy hair and neat goatee were natural or if he did whatever people do to combat the yellow tint that afflicts so many when they start graying.

"I don't actually know where he is," I said aloud. "I doubt if he's in his room—he said he needed to concentrate, and there's a rehearsal going on there. He put me in charge of conference logistics, you know—is there anything I can help you with?"

"I doubt it." Frogmore actually met my eyes, now that they were on the same level as his.

"If it's about your handouts, Dr. Czerny is off taking care of that," I said.

"The hell with the damned handouts," Frogmore roared. "Where's Blake? Have him paged."

"I'll see what I can do," I said. "May I tell him what it's about?"

"Hmph." He raised his eyes with a "give me patience" expression and stomped off down the hallway, elbowing aside the occasional person who wasn't quick enough to get out of his way.

"Don't let him get to you."

I turned to see a tall, angular woman in khakis and a teal blue Blake Foundation sweatshirt, her graying hair pulled back into a rough French braid. Dr. Vera Craine, another of Grandfather's distinguished attendees.

"Don't worry," I said. "Remember, I'm used to putting up with Dr. Blake. Frogmore's annoying, but as a curmudgeon, he's bush league compared to Grandfather."

"Ha!" Her laugh was loud and staccato, and accompanied with a sharp slap to her thigh. "I like your style. I'm heading for the bar—are you going there?"

"Do I look as if I need to?"

"You look as if you could use a few minutes off your feet," she said. "I know you're busy, but I can probably tell you what Frogmore's on about now, and then you can warn your grandfather."

With that she turned and exited the conference area for the lobby, where the entrance to the Mount Vernon Grill, the hotel's bar and restaurant, could be found.

I texted Grandfather that Dr. Frogmore wanted to see him. I was torn—I should probably hang around to take care of any problems. And I did have to put in all those changes to the banquet program. But I didn't want to pass up the chance to hear what Dr. Craine had to say about Frogmore. And for that matter, I wouldn't mind the chance to learn a little bit more about her. Grandfather thought very highly of her, but since she'd been one of the few completely cooperative and undemanding panelists at Owl Fest, I'd had no chance to talk to her. So I left the conference area and crossed the lobby to the Mount Vernon Grill. I joined Dr. Craine at a table just inside the door. Eduardo, the duty bartender, spotted us and hurried over.

"How is the conference going?" His face looked worried, and his voice was solicitous.

"About the same," I said.

"I'm so sorry." He shook his head. "But courage! It will improve. Your usual?"

"Please."

"And you, madam?" He turned to Dr. Craine.

"I'm not sure whether I should be impressed or worried that you have a 'usual,'" she said to me. "Mind if I ask what it is?"

"An Arnold Palmer," I said. "At least that's my usual when I'm working the conference and need to keep my wits about me."

"Very wise." She smiled up at Eduardo. "Make that my usual, too."

Eduardo bowed and hurried away.

"So why does Dr. Frogmore want to talk to my grandfather?"

"That's easy." Dr. Craine leaned back in her chair and fixed me with a steady gaze, as if assessing me. "He knows Monty's preparing for a presentation, and he wants to interrupt him. Annoy him. He's under the delusion he can throw your grandfather off his stride and make him screw up his presentation."

"As if," I said.

"Exactly. The man's an idiot. Of course, even Ollie the Frog has to have some plausible excuse for badgering Monty. Pretty sure he's going to make a big fuss about wanting to have his minion added to tomorrow's panel on pesticides."

"His minion?"

"Ned Czerny. Junior member of Frogmore's department at Buckthorn."

"Oh. Him."

"Indeed."

I flipped through the program to find the panel in question: Measuring the effects of insect- and rodent-control pesticides on the Strigiform food chain. Sounded like a real snooze fest. "Is Dr. Czerny an expert on the topic?"

"He's not an expert on anything other than sucking up to Frogmore," Dr. Craine said. "Which is why your grandfather didn't put him on any panels. But if you have to give him a panel somewhere—which Frogmore seems to think is necessary—the pesticide one's probably the closest to something he can talk about without looking like a total idiot. And Frogmore's on that panel, so it's not as if anyone else will have much of a chance to say anything."

"I'll warn Grandfather." I pulled out my walkie-talkie and hit what I hoped was the right set of buttons to reach him.

"What now? I'm busy." Even through the static there was no mistaking his voice. Or his state of mind.

"And Dr. Frogmore is trying to hunt you down," I said. "Probably to badger you about adding Dr. Czerny to his panel tomorrow."

"It's his wretched panel." I could almost hear his shrug. "If he wants to add Czerny, fine by me. That should make sure no one shows up for it. Just keep him out of my hair. I'm hiding out in your parents' cottage. Over and out."

Dr. Craine had been silently laughing during my conversation with Grandfather. Eduardo set down our Arnold Palmers and she took a long pull on hers.

"I gather you're not a fan of Dr. Frogmore, either," I said when I'd taken a swig of mine.

She snorted.

"No, not a fan. Not surprising, given our history."

Chapter 3

"Given your history—you have a history with Dr. Frog-more?"

"Eww." Her grimace was eloquent. "When you put it that way, it sounds as if we were romantically involved. What a revolting thought. Our history, if you want to call it that, is purely academic. I gather your grandfather hasn't filled you in on that."

"He's more apt to gossip about the lives of owls and meerkats than mere human goings-on," I said.

"I should fill you in, then." She leaned back in her chair and fingered the condensation on the outside of her glass. "So when I say something about Frogmore you'll know how many pounds of salt to take it with. I started my academic career at Buckthorn College."

"Under Dr. Frogmore?"

"No, he'd only just achieved tenure then. A mere rank-and-file professor when I got there. Unfortunately, he was already starting his meteoric rise to power. By the time I was up for tenure, he had enough clout to derail anyone he didn't want around."

"He kept you from getting tenure?" I could feel myself getting angry on her behalf. I remembered how tense it had been when Michael had been up for tenure at Caerphilly College. He'd had a rocky time, mainly because back then Drama had been an unloved subsection of the English department, whose senior professors had looked down their noses at anyone, however brilliant, whose résumé included stints on a soap opera and a cult-hit fantasy TV show. Michael's tenure battle had had a happy ending, and he was now the heir apparent to the chair of the recently liberated drama department, but to this day, I had to make a conscious effort to be polite to a few of the dinosaurs, as we called them. "Since I'm a faculty spouse, I can imagine how you feel about him," I said aloud.

"Yes." She nodded slightly. "And believe me, I was not a marginal tenure candidate. I had more publications—and more prestigious publications—than any of the other hopefuls. My student evaluations were solid. I'd done twice as much committee and volunteer work as anyone else in the department. Your grandfather mentioned that, when not running conferences for him, you're a blacksmith, so I'm betting you know what it's like to be a woman in a male-dominated field. You have to work twice as hard just to get taken seriously. I'd done that. I was well-respected in my department and in my field. But Frogmore didn't want a tenured woman in his department—he was already referring to it as his, even though it took him another five years to backstab his way into the chairmanship. He didn't want any women, and for sure not one whose academic record rivaled his. So he started a smear campaign. Accusations that I'd fudged my research or stolen other people's data. Rumors that passages in my dissertation were oddly similar to various other researchers' papers. Rumors that I'd slept with the editors of a couple of the journals that published me. He even got a handful of students to file complaints about me. I'm not sure anyone on my tenure committee believed all of it. But there was so much of it."

"If you throw enough mud, some of it will stick," I said.

"Yes." She took another gulp of her Arnold Palmer.

"It scared them off. So there I was, thirty years old, still trying to make a dent in a student loan debt bigger than most people's mortgages, and positive I'd never get another job in the profession I loved. I was feeling . . . well, to be blunt, suicidal. I'd actually started thinking about ways and means. And then I got the call from your grandfather. I wouldn't be here now—not just at Owl Fest but on this earth—if it wasn't for him."

"He helped you get another job?"

"He browbeat every biology department chair he knew to interview me, and made sure they got the scoop on just why I was in the job market. It helped that, even back then, Frogmore's reputation was starting to get around. Helped even more to have Dr. J. Montgomery Blake tell them I was brilliant and they were idiots if they didn't hire me. Wish I could have seen Frogmore's face when I landed the post at Cornell."

Her smile radiated pride, triumph, and maybe just a smidgen of completely understandable malice. I could relate. She'd probably gotten a belated start on her career, thanks to Frogmore, but she'd made good. Buckthorn College had a decent reputation in the biological sciences, but it wasn't in the top echelon, like Cornell.

"And all these years later, Buckthorn's still in the dark ages when it comes to diversity of any stripe," she said. "Not that the rest of the academic world is going great guns. Nationwide, almost half of all graduate biology students are women, but we make up only a third of the assistant professors and less than a fifth of the full professors. Pardon my soapbox—"

"Preach it," I said. "Because it's true."

"And Buckthorn College makes everyone else look enlightened. Only twenty percent of their graduate students are women, and last time I looked they had only three women on the faculty, one assistant professor and two adjuncts. And don't even get me started on their abysmal record on minority hiring. All Frogmore's doing."

"Lovely," I said. "He just took what is probably an unbeatable lead in my award judging." I explained about the Most Annoying Conference Participant Award.

"Frogmore's a shoo-in, no question," she said with a laugh. "Czerny's merely the acolyte. Anything you say to him, you can be sure he'll go running to tell Frogmore—and put the worst possible spin on it. But he's merely weak, not malicious. If Frogmore dropped dead during one of his epic temper tantrums, it might be the saving of poor Ned Czerny. He might find a better mentor, some decent soul who'd turn all that energy and loyalty to good use instead of bad. He wasn't nearly as useless before Frogmore got hold of him."

"I wish I'd talked to you a couple of months ago," I said. "I could so easily have managed to lose both of their registration forms."

"Ha!" She slapped her thigh and threw back her head with another hoot of laughter. "I like the way you think. But you know the one good thing about Frogmore?"

I shook my head.

"I've never been at an event with him without taking home at least a couple of new stories about outrageous things he's done," she said. "You survive Frogmore, you get bragging rights."

"As Grandfather says, even hissing cockroaches and naked mole rats have their place in the great scheme of things. And that reminds me—I should go." I stood and made a quick gesture to Eduardo, who nodded. "Right now my place in the scheme of things is keeping Grandfather and the conference on track, and he completely revised the program for tonight's banquet. I won't have time to get him to approve it and then have it photocopied if I don't get the changes done before lunch. No, don't bother leaving money. Eduardo's already got your Arnold Palmer on my tab."

"I owe you one, then." We ducked out of the Mount Vernon Grill and headed across the lobby. "And I need to get back to the conference, anyway. Dr. Arai and Dr. Kelner are going to argue about whether the flammulated owl belongs in the genus *Otus,* or whether they should be moved over into *Megascops* with the screech owls. Better than a circus when those two get going."

"Just tip off whoever's at the information desk if anyone starts throwing punches," I said. "They'll have a walkie-talkie and can summon hotel security. And—what's wrong?" I'd noticed she was staring out a window—not the huge wall of glass that showed only snow, but a smaller window on the other side of the lobby.

"Someone should go drag Ben back inside before he gets frostbite," Dr. Craine said, strolling over to the window and peering out.

Ben, I realized, was Dr. Benjamin Green, another of the ornithologists. One of the nicer ones, if a little weird. He'd spent almost an hour Friday morning talking to Rose Noire, exchanging views on the owl's role in folklore and mythology. He got points for that in my book. But now he was standing a few feet outside the door leading into the President's Garden, which was the Inn's fancy name for the small open-air courtyard between the main body of the Inn and the three cottages normally reserved for important guests. The snow made it hard to see well, but he seemed to be just standing and looking around as if lost.

"What's he doing out there?" I asked.

"I'm sure even he doesn't know," Dr. Craine said. "He's the original absent-minded professor. Rumor has it he showed up for his morning class in pajamas one time, holding his toothbrush. Even tried to write on the white-board with it."

I usually suspected such extreme absent-mindedness was exaggerated for effect. But regardless of whether he knew what he was doing, Dr. Green was definitely standing outside in twenty-degree weather wearing only a windbreaker. No heavy coat, no hat, no scarf, no gloves—and clearly no common sense.

"I'll go see what he's up to." I grabbed my coat, which I'd left in the lobby behind the reception desk for just such occasions, and went outside. The staff had been shoveling recently, which meant the quaint cobblestone paths leading to the cottages were merely slick and treacherous, not downright impassable.

"Dr. Green?" I called as I drew near his tall, bearlike figure.

He started and whirled around, with what almost looked like a guilty expression on his face.

"Yes? What is it?"

"You should come back inside," I said. "You'd be surprised how fast frostbite can happen in conditions like these."

"You're right," he said. "Only . . ."

He frowned, and studied the cobblestones at his feet.

"Were you going somewhere?" I asked.

"Outside."

"Why outside?"

He sighed, looked up at the sky, blinked as the snow-flakes landed on his eyelashes, and finally spoke.

"I found a . . . um . . . a bug in my room," he said. "I was going to do what I usually do in such cases—take it outside, ask it politely not to come back in, and release it into the wild."

I wasn't sure the well-manicured grounds of the Caerphilly

Inn bore the slightest resemblance to anything you could call "the wild." And for that matter, I had no idea what to think of a scientist who held conversations with bugs. I simply nodded.

"I hadn't been out," he said. "I'd heard it was snowing— seen it occasionally from the windows, of course—but I had no idea it was this bad. I'm from California, you know."

I could probably have guessed that.

Another cold blast of wind drove clouds of snow through the narrow little courtyard and we both braced against it for a few seconds.

"I'm not an entomologist," he said. "I have no idea whether the poor creature could even survive out here. And frankly, unless I took it rather far from any of the buildings, I'm sure it would just come back inside."

I was getting cold. And annoyed. If I'd known I'd be having a lengthy heart-to-heart with Dr. Green, I'd have put on more than my coat to come outside. And the fact that we were standing here in the blizzard discussing the fate of a bug didn't improve my mood. I drew on the stores of patience I usually saved for dealing with Grandfather and Dad.

"Maybe you could release it near one of the outbuildings," I suggested. "The garden shed, perhaps. I could get one of the staff to guide you there. Or the gazebo. Both would offer some shelter from the cold, and I'm sure they find plenty of bugs in them."

"Oh, no," he said. "That would be a bad idea. A very bad idea."

I was going to ask why but it was getting hard to keep my teeth from chattering.

"Why don't we step inside and discuss this?" I said instead.

He frowned, and looked over his shoulder at the hotel.

"Let's go into one of the cottages," I said. "There's a rehearsal going on in the Jefferson Cottage—that's where Grandfather's staying—but Michael and the boys and I are in the Madison. We can talk privately there."

He nodded, and followed me down the path. We passed by the Jefferson Cottage, which was a smaller-scale reproduction of Monticello—the central portion, at least. Evergreen garlands woven with strands of fairy lights lit up the sheltered space under the portico, and electric candelabra gleamed behind the multi-paned front windows. It looked festive, warm and welcoming, especially since, even above the wind, we could hear laughter and the strains of "I'll Be Home for Christmas."

Dr. Green stopped and stared at the Jefferson Cottage with a puzzled expression.

"Rehearsal." I took his arm and set him in motion again. "The entertainment for tonight's banquet."

A little farther down the path was the Madison Cottage, a faithful half-sized replica of Montpelier, James Madison's home. We took shelter on the diminutive white-pillared portico that sported its own collection of evergreens, fairy lights, and candelabra. I slid my key card through the door lock to let us in. As soon as we entered I heard voices coming down the hall from the cottage's living room.

"No! Not more sheep!"

"Aha! Soon I will own all the sheep in the world!"

"How about trading me a sheep for two rocks?"

Dr. Green's face wore a puzzled frown.

"You have sheep here?" he asked, looking around warily.

I restrained the impulse to ask why someone who regularly rescued bugs would have a problem with a few sheep.

"My husband, Michael, and our twins are playing *Settlers of Catan.*" Seeing his look of incomprehension, I added "It's a strategy board game—no live sheep involved. They'd love to show it to you if you're interested, but first let's talk in the study."

Yes, the Madison Cottage had a study—although since two of the mahogany bookshelves lining its walls actually slid aside to reveal Murphy beds, it could also serve as a second bedroom when needed. The boys were sleeping in it this weekend—at least I hoped they would be sleeping tonight instead of once more spending half the night trying to fold each other up in the Murphy beds. I waved at Michael and the boys before following Dr. Green into the study.

He sighed with what I assumed was contentment at being warm again—warm, and in the presence of books. Then with a guilty start he tore his eyes from the shelves and retrieved a small jar from one of his pockets before sprawling on the nearest leather couch. A jar with tiny holes punched in its lid. Clearly he was serious about this bug-rescuing gig. I hoped it wouldn't turn out to be a cockroach. Or worse, a bedbug. Ekaterina would be furious.

"I think it's lovely that you're so concerned about protecting all creatures, even insects." Actually, I didn't think it was lovely at all. Probably a character flaw, but my sympathy for living creatures didn't extend much beyond birds and mammals. With a few exceptions, like butterflies, the invertebrates left me cold. "If you think conditions outside are unsuitable and you don't want to turn it loose in one of the outbuildings, how about leaving it in its jar until the weather improves?"

"Could be a while." He glanced at the window. "I wouldn't want the poor thing to starve."

"There are nearly two hundred biologists here," I said.

"I'm sure some of them are knowledgeable about things other than birds. Grandfather, for instance. If he doesn't know what your bug eats, I'm sure he'd know how to find out. Why don't we show him your—oh, my God! It's a black widow spider!"

Chapter 4

I'd jumped back on seeing the spider. I hadn't actually shrieked, but my voice had gone up almost an octave and become noticeably louder. Evidently Michael and the boys heard me and were on their way to the study, to judge by the thundering footsteps now approaching. The study door opened about a foot, and two tousled heads peered around the corner.

"Mom? You okay?" Jamie asked.

"Who is this guy?" Josh demanded.

Michael appeared behind them, pushed the door all the way open, and stepped inside, frowning slightly.

"Nothing's wrong," I said. "Dr. Green was showing me the unusual bug he found in his room."

"A black widow spider." Dr. Green held up the jar, looking very pleased with himself. The boys descended on him.

"Whoa! Look at that monster!" Josh's nose was almost touching the jar.

"Awesome!" Jamie had joined his twin. "He's a big one."

"Probably she," I said. "Only females have that distinctive red hourglass marking. Males have much less memorable markings of various colors."

"So the male could sneak up on us and bite us without our even realizing it was a black widow?" Josh asked. "Cooool!"

"He could, but since only the female's bite is danger-

ous, the male can sneak up on us and bite us all he likes,"
I said. "What do we care?"

"But this one's a female," Jamie said. "She could kill us."

"Unlikely," I said. "They aren't really that poisonous. A
bite would be painful, but unlikely to be fatal."

"Too bad." Clearly the spider was losing a little of its
cachet in the boys' eyes.

"You know a lot about black widow spiders." Dr. Green
sounded impressed.

"Just a few bits and pieces I've picked up from my grandfather," I said. "He's *very* knowledgeable—you know how
fond he is of predators of any size. Which is why I suggest
we let him handle your find. He can figure out someone
qualified to care for her, and when the storm's over we
can take her out to his zoo and give her a new home in the
insect exhibit."

"Perfect," he said. "I leave her in your care."

He stood and held out the jar to me with both hands,
bowing slightly. I'd seen a very similar ritual done with a
katana in at least one of the samurai movies my brother
loved to watch with the boys. I had to steel myself to re-
ceive the jar with something resembling dignity. At least I
managed not to flinch.

"Oh, while I'm thinking about it—where did you find
her?" I asked.

"In my bathroom," he said. "In with the towels on the
rack under the sink. Well, I should be getting back. I think
I have a panel soon."

He looked much more cheerful at having handed over
his charge. He struggled into his windbreaker, realized he
had it on inside out, corrected the error with much help
from Michael and Josh, and hurried off.

I waited until he was out of sight before testing to make
sure the lid of the jar was on tight. And peering at the

holes to make sure they were much too small for the spider.

"Mom, why don't you let us take care of him?" Jamie tried to sound disinterested and helpful.

"Her," Josh said.

"No," Michael and I said in unison.

"But—"

"I'm going to find Grandfather and make him deal with this," I said. "You get back to your game."

"I'm sure Great will let you visit the spider," Michael said, using the boys' favorite nickname for Grandfather. "Now go back to the game, or I'll declare a special tax and confiscate all your sheep."

"You can't," Josh said. "It's not in the rules."

But they hurried back to the living room anyway, only casting a few longing glances over their shoulders at the jar I was holding.

"They are not visiting the spider," I said. "And I hope Dr. Green doesn't suspect anything when he comes back to his room and finds it smelling of bug spray. I'm going to deliver this spider to Grandfather, because Dr. Green might care enough to check on her, but if she has any brothers and sisters or—ick!—offspring, I think Ekaterina will want to put them out of their misery soon."

"At least it wasn't bedbugs," Michael said.

"Not much chance of that," I said. "Ekaterina has Dagmar Shiffley out every week with one of her bedbug-sniffing dogs."

"Nice to know," he said. "I'll get back to the game. Courage!"

I found a small paper bag from the hotel coffee shop to hide the jar in, since I didn't think walking around the hotel with a visible black widow spider was a good idea. Then I grabbed my walkie-talkie and buzzed Ekaterina.

"Yes, Meg?"

"We have a problem," I said. "Can you meet me someplace?"

"The lobby?"

"Someplace more private."

"Oh, dear. My office, then," she said. "I will go there as soon as I finish talking to your grandfather."

"Bring him with you," I said. "He could be useful in solving the latest problem."

"I will try." Her voice suggested she expected to fail.

"Tell him I have something he's going to want to see right away," I said. "Mention the word 'predator.'"

Ekaterina's office—as opposed to the lush public office right behind the front desk—was hidden away off a side corridor lined with cleaning equipment, supply cabinets, and storage rooms, so people were unlikely to find it by accident. You'd never expect, from the outside, what a cool, serene, modern space she'd created out of an old supply room.

I found her there, sharing a plate of Christmas cookies with Grandfather.

"What is wrong?" She indicated a chair and shoved the cookie plate in my direction.

"One of our conference attendees found this in his bathroom." I plunked the jar down on her sleek, almost bare desk. She recoiled. Grandfather's face lit up.

"*Latrodectus mactans!*" His face it up with enthusiasm. "And a remarkably large, healthy specimen."

"Is it not a spider?" Ekaterina looked a little wild-eyed.

"A black widow spider!" Grandfather was tapping gently on the side of the jar. "Where did you find it?"

"Dr. Green found it in his bathroom."

"In one of my bathrooms!" I was relieved to see that Ekaterina didn't look freaked out anymore. She looked furious. "Which room?"

"I don't know the number, but look for Dr. Benjamin Green."

I spelled the last name and her fingers rattled over her computer keyboard.

"Room 506. I suppose we should also treat the adjacent rooms." She was already pressing buttons on her walkie-talkie.

"I told Dr. Green that you'd find someone to take care of her," I said to Grandfather. "Until we can deliver her to the insect pavilion at your zoo."

"We don't really need any more black widows at the moment," he said.

"Humor him," I said. "He's one of the well-behaved ones. And it's not as if she'll take up much room."

"If you like." He shrugged. "She can eat a few of the crickets I brought as owl food. First let's make sure she's all alone." He turned to Ekaterina. "I'll go along with your staff and see if there are any signs that the spiders have established themselves."

"Heads will roll if they have," she muttered. "But yes. I would be grateful for your assistance. What if she's laid eggs?"

"Unlikely," Grandfather said. "They mate in the late spring and summer."

"That relieves the mind a little." Her fingers were flying over the keyboard again. "Meg, the occupants of those rooms—Dr. Frogmore in 504, Dr. Green in 506, and Dr. and Mrs. Voss in 508—are they likely to be in their rooms in the next hour or so?"

I checked the conference schedule.

"It's ten forty-five." I almost said "only ten forty-five"— the day already felt as if it had been going on for much longer. "Both Voss and Frogmore are on eleven o'clock panels, so by the time your crew gets up to their rooms they'll be down in the conference area. No idea where

Mrs. Voss will be, but I'd be astonished if she objected to having her room de-spidered. And Dr. Green seems to think he has a panel, so he's probably lurking down there, already. Total space cadet, so if he turns up at the room before you're finished, look at your watch and tell him to run to the Hamilton Room before he misses his panel."

She nodded and dashed out. Grandfather rose to follow her.

"Grandfather."

"I know," he said over his shoulder. "I only have fifteen minutes to get to my panel. This won't take long."

"I have a quick question."

He paused in the doorway.

"I think someone on the hotel staff would have noticed before now if the south wing were infested with black widow spiders. Where did this one come from?"

"Who knows?" He shrugged. "Maybe she came in on Ben's suitcase. If he keeps it in a dark corner of his basement, attic, or storage shed, she could have hitched a ride."

"Maybe," I said. "Or maybe someone brought her deliberately."

"You're sounding like your father now." He was referring to Dad's insatiable love of mystery books. "If you're thinking someone was trying to knock off Green, remember—"

"Black widows aren't that lethal," I said. "I'm not thinking murder—but what if someone wanted to disrupt your conference?"

He frowned at that.

"Are any of your ornithologists also keen on entomology?" I asked.

"Undoubtedly. I'll try to remember which ones."

With that he vanished.

I studied the spider for another minute or so. She wasn't

moving much. Maybe that was a bad sign. Or maybe black widow spiders hibernated in the winter. I decided they probably did, although maybe entomologists called it something else. When reptiles did it, the herpetologists called it "brumation," so perhaps the entomologists also demanded a word of their own.

Maybe if I put the spider in a dark place she'd go back to sleep. I tucked the jar back in the coffee shop bag, put the bag right in the center of Ekaterina's enviably tidy desk. And then worried—did the bag look too much as if it might contain some treat worth swiping? Well, if anyone tried, I suspected we'd hear about it before long.

I took a couple of calming deep breaths before heading back down to see what else was going wrong at Owl Fest. And to make those changes to the banquet program. I'd left my laptop in the closet-sized cubbyhole behind the registration desk that currently served as the convention office. With any luck, Rose Noire would be staffing the desk, and I could guilt-trip her into doing the revisions.

I strode across the lobby, noticing that the Ackleys were back, sitting near the fireplace, glaring from time to time at Sami. They really did look like the Grinch and his wife, sitting among the evergreens and poinsettias with such sour faces.

Suddenly the Inn's front door opened and a snow-covered figure staggered in.

Chapter 5

"Who in the world would be out in this weather?" Sami exclaimed.

For just a moment, I found myself imagining Santa, struggling through the storm with his present sack. Although surely even in this weather the reindeer and sleigh could cope.

After staring for a few moments, Sami dashed over to greet the newcomer. Normally there would have been a doorman on duty—two at busy times of the day—but when it had become obvious that the roads were impassable, Ekaterina had reassigned the doorman to snow removal duty. New arrivals were the last thing any of us expected.

I followed Sami, eager to see who had been brave or foolhardy enough to make the trip to the Inn in the middle of a blizzard.

"Let me help you . . . er . . ." The figure was so bundled up that Sami couldn't immediately tell whether to use "sir" or "ma'am." He settled for easing him or her onto the bench just inside the door and started to brush off some of the snow.

"I didn't think I'd make it," croaked the new arrival. The voice was male—and familiar.

"Horace?" I exclaimed. "What are you doing here?" My cousin Horace Hollingsworth was an officer in Caerphilly's consolidated town police force and county sheriff's department, so normally I wouldn't have questioned his appearing anywhere at any time. But according to Sami, who had been monitoring both the NOAA weather and the Caerphilly police radio systems, it had been over an hour since the chief had told his troops that conditions were so bad he was suspending operations until further notice. "Didn't you get word from the chief to either go home or shelter in place?"

"Looks like I'll be sheltering in place here," he said. "I was out near the county line when the chief gave the word. Thought I could make it back to town. Thought wrong. Car got stuck just outside the Inn's driveway."

"And you walked all this way!" Sami exclaimed. The Inn's driveway was about a mile long.

I had already pulled out my walkie-talkie and was calling Dad.

"Meg, you're missing a fabulous panel on owl pellets," he said in lieu of hello.

"I hate to tear you away from it, but we could use your medical skills in the lobby," I said. "Horace just staggered through the front door after walking the whole way from the road."

"I'm fine, really," Horace murmured.

"You could have frostbite and not even know it," I said—to Horace, but audible to Dad. "Right, Dad?"

"The temperature's in the twenties," Sami said. "You can get frostbite in as little as half an hour when it's that cold."

"Oh, dear," Dad said. "On my way."

"As little as ten minutes if there's a strong wind on top of the subfreezing temperature," Sami went on.

"Drink this." Ekaterina appeared holding a steaming mug of coffee. "I will make arrangements for a room." From the slight frown on her face, I deduced that finding a room wouldn't be easy—Grandfather's conference had filled up most of the guest rooms, and I suspected the rest were filled with the various staff members who'd agreed to sleep on site to be available to work through the storm. Housing Horace would almost certainly mean ousting at least two staff members to less comfortable quarters.

"Horace can stay with us in the Madison Cottage," I said. "There's plenty of room. He can choose between one of the Murphy beds in the study and one of the sofas in the living room."

"I will have hot food and some dry clothing sent there." Ekaterina, looking relieved, stepped briskly across the lobby, already speaking into her walkie-talkie.

"Even Osgood and Beau have given up." Horace was referring to Osgood and Beau Shiffley, who owned and operated the county's two snowplows.

"Given up?" I said. "I thought they were stuck."

"That too. But now they've given up trying to dig themselves out. Their cousin Randall had to rescue them with his snowmobile."

News to me that Randall Shiffley, Caerphilly's mayor, had a snowmobile. Potentially useful news if it took a while for Osgood and Beau to dig their plows out.

Sami and I peeled Horace out of his outer layers of wraps. The Ackleys had left their place by the fire and were watching with horror-struck expressions. Good—maybe getting an idea of exactly how bad it was out there would convince them to stop giving Sami such a hard time.

Dad arrived with his black medical bag in hand, and he and Sami helped Horace through the lobby, with Ekaterina trailing along to carry the discarded wraps and open up the cottage door.

Almost as soon as they left the lobby, a uniformed staff member appeared with mop and pail and erased all traces of snow, ice, and water. By the time Sami returned, the lobby was back to normal.

"Horace will be fine," Sami said. "Your father says he

does have a touch of frostbite, but with proper treatment he should have no lasting ill effects. A good thing Dr. Langslow was here this weekend."

I nodded. Having Dad here was good. He'd be able to handle any minor medical emergencies. But somehow Horace's arrival brought home how isolated we were until the storm was over. What if someone had a heart attack? Or slipped on the icy cobblestones and cracked his skull? Or—

At least having Horace here would take care of one what-if that had been bothering me—what if the squabbling among the ornithologists escalated beyond shouting and the odd shoving match? At least for the time being, we had a duly sworn law enforcement officer on the premises to arrest anyone who crossed the line.

And maybe when Horace had recovered from his journey I'd sic him on finding out who had put the black widow spider in Dr. Green's room. Yes, and I'd recruit Dad, too. After all, didn't planting a dangerous spider in someone's bathroom count as some kind of crime? Probably not attempted murder, but maybe reckless endangerment?

Or had I been watching too many crime shows lately?

I could ask Horace later. Meanwhile, I made my way through the lobby and reentered the conference area. Unfortunately Rose Noire wasn't at the reception table. In her place sat a young black woman with long, elaborately beaded braids. She looked vaguely familiar—but only vaguely, even though she was wearing a yellow volunteer ribbon on her badge. Probably one of the grad student volunteers from Caerphilly's biology department. She was folding a stack of the bags we'd been giving away to all registrants—a rather attractive black canvas tote bag with a snowy owl screen-printed on it, along with the conference name: OWL FEST 2019. For some reason the 2019 part always reminded me of the daunting prospect that there might be more Owl Fests in our future. I pushed the thought to the back of my mind, stopped in front of the desk, and cast a surreptitious glance at the young woman's name tag. Melissa McKendrick.

"Hi, Meg," she said. "Can I help you?"

"I was looking for Rose Noire," I said. "But I bet she went to Grandfather's owl pellet panel." I glanced over at the door to the Hamilton Room, from which gales of laughter were emerging.

"Actually, she's giving Dr. Green a tarot reading." Melissa nodded toward the far corner of the Gathering Area. Rose Noire had spread out her cards on one of the tables and she and Dr. Green were bent over them, heads almost touching. Perhaps they needed to be close to hear each other over the frequent bursts of merriment from the Hamilton Room. Still, given the way he was hanging on her every word . . .

"I hate to disturb them," I said.

"Anything I can do?" Melissa asked.

"Dr. Blake gave me a bunch of changes to the printed program for the banquet," I said. "And I keep getting interrupted every time I remember I have to do them."

"Let me do them, then," she said. "I'm just sitting here anyway. Unless you're using some exotic program I haven't learned yet. I could fetch my laptop from the room unless you have a computer here."

"My laptop's back there." I pointed to the doorway of the conference office. "And the program's just done in Microsoft Word."

"No problem, then," she said. "Well, with the possible exception of trying to decipher Dr. Blake's handwriting if he wrote them himself."

"Tell me about it," I said. "I had my cyber-savvy nephew install some dictation software on his phone. Figured it would be much easier for everyone. Now all we have to do is talk him into using it."

"Well, I've had some experience decoding his scribbles," Melissa said. "I volunteer in the aviary out at the zoo."

"You're perfect for the job, then." I fetched my computer from the tiny office and she booted it up while I rummaged in my own tote bag for the marked-up program copy.

More laughter from the Hamilton Room. Mostly silence from the Lafayette Room.

"Who's unlucky enough to be competing with the owl pellet panel?" I asked.

"Dr. Frogmore presenting some kind of research project that next to nobody wants to hear about."

"Damn." I winced. "I'm sure he'll be in a foul mood by lunchtime."

"Is he ever in a good mood?" she asked. "And to think I almost ended up studying under him."

"What made you change your mind?" I asked.

"Not getting accepted." She laughed, a little sardonically. "I thought I was a shoo-in. B.S. in biology from Duke, summa cum laude, tons of relevant work experience. And if you're looking to punch your diversity ticket, which most places are these days, I'm a double threat. But apparently I didn't quite have what it takes to make the grade at Buckthorn."

"I hear it takes a Y chromosome," I said.

"Pretty much." She smiled. "Also helps having a lot less melanin than I have. Took me a while to realize what a narrow escape I'd had. I'd have been such a fish out of water at Buckthorn. Sometimes life has a way of looking out for you. I moped for a few months, kicked myself back into motion, and applied here at Caerphilly. Best decision ever—especially once I got past being scared of Dr. Blake and started volunteering at the zoo." When she said Grandfather's name, her face lit up in a way I'd so often seen when his students or colleagues talked about him.

"Yeah, he can be scary till you get used to him," I said. "But he's not a misogynist—just an all-purpose misanthrope."

"About the only thing he's prejudiced against is stupidity," she said. "I like that in a person."

I nodded.

"Seeing Dr. Frogmore this weekend has made me realize all over again what a lucky escape I had." She glanced toward the door of the Lafayette Room. "I could have ended up like poor Ned Czerny."

"Somehow I doubt it," I said. "You seem to have a backbone."

"He wasn't a bad guy before Frogmore got hold of him," she said.

"You know him?"

"Knew him," she said. "Slightly. Not that he'd remember me. He was a teaching assistant at Duke when I was an undergrad there. Nice enough guy back then. Too easily influenced, maybe. It was turning into Frogmore's acolyte that ruined him. Speak of the devil."

Frogmore emerged from the Lafayette Room with Czerny on his heels. Frogmore cast a malignant glance across the room at the Hamilton Room—from which more laughter erupted—and stormed across the Gathering Area to disappear into the lobby. Czerny stood irresolute for a few moments, then departed in the opposite direction—down the hallway toward the ballroom.

To my surprise, a third person came out through the door of the Lafayette Room.

"He had an audience after all," Melissa said, under her breath. "Will wonders never cease?"

Not, however, a very appreciative one.

The man strode over to where we were sitting and I managed to read his name tag: Dr. Nils Lindquist. He was fiftyish, tall, lanky, and fit, with sharp cheekbones and hair of such a pale blond shade that any gray hairs were hardly noticeable.

"I'm going to file a complaint," he announced. But instead of launching into his complaint, he stormed through the Gathering Area, jerked opened the door to the lobby, and left without looking back.

"I should probably see what he's so upset about." I stood to follow.

"No problem," Melissa said. "I'll hold down the fort here while I'm making those changes to the program."

I glanced again at Rose Noire and Dr. Green, who were now sitting with their eyes closed, presumably meditating together about whatever the outspread cards had revealed. Truly birds of a feather. Then I headed for the door to the lobby.

Chapter 6

In the lobby, Dr. Lindquist was striding over to the registration desk, where Sami was awaiting him, wearing a cheerful, helpful, welcoming expression that probably belied how he really felt at seeing the angry scientist approach.

"It's a disgrace," he announced to Sami. "I intend to file a complaint."

"I'm so sorry," Sami said. "What's wrong, and what can I do to resolve it?"

"That man is completely unsound on the barred owl!" Dr. Lindquist exclaimed. "Ludicrously so!"

It took a lot to unsettle Sami, but this outburst, which must have been incomprehensible to him, clearly had him shaken. He stole a glance at me.

"Now, now," I said. "I understand how you feel, but I'm sure by the end of the conference you'll have made some progress toward sorting that all out."

"I'm glad you're sure." Dr. Lindquist frowned at me. "Because I'm not. Not while lunatics like Frogmore are given scope to spread their idiocy."

I thought of pointing out that Grandfather had scheduled Dr. Frogmore opposite his highly popular owl pellet panel, thereby ensuring he'd have almost no audience, but I didn't think that would do much to calm him.

"You're distraught," I said. "Why don't you let me get you some coffee? Or—"

"Coffee, be damned!" Dr. Lindquist drew back as if I'd insulted him. "This calls for a drink!"

He strode off toward the Mount Vernon Grill and disappeared inside.

"What does he mean by 'unsound on the barred owl' anyway?" Sami asked. "In fact, what is it about the barred owl that upsets all these scientists? Seems like all you have to do to is mutter 'barred owl' at them and they go ballistic."

"Do you really want to know?" I asked. "It's kind of a long story."

"Are any of us going anywhere anytime soon?" He jerked his head toward the glass wall, as if to remind me of what was going on outside. Did he think I needed reminding?

But he had a point. And if I stayed here and explained the whole barred owl thing to Sami, it would give me a good excuse not to run after Dr. Lindquist and try to placate him.

"You're probably too young to remember the whole spotted owl controversy," I said.

"I thought it was barred owls that guy was upset about."

"Bear with me," I said. "Back in the 1980s and 1990s, there was a big brouhaha in the Pacific Northwest. Conservationists were trying to save the northern spotted owl. *Strix occidentalis caurina.*"

"You're starting to sound like them," he said. "The scientists, I mean. Save the spotted owl from what?"

"Habitat destruction," I said. "That's what put the spotted owl on the endangered species list. It can only live in old-growth forest, and there's not as much of that as there used to be in the Pacific Northwest, thanks to the logging industry clear-cutting forests."

"Can't they just make the loggers plant new trees?"

"They do, but it would take a century or so for that to

be of any use to the spotted owls. They only eat certain kinds of prey that only live in old-growth forest. There's a term for that—"

"Picky eaters?" Sami suggested.

"A scientific term," I said. "But you get the idea. You cut down the old-growth forest and their prey disappears, and they don't adapt well. Conservationists and the timber industry have been at each other's throats over this for decades now, and from what I can tell, neither side is happy. The timber barons resent the restrictions on where and how much they can log, and the conservationists don't think the restrictions go far enough. And the spotted owl is declining faster than ever, and the ornithologists have figured out it's because the barred owl—*Strix varia*—is muscling in on their territory."

"You're kidding, right?" Sami said.

"Nope. Barred owls used to live only east of the Mississippi, but in the last hundred years or so they've been moving into the Pacific Northwest. Out there, they count as an invasive species. They're twenty percent bigger than the spotted owls, they breed faster, and they're not picky eaters at all. They'll eat anything they can catch—including spotted owls."

"Uh-oh," Sami said. "So what's going to happen? Is there anything the owl guys can do about it?"

"That's what they're arguing about," I said. "Apparently there was a small pilot program in Northern California where they removed as many barred owls as they could from a forested area. And sure enough, the spotted owl population began to rebound."

"Then what's the problem? They just do the same thing on a larger scale until—wait. I bet it's money. They'd need buckets of money to remove all the barred owls in the whole Pacific Northwest."

"I'm sure that would be a problem. Plus a lot of spotted

owl habitat is on state or federal land, so they'd have to convince three state governments and who knows how many federal agencies to cooperate. And a lot of the habitat is pretty remote, which could make it hard to find all the barred owls. But the biggest reason they're not going ahead with a region-wide program of barred owl removal is in this case removing the owls is a euphemism for shooting them."

"Shooting them?" Sami's mouth fell open. "They can't just do a trap and release program?"

"I don't know," I said. "I'm kind of afraid to ask. I don't want to set them off again. Oh, and if you hear them talk about harvesting the barred owls, it's the same thing."

"Shooting them. Okay, I see why they're arguing."

"Well, it's not the only thing they're arguing about," I said. "They're also perfectly capable of getting worked up over where various prehistoric owl fossils fit into the Strigiform family tree. Or whether the eastern barn owl is a regional variation or a separate species. And don't even think of getting them started on what should be done about the fact that the great horned owls' diet includes Pacific pocket mice, marbled murrelets, and several dozen other highly endangered species."

"Wait—are you saying that all these species are going extinct because the great horned owls are eating them?"

"No, they're going extinct for all the usual reasons— habitat destruction, climate change, introduction of new diseases, and so on. Problem is, if a species is down to a only a few dozen individuals, it can be really devastating to have a nesting pair of great horned owls move into the neighborhood and start picking off the rare critters one by one—but what can you do? It's not as if you can discuss it with the owls—'Hey, why don't you leave those endangered rodents over here alone and pick on those equally delicious but completely unendangered field mice over there.' Not going to work."

"You seem to know a lot about owls." He didn't have to sound so surprised.

"Most of it picked up this weekend while standing by to keep various irate scientists from punching each other in the nose." Okay, I was exaggerating—I'd also learned quite a lot while helping Grandfather plan Owl Fest. Sami was frowning and seemed to be working up to posing a question.

"Are all owl experts this . . . um . . . excitable?" he asked finally.

"I've been wondering that myself," I said. "Maybe it's just the ones Grandfather knows and likes enough to invite to Owl Fest. When it comes to animals, he makes no secret of his fondness for predators. Most of us look at a koala and say 'oh, how cute!' Show Grandfather a koala and he'll wax eloquent about its long, sharp claws, its powerful jaws, and its antisocial personality. Maybe he feels the same way about scientists. Favors the truculent ones."

"So maybe he deliberately picked a whole bunch of scientists who disagreed with each other and cooped them up together in the Inn for fun."

"Well, the cooping up is mainly because of the snowstorm," I said. "Things were better yesterday when they could all go off hiking in the woods to cool off between squabbles. And I have this sneaking suspicion that he was hoping for a more congenial kind of argument. Debates over whether greedy developers and the CEOs of corporate polluters should be drawn and quartered in public or quietly euthanized. Followed by team-building sessions in which they all vilify climate change deniers together. And lots of strenuous bird-watching hikes through the surrounding woods to blow off steam. I have a feeling the whole debate over the barred and spotted owls isn't nearly as much fun as what he had planned."

"The weather's rearranging everyone's plans," Sami said.

"Yeah." I glanced over at the glass wall, currently solid white with snow, and then quickly back to the small Christmas tree on the reception desk, which was much more comforting to contemplate at the moment. "You know the weird thing? I could have sworn Dr. Lindquist and Dr. Frogmore were on the same side of the whole barred owl debate. Both in favor of shooting the owls, that is. I must have gotten it all wrong."

"Meg?" I turned to see Ekaterina had joined us. "I could use your assistance."

She was frowning fiercely. Fortunately, I knew her well enough not to worry that she was upset with me. As the Inn's manager, she'd only get that look if someone was threatening the orderly running of the hotel or the well-being of its employees.

"Is one of my flock causing problems again? Not more black widow spiders, I hope."

"No, your grandfather saw no signs that we have a spider infestation, and my staff have already sprayed Dr. Green's room and the adjacent ones. I'm sure they will all complain about the smell, and what have you." She shrugged. "That's not what I wanted you to help me with. One of the attendees has taken it upon himself to inspect all the food. My kitchen staff are trying to get the buffet ready for lunch, and he is interfering with their efforts."

"I'll deal with him," I said. "In the ballroom?"

She nodded. We hurried back to the conference area, and then down the corridor to the double doors that led to the ballroom. A few convention attendees were loitering nearby, probably hoping to be the first inside. They all looked up eagerly when they saw me open the ballroom door, but Ekaterina paused in the doorway, drew herself up to her full height, and favored them with a withering gaze. Nobody tried to follow us.

Inside, all the tables were topped with spotless white tablecloths, and each was decorated with cluster of tiny red poinsettias in the middle. Along one side of the room the buffet table was set up—stacks of red plates, sets of flatware wrapped in green napkins, a forest of gleaming glasses, large bowls of salad, and a row of empty steam tables that should have been already filled with the vegetables and entrees.

Nearby a hotel staff member was standing beside a cart loaded with long, rectangular covered dishes bound for the steam tables, arguing with someone who was trying to pick up the cover of one of the dishes.

"You're not supposed to be touching that," the hotel employee was saying. "You're not even supposed to be in here."

I recognized the shabby, stoop-shouldered figure leaning over the cart.

"Dr. Czerny!" I snapped, as I drew closer.

He jumped and whirled, shrinking slightly. Then he appeared to regain his courage. He lifted his chin and his face assumed a combative expression.

"I insist that you let me finish my inspection." His high, nasal voice was downright annoying.

"Inspection? I was unaware that we had a new hire in the Caerphilly Health Department."

I took a position facing him and crossed my arms. He took a half step back. If he chose to interpret my stance as menacing . . . he had more common sense than I'd previously given him credit for.

"I have to make sure that the food is safe for Dr. Frogmore to eat," Czerny said. "He has serious allergy issues."

"Did he report them on his registration form?" I said.

"Because I can assure you, we took all food allergy notifications seriously."

"How would I know?" Czerny asked.

"Then perhaps we should go and talk to Dr. Frogmore," I said. "I'll go and catch him before lunch, so we can make sure we can accommodate his needs, even if he didn't think to report them. If you'll come with me—"

"No." Czerny paled, as if the idea of having me bother the great man terrified him. "You don't need to ask him. I can tell you what he's allergic to—"

"Mushrooms," Ekaterina said, looking up from her phone. "I have it right here in the database."

"Good." I took Czerny by the arm and tried to steer him away from the cart. "Then we won't have a problem."

"We will if Dr. Frogmore eats so much as a bite of mushrooms." Czerny was digging in his heels, but at least with me distracting him the hotel employee managed to get her cart moving again toward the steam trays.

"Impossible," Ekaterina said. "There are no mushrooms in any of the dishes we are serving in today's buffet."

"Or in any of the other meals we're serving during the conference," I added. "Grandfather insisted."

"He must really hate mushrooms." Ekaterina's voice sounded just a little annoyed—okay, maybe a lot annoyed—and I realized no one had explained the reasons for Grandfather's fiat.

"Actually, he does rather dislike them," I explained. "But more importantly, he distrusts them. A few years ago a biologist he knew—someone who fancied himself a mushroom expert—poisoned himself and two other colleagues with an omelet full of *Amanita phalloides*. Grandfather was the only one rude enough to turn up his nose after a single bite—and also the only one who didn't end up in the hospital or the morgue. Ever since then he's taken against mushrooms in a big way."

"Ah." Ekaterina nodded. "So that is why he so vehemently vetoed the idea of a grilled Portobello mushroom for the vegetarians."

"So Dr. Frogmore is in no danger of consuming any mushrooms if he's eating the official conference meals." I turned back to Czerny and tugged at his arm again.

"And since he's a grown-up, I assume he makes the waitstaff aware of his allergy if he's ordering food in the restaurant." Ekaterina took Czerny's other arm and between the two of us we managed to get him moving toward the door.

We let go of Czerny just inside the door, and Ekaterina pushed it open and held it for him.

"On your heads be it if anything happens to him, then." Czerny clearly didn't like it, but he walked through the doorway, pausing slightly halfway, like a cat who wants to test its owner's patience, before finally leaving.

Chapter 7

"What a nuisance." I waited until the door was shut behind Dr. Czerny. "Although I suppose we should cut him some slack. Maybe Dr. Frogmore's had problems before with places that aren't as meticulous about food allergies as the Inn is. And Czerny's nothing if not protective of his mentor." I almost said "lord and master."

"He should know by now that we are not the least bit careless about food allergies."

Yes, I knew that. Ekaterina had contacted every single conference attendee to ask about any food allergies or restrictions and we'd designed all of the conference meals accordingly. We'd had about the usual trouble getting Grandfather to understand that quite a few attendees would have religious, ethical, or health objections to consuming bacon-wrapped filet mignon. And thank goodness none of the attendees seemed to be keeping kosher, since the hotel's usual solution was to have meals brought in from Caerphilly's well-regarded kosher restaurant and deli, which would have been difficult on Friday and impossible today.

Ekaterina was already typing on her phone. "I will issue instructions that no mushrooms should be served to Dr. Frogmore or anyone at his table, even if they demand them. In fact, we will take mushrooms completely off the hotel menu until he leaves. We can say that due to the inclement weather our mushroom supplier was unable to deliver."

"You're thinking maybe if he's feeling suicidal he might just call room service and request an *omelette aux champignons*?" I turned to see how the waiters were doing.

"More likely he would order it, take one bite, claim it made him deathly ill, and sue the hotel," she said. "I've seen it happen before. By the way, while we're talking about food, there is a situation that must be dealt with."

"What's that?" I braced myself, and hoped this would turn out to be a situation that I could deal with after lunch. I needed a break.

"Sami has been monitoring the forecast on my weather radio," she said. "The storm may be slowing down."

"Oh, great."

"Not great at all—if it slows down—"

"It will have time to dump even more snow on us. Definitely not great—I was being sarcastic." And should have known it would be lost on Ekaterina in full-blown crisis mode.

"Ah. Yes, more snow, and they continue to forecast temperatures in the twenties for at least the next week. It begins to look very possible that we could still be snowbound on Christmas Eve. Even Christmas Day."

Had she only just noticed this possibility?

"Very possible," I said aloud.

"We must make plans to feed them." Her tone was solemn, yet fierce.

"Feed them? I thought you said the Inn had plenty of supplies if we were snowbound for weeks, even months. If there's—"

"Of course we do," she said. "That is not the issue. We must figure out what to feed them for *Christmas*. What they will be homesick for if they cannot go home. If they were all Russians, I would know what to do. For Christmas Eve we would have *kutya, borscht, zakuskie, pirozhki*, beans for prosperity, maybe *pagach* if that is their tradition, and *vzvar* with *pryaniki* and *kolyadki*." Her face took on a blissful expression.

"I have no idea what any of that means," I said. "Except for the beans and the *borscht*. But I gather it must be delicious."

"Well, not all that delicious," she said. "It's a meatless meal, of course, since it's the last day of Advent. Which means, in a strict Russian Orthodox household, no fish, vegetable oil, or alcohol allowed, either. I can think of more delicious meals. But it's tradition! It brings back the memories. Eating it would not entirely make up for not being able to go home, but it would help. Possibly a good deal. So we must figure out what these poor scientists will be missing if they do not go home to their homes for Christmas."

"Some of them will be missing Hanukkah instead of Christmas, and that starts tomorrow night," I said. "We should work on that, too."

"Precisely," she said. "So what should we be serving them? Start with Christmas—what is the standard American Christmas dinner?"

"I think starting with Hanukkah would be easier," I said. "I'm not sure there is any standard American Christmas dinner. Everyone I know does it differently. It depends on where people live, and where their ancestors came from, and just what they like to eat. There isn't even a rule on whether you have it Christmas Eve or Christmas Day or both."

"Then you will have to find out what each of them is accustomed to eating for their various holidays," she said. "And then I can determine what to serve to bring happiness to as many of them as possible."

Was she serious? She wanted me to ask every single one of the two hundred scientists what they wanted for Christmas and/or Hanukkah dinner?

Then again, perhaps I could recruit Mother. And Rose Noire. They might even enjoy it.

"Let me see what I can do." I hoped that didn't sound like a promise.

"Good. I think we can open the doors now."

"I'll go share the glad tidings with the ravening hordes."

I didn't need to go far. Evidently the panels had ended while we'd been dealing with Dr. Czerny. Nearly everyone attending the conference was milling around in the hallway outside. Though they were all in a remarkably cheerful mood—clearly scheduling the owl pellet panel just before lunch had been a stroke of genius on Grandfather's part. We opened the doors and stepped aside to let them in.

"I can supervise the buffet if you would rather eat with your family," Ekaterina said. "I sent plenty of food to the cottage. And you could check on your cousin."

"I'll take you up on that," I said. "Thanks."

"And let me know what he has to say about conditions outside."

"Will do."

"What are those things they're putting on the tables?" Ekaterina pointed to the nearest table, which was littered with small dark objects, most either round or Vienna sausage-shaped.

"Ah," I said. "Evidently the owl pellet panel gave out samples."

"Owl pellets?" She looked puzzled. "Owls eat those? I thought they caught mice."

"No, owl pellets are what they do with the bones, fur, teeth, feathers, and other indigestible parts of their prey."

"You mean it's owl poop? They are putting owl poop on my tables?"

"No, no," I said. "It's not poop. Owls regurgitate the pellets."

"That is only a small improvement," she said. "What are we supposed to do with them if they leave them behind?"

"They won't," I said. "Or if anyone does, someone else is sure to snatch them up. They're highly prized."

"*À chacun son goût*," she murmured. "Go see your family. I will keep an eye on these barbarians."

I was tempted. But I also didn't want to leave Grandfather in the lurch. If he needed help fending off Frogmore, or Czerny, or any of the other annoying attendees . . .

But then I saw him going through the buffet line, accompanied by Dr. Craine. Rose Noire, her plate piled high with vegetables, was waving at them to join her at a nearby table. Dr. Green was already sitting beside her, and it dawned on me that this wasn't the first time I'd seen them eating together during the conference. In fact, I was pretty sure he'd been glued to her side at every meal.

I made a mental note to ask Grandfather what he knew about this Dr. Green. What if his absent-minded professorial manner was camouflage for his real character as a conference Lothario? Of course, all Grandfather would care about was Dr. Green's scientific abilities. Maybe I should ask Dr. Craine. Or, better still, sic Mother on the question.

Meanwhile, Grandfather would be fine. And Owl Fest would survive if I spent the lunch hour with Michael and the boys.

I left the conference area, slipped back into the lobby again, and breathed a sigh of contentment. I felt as if I'd crossed from the contentious world of Owl Fest back into the warm, welcoming world of Christmas Land. The large-screen TV over the mantel in the lobby, usually tuned to CNN, was now showing *How the Grinch Stole Christmas*. Of course, the real reason for this was that the hotel's cable was out, but at least they were prepared with a DVD player and some seasonally appropriate fare. I made a mental note to ask Ekaterina if I could borrow it to watch with the boys.

Christmas Land was intensified in the cottage, and I could have sworn that some of the decorations were ones that I'd have expected to see back at home. One evergreen garland looked pretty much like another, although these did have the oversized red velvet bows Mother was so fond of using, and Mother had been advising Ekaterina on the hotel's decor. But the gold tinsel mobiles representing the twelve days of Christmas, now fluttering overhead in the breeze that had followed me into the cottage—those were pretty distinctive. I'd last seen them in the front hall of our house. And the tree that had suddenly appeared beside the fireplace, completely blocking the soaring multi-paned window—I could spot one-of-a-kind ornaments that I remembered hanging on our tree at home just a few days ago.

"I had some of our old, familiar decorations brought over before the snow started," Mother said when she noticed me staring at the tree. "As bad as this storm is, we might not be able to leave for a few more days, so I thought we should make ourselves as much at home as possible."

"And what if the snow cleanup goes faster than expected and Ekaterina kicks us out tomorrow or Monday?"

"Then I'll have it all moved back," she said. "Don't worry—I know you'll be exhausted from the conference. You won't have to lift a finger."

"In that case, let's enjoy the tree," I said.

Ekaterina hadn't been kidding about sending more than enough food. The Madison Cottage's dining table was covered with plates and bowls. Caesar salad and pasta salad. Several pizzas. A platter of ham, turkey, roast beef, and assorted cheeses. Fresh baked bread. French fries and onion rings. Stir-fried vegetables. Fresh-cut fruit salad.

And half a dozen desserts—Christmas cookies, brownies with red and green candies on top, three kinds of pie, and some little cups of crème brûlée that were calling my name. Michael, Dad, and the boys were already digging in. I began filling a plate, and secured two of the crèmes brûlées before they could disappear.

Horace was sitting on one of the sofas with warm wet washcloths draped over his hands and bare feet—no doubt part of Dad's treatment for frostbite. Mother was feeding him tidbits.

His police radio was sitting on the end table, plugged into the wall to charge. He came to attention whenever it made any noise, but all I'd heard so far were occasional bursts of static.

"Pretty bad out there?" I asked as I took a seat on the other sofa.

"Power and telephone lines out everywhere," Horace said. "And anyone who didn't already get where they're going by now is out of luck."

"Randall Shiffley was convinced this was going to be an epic disaster," Michael said. "He had his workmen set up generators at the town hall and at the various local churches, so they could be used for shelter. And made sure each of the churches had a satellite phone, so they could stay in communication."

"Good for him!" Mother exclaimed.

"And having those helped us convince a lot of people to come into town," Horace said. "It could take a while to dig out from this."

Of course, not everyone could simply drop everything and take refuge in town. There were plenty of farmers who couldn't abandon their livestock. Just for a moment, I felt a twinge of guilt, sitting here in a warm room, feasting on such a delicious spread with all my family around me.

"We'll get through this," Mother said. "All of us." Was

she reading my mind, or was it just that my dark thoughts were all too visible on my face? "I'm sure there will be much to do when the storm is over, but for now, let's all be thankful that we're all here safe and sound together."

"Hear, hear!" Michael said, and we all clinked glasses as if it were a toast.

"And God bless us every one," Josh and Jamie chorused. Even though Michael's traditional one-man staged reading of *A Christmas Carol* had been postponed due to the snow, the boys had seen a rehearsal and were uttering Dickensian quotes at the slightest opportunity.

We went back to eating and talking. Every so often Horace's radio would erupt with bits of news. Chief Burke, his wife Minerva, and the three orphaned grandsons they were raising had moved into the New Life Baptist Church for the duration. Adam, the youngest grandson, was one of the boys' best friends, and while the chief wouldn't let the three of them talk on the police radio, he gave us the number of the satellite phone he'd brought along to keep in contact with the outside world—at least that part of the outside world who were either also equipped with satellite phones or were located west of the Mississippi and thus out of the storm's reach. Deprived for hours now of their ability to text each other at will, all three boys were delighted at the prospect of a lengthy conversation after lunch.

"And you can give me some hints about what you're giving me for Christmas," Adam said. "You'll never guess what I'm giving you."

I wondered if Chief Burke, in the background, was repressing the same conspiratorial smile I was trying to hide. Michael and I had conferred with Chief Burke and Minerva at great length about the boys' presents to each other. Josh and Jamie were joining forces to give Adam the expensive new bat that Michael and the chief agreed would be perfect for the coming year's baseball season, and Adam was giving Josh and Jamie tickets to a home game between his beloved Orioles and their arch-rival Yankees. Still to be determined was whether Michael and I would tag along to help out or whether the chief and Minerva would really try to cope all by themselves with our two on top of his own crew, which included not only Adam Jones Burke but also Frank Robinson Burke, Junior, and Calvin Ripken Burke. I'd blocked the relevant dates out on my calendar, just in case. Curious how comforting it was, in the middle of the snowstorm, to think that pitchers and catchers would report in a mere seven weeks.

All too soon it was time to head back to Owl Fest. I took one last look around the cottage, kissed Michael, reassured the boys that I would not insist on kissing them, and went back out into the storm.

Chapter 8

As I entered the lobby, I braced myself. So far I hadn't received any frantic walkie-talkie calls from Rose Noire, but that didn't necessarily mean nothing had gone wrong. She could just be trying to keep me from being bothered over lunch.

I brushed the snow off myself and waved at Sami, who waved back with a candy cane.

"Want one?" he called. "We also have gingerbread people!"

"How modern." I drifted over to the reception desk and studied the plate of gaily decorated cookies. About half of them were the traditional gingerbread man shape—the others had longer hair and appeared to be wearing skirts. "I'm fairly stuffed, but if I could just have that foot that one of them seems to have lost."

"It's yours," he said. "Trying to add a little seasonal cheer for the guests who don't have your grandfather's conference to keep them busy."

"Are there that many?"

"Not many," he said. "The Ackleys, a professor who's here to interview for a post at the college and having serious doubts about leaving Arizona, and a handful of conference attendees' spouses who came along for sightseeing and shopping and weren't too happy about the change in plans. But after Ekaterina gave them all coupons for deep discounts and free services at the spa, they've gotten pretty mellow. Mrs. Ackley, too. And your grandfather issued an open invitation to anyone stuck in the hotel to attend his conference if they want to."

"Anyone taking him up on it?"

"So far, just Mr. Ackley," Sami said. "Who doesn't look as if he's exactly having the time of his life. But I've been thinking of trying it myself, if I can figure out what some of the panels are about. Some of them have me baffled." He held up a copy of the conference program.

"You and me both."

"Just what is that anyway?" He pointed to something in the program. I peered at the line in question, which read "*Tyto alba*: some taxonomic considerations."

"Not one I'd recommend for a layperson."

"That's the one that was going on in the Hamilton Room at half past nine this morning, when I looked in during my break," he said. "The one with all the shouting."

"That's right."

"But why?" he asked.

"Why the shouting?" I countered. "Or why the panel?"

"Yes. Both."

"Well, you know what taxonomy is," I said.

"Giving things the proper Latin names," he said. "Like *Homo sapiens* and *Canis lupus*."

"It's a little more than that," I said. "The names show how they fit into the whole family tree of living beings. The modern system got started in the 1700s. But back in the old days, all they had to go on was what the animals looked like. The whole system has been gradually evolving over the centuries, as they get better at figuring out how various living things are related. I mean, if you'd never seen them before, would you ever think that Chihuahuas and St. Bernards were closely related?"

"No." He chuckled at the image. "DNA must have been a big help."

"So I gather. But there are still a lot of arguments about

how much of a difference it takes to call something a separate species. If it's not different enough, it's a subspecies, or maybe just a regional variation. Apparently there are a lot of unresolved questions of that kind about barn owls, aka *Tyto alba*."

"Okay," he said. "I get how it's maybe important to get that all sorted out if you care about that kind of thing."

"Like if you're the kind of person who alphabetizes her spices."

"But why do they get so worked up about it? I mean, from the amount of shouting that goes on you'd think it was a political meeting or something."

"I don't get it, either," I said. "Clearly you and I were not meant to be ornithologists."

"Yeah." He shook his head. "I don't think our meetings are like that. The American Meteorological Society, that is. At least I hope not. I'm going to my first one in a few weeks, in Boston. I'm starting to get a little worried."

"I'm sure it will be much saner than this," I said. "Besides—"

The door to the conference area slammed open and Dr. Frogmore stormed out and across the lobby. He, too, was carrying a conference program, although unlike Sami he did not appear to be studying it with bemused interest. I thought at first he was headed toward us. I braced myself, and I noticed Sami did, too. But instead of approaching the registration desk he steered toward the door to the hotel office

"A hotel problem, then, rather than a conference one," I said, *sotto voce*, as we watched Frogmore jerk the door open. "Is Ekaterina in there?"

"No, I think your grandfather was using it."

"Blake!" Frogmore's shout probably carried back to the conference area. "What the hell do you mean by this!"

"I should go referee," I said, as I headed for the office.

"'This' would be the conference program." Grandfather's voice was surprisingly mild. "Latest printed version thereof—any last-minute changes are posted on the message board in the conference center."

"I mean, what is this. Hirano? *Hirano?*"

"Yes, Dr. Hirano's giving the keynote at tonight's banquet."

"What I want to know is why the hell you didn't ask *me* to do the keynote address?"

"My conference, my choice," Grandfather said.

I increased my speed and stepped into the room. Frogmore, who was pacing up and down, looked red-faced and furious and barely glanced at me. Grandfather, seated at Ekaterina's desk, looked calm. In fact, I could swear he was enjoying himself. He nodded at me, then turned his attention back to Frogmore.

"Hirano's English is practically nonexistent," Frogmore said.

"Which is why Dr. Arai is going to translate for him," Grandfather said. "And Dr. Hirano says he plans to keep it short and sweet. I like that in a speech."

"I'm a hell of a lot more well-known than Hirano," Frogmore said.

"If you say so." Grandfather sounded amused. "Doesn't matter. I asked Hirano. Asked him months before you invited yourself to my conference. I'm not going to unask him just because you feel like strutting around like a peacock in front of a captive audience."

I expected an explosion from Frogmore. He narrowed his eyes and got even redder in the face. But just as I was bracing myself for a loud blast, he spoke, his voice low and venomous.

"You're going to regret this." With that he turned on his heel and stomped out of the office, slamming the door behind him.

With Frogmore gone, I was expecting Grandfather to say something snarky. Instead he sighed and began massaging his eye sockets with his thumbs, in what I recognized as his favorite technique for easing a headache.

Damn Frogmore anyway. He must be really getting to Grandfather.

"I should have held this conference earlier in the year." Was this a non sequitur, or did it have something to do with Frogmore? "In the middle of everyone's fall semester. Maybe Frogmore would have been too busy to come."

Ah. "That would have been nice," I said.

"I tried, you know."

I nodded. Unfortunately, he hadn't involved me or Mother or any other well-organized person in his initial planning, and therefore didn't realize that the date he'd originally picked had conflicted with Rosh Hashanah. By the time half a dozen potential attendees had pointed this out to him, there weren't many other weekends available. Of course, this weekend had conflicted with a family reunion that Trevor Ponsonby-West, Grandfather's assistant, had been planning for three years, which was how I'd ended up running the conference. With luck the whole process of rescheduling had been painful enough that he'd remember to ask us the next time he decided to throw a conference. Maybe he'd even listen to our suggestion to hold it someplace warm next time.

"And there was a reason I decided to hold this conference here in Caerphilly," Grandfather said, as if reading my thoughts.

"You mean apart from the fact that having it here meant you wouldn't have to travel in the middle of the winter, and you'd have an excuse to stay here in the Inn in great luxury, and you could draft all your family and friends and the entire Caerphilly College biology department to run it for you?" I asked.

"I could have had it in the Pacific Northwest," he went on, ignoring me. "That would have been a lot more convenient for the Japanese and the Australians. Better weather, too. But I was hoping if I had it on the East Coast, all these idiots who are busy feuding over what to do about the spotted and barred owls would stay put on the West Coast."

"I thought you invited them," I said.

"I did. Had to. Wouldn't have been polite to leave them out. But I didn't expect very many of them to come. And I certainly didn't expect them to bring their wretched squabbles here."

"Just what's your take on the issue, anyway?" I asked. "You've been uncharacteristically reserved on the subject— maybe a good thing, since you're playing host to all of them. But what do you think—shoot the barred owls, or let nature take its course?"

"I think before we go around shooting a whole bunch of healthy predators we should spend a little effort trying to figure out if there's a nonlethal method of encouraging them to go back to their original habitat. A habitat that's under increasing pressure itself, you know. The barred owls might be invasive on the West Coast, but here on the East Coast they're being displaced in many areas by the great horned owls."

I had a brief vision of the various owls as aggressive warring tribes, ceaselessly invading each other's territories, like so many feathered Genghis Khans. "Nature, red in tooth and claw," I muttered.

"What's that?"

"So you're in favor of trying to find a compromise," I said aloud.

"I'm in favor of trying to find a less drastic and bloodthirsty solution to the problem." He sighed. "The whole thing is particularly ironic considering how closely related the two species are. They can actually interbreed, you know."

"Barred and spotted owls?"

"Yes." He chuckled. "And unlike many hybrids, the offspring are fertile."

"So they could eventually become one species."

"It's possible," he said. "Or what's left of the spotted owls could just be absorbed into the barred owl population. No one knows what's going to happen."

He fell silent as if pondering deeply over the unsettled fate of the barred and spotted owls.

"So what do they call them?" I asked after a few moments.

"Call what?"

"The hybrids of the barred and spotted owls? Sparred owls? Botted owls?"

"I don't actually know." He frowned. Grandfather didn't like to be asked questions when he didn't know the answers.

"I bet they're still arguing about it," I said. "I bet before the conference is over, we'll have three or four of them throwing things at each other. 'Sparred owls!' 'No, botted owls!' Good thing Horace is here in case we need him to break it up."

"I think you have our number," Grandfather said with a chuckle. "I'm going to put my feet up for a half hour or so before my next panel. Call me if you need me."

"I'll try not to," I said. "If the SPOOR folks are still rehearsing in your cottage, tell them to go next door to the Madison or the Washington."

"Rehearsing?"

Oh, dear. SPOOR—Stop Poisoning Our Owls and Raptors—was a local bird conservation group. They were famous—or maybe infamous—for dressing up in rather ridiculous bird costumes and performing humorous conservation-themed skits or musical numbers. In honor of the season, at tonight's banquet they were planning to do a few Christmas carol parodies filled with owl puns: "O Owly Night." "What Owl Is This?" "Owl Be Home for Christmas." And maybe one or two others that I'd blotted out of my memory. Dad's idea, but I could have sworn he'd gotten Grandfather's assent.

"They're singing some Christmas carols at the banquet, remember?"

"Of course I remember. Are you saying they actually rehearse for these shindigs? I always assumed they just got up on stage and made it up as they went along."

Having seen SPOOR in action, I could understand why he thought that.

"For you, they're rehearsing," I said. "By the way, I thought Dr. Lindquist was on Dr. Frogmore's side."

"No one's on Frogmore's side," Grandfather said. "With the possible exception of Ned Czerny, and he's soft in the head."

"On the plight of the spotted owl," I explained. "I could have sworn they were both in favor of shooting the invading barred owls."

"Oh, yes." Grandfather nodded briskly. "Nils is in favor of barred owl removal. Must drive him bonkers to have Frogmore ostensibly on his side."

"Ostensibly?"

"Nils's theory is that Frogmore's secretly in favor of just letting the barred owls take over," Grandfather explained. "But that Frogmore also realizes that if he's for it, a lot of people will take the other side, just to be contrary. So he goes around supporting barred owl removal—but in such a pig-headed, over-the-top way that it makes the whole proposal look bad. Like his idea of paying exorbitant bounties for barred owl carcasses—will that result in a controlled, orderly removal of barred owls from the spotted owls' territory? Or will it turn into open season on anything that vaguely resembles a barred owl?"

"Including the few remaining spotted owls."

"Exactly. Bad idea. Frogmore goes around spouting off stuff like that and it taints the whole barred owl removal camp by association."

"So Dr. Lindquist and the other sane barred owl removalists hate him because he makes them look bad, and the anti-removalists hate him because they think he's a heartless monster who wants to slaughter vast quantities of their beloved owls."

"Pretty much." He nodded. "Whole field would be a lot more congenial if he were out of it."

"So if he gets the crazy idea to go on an owling expedition in the middle of the blizzard, I should let him do it for the good of the whole field?"

Grandfather grinned at the idea, then his face grew serious and he shook his head.

"No, you should tackle the bastard and drag him back inside," he said. "Because if one of our own, even Frogmore, got lost in a blizzard, a lot of good people would risk their lives trying to save him. And now I'm going to take my nap."

Although it wasn't five minutes before I got a text from him. I wondered, not for the first time, if I should be grateful to the boys for having taught him how to text or worried that they had created a monster.

Chapter 9

"Have you fed Percival?" Grandfather's text read.

I took a deep calming breath. Percival was a great horned owl—the one owl officially authorized to be in the hotel. We were keeping him well out of sight to avoid complaints from ornithophobes like Mrs. Ackley. Or for that matter, from the various scientists who were still sulking because we'd confiscated the various owls they'd brought along for what they no doubt thought were good reasons.

Grandfather had originally planned to use Percival as part of a demonstration on the medical issues involved in owl rehabilitation, given by the vet who tended all the exotic animals at his zoo. But Dr. Clarence Rutledge, the vet, was snowed in by now, with not only his own pets but also any patients staying at the Caerphilly Animal Hospital who could not easily go home and the entire current population of the Caerphilly Animal Shelter. We'd canceled the demonstration, and Percival had been demoted from program participant to non-paying guest. Grandfather had wanted to keep him in one of the cottages, but I'd vetoed that, so Ekaterina had found a place for us to hide his enormous cage in a well-heated and -ventilated hotel storage room. But surely Grandfather had tasked someone with feeding him.

"Was I supposed to?" I texted back.

"No, I was supposed to, but I keep getting interrupted."

I sighed.

"I'm not doing mice," I replied. "I'll give him some crickets. That should hold him till you have time."

"Fine."

So I headed for the storage room. In good weather it would have been only a five-minute walk from the cottages down to the side door nearest the storage room. Given the snowstorm, getting there right now required taking an elevator down to the basement, using the key card Ekaterina had given me for getting into staff-only locations, and following a series of long, dimly lit, utilitarian corridors that snaked their way beneath the hotel. The basement was the one part of the Inn that Ekaterina had not yet brought into line with her high standards of efficiency and order, probably because doing so would mean a lot of expensive remodeling, and she hadn't yet convinced the owners it would be worth doing. In the long run, my money was on Ekaterina, but for now the basement still revealed the fact that the Inn had been added on to half a dozen times over the century or so of its existence. My path wound past the food storage rooms, the staff locker rooms, the immense laundry rooms, and other unidentified but doubtless useful areas. I finally arrived at the wider area at the end of the corridor from which a battered, unmarked door opened into a huge warehouse-like space.

Rather a creepy space. A lot of it was filled with furniture and decorations that were coming or going. Old furniture that hadn't yet been hauled away for sale, donation, or disposal. Repairable bits of current furniture awaiting the next visit of the furniture doctor. Brand-new duplicates of many of the current standard items, all ready and waiting to be deployed within minutes if something dire happened in one of the rooms. Seasonal items, like the patio tables and umbrellas. Two or three flatbed dollies big enough to haul any large items of furniture—or Percival's cage, when I'd had to bring it down here. A collection of vacuum cleaners—new ones ready to be put in service when the current ones began to wear out, and malfunctioning ones that could be scavenged for parts. It was a lot better organized than it had been before Ekaterina had taken over as manager, but even she was finding it took time to figure out what could go and what needed to stay.

Percival's enormous cage stood in the middle of an open space to the right of the door. He was facing away from the door, but when I came in he swiveled his head 180 degrees to look back at me and blinked sleepily.

"Hey, Perce," I said. "Cricket time."

He came to attention when I went over to the collection of terrariums and cages where his meals lived. I tried to not even see the cage of mice. If he'd been a reptile, and willing to eat frozen mice, I might have obliged. But owls, I'd been told, only ate live prey. Not happening today. I peered into the other crates—aha. Plenty of crickets. I opened a little door in the side of the cricket cage, shook out a cricket, and quickly snagged him with the ice tongs I'd brought down after the last time I'd done this. It's not as if I couldn't pick up a live cricket if I had to, but if I didn't have to . . .

Percival flapped his wings—you could see that the injured one wasn't quite healed yet, but he looked a lot better than the first time I'd seen him.

"Knock your socks off," I said, and flicked the cricket at his head.

He caught it very neatly, swallowed it whole, and looked expectantly at me.

I continued tossing crickets at him until he began to seem less keen.

"That will have to do you for now," I said. "I'll send Dad or Horace down later to do the mice."

He rustled his wings, settled down on his perch, pulled his head closer to his body, and closed his eyes.

"Merry Christmas, Perce," I said.

I heard rustling somewhere nearby and jumped slightly. Percival opened one eye, decided it was nothing interesting, and closed the eye again.

"Not mice, then, I hope." At least not any mice other than the ones sleeping in their cage. Although it would be a miracle if the storage room didn't have mice of its own. I'd suggested to Ekaterina that we turn Percival loose in here for a while, just to make sure, but she hadn't been thrilled by the idea. I suspected Grandfather had been doing it anyway when he came down here, letting Percival take short hops to test his almost-healed wings. What Ekaterina didn't know wouldn't hurt her.

The rustle came again, but this time I could tell it was outside the storage room. I made sure Percival's water supply was full and left.

And immediately spotted someone at the other end of the hall.

"Hello?"

The figure turned and I recognized Mr. Ackley.

"Thank God," he said. "I thought I heard a noise down this hall. Do you know the way out of here?"

"Yes," I said. "What are you doing down here, anyway?"

"Long story," he said.

"Long way back to civilization." I reached the part of the hall where he was standing. "We've got time."

"Don't tell my wife," he said. "I was looking for someplace to smoke a cigarette. I've technically quit, you understand. But sometimes when things get stressful I backslide a little. Just one. Two at the most. Helps the nerves. And this whole storm thing has been stressful."

"Not a smoking zone down here." I set off along the route that would eventually lead to the elevator.

"Didn't figure it was," he grumbled as he fell into step beside me. "I was trying to find the loading dock. Figured smoking there would be okay. Couldn't find it on the main floor, so I thought maybe it was down here."

"It's on the main floor," I said. "But they've rolled the security door down, so even if you found your way there it probably didn't look like a loading dock. And you couldn't smoke there if the door's not open."

"Figures."

"If you can't do without a smoke, go out the front door," I said. "Technically the hotel has a rule that you have to go to the gazebo to smoke, but I doubt if they've bothered to shovel a path to it, and I can't imagine anyone would care or even notice you smoking out front in this weather, as long as you bring the butts back inside and throw them away discreetly."

"Tried that," he said "Took about thirty seconds before I came back inside to look for a warmer option. And to top it all off I dropped my cigarettes somewhere down here. Got turned around looking for them. You haven't seen them by any chance? Almost full pack of Marlboro Reds?"

I shook my head.

"And I bet the hotel gift shop doesn't sell tobacco products." No, thanks to Ekaterina's disapproval, it didn't. "Guess I'll have to wait for my nicotine fix till the storm breaks."

I was glad to note that he sounded reasonably philosophical about this.

"How'd you get down here, anyway?" I said.

"Found a door propped open. Thought I'd had a bit of luck, but pretty soon I figured out all the doors down here were locked. Except for a couple that led outside, into the snow, and that wasn't happening. Couldn't even figure out which door I'd come in by—I guess someone noticed it was propped open and shut it. This is a staff-only place, right?"

I nodded.

"Then I'm going to file a complaint about the staff member who ran away instead of helping me."

"Staff member?" Running away didn't sound like something any of the Inn's staff ever did. "Are you sure it was a staff member? Did you see them well enough to give a description?"

"No. They were at the other end of a long corridor, and the lights were so dim all I saw was a figure. I shouted for help and whoever it was ran away. I assumed it had to be a staff member, with everything around here locked up."

"Maybe it was someone else who'd gotten in through the same propped-open door you used," I pointed out. "In which case they might have run away because they thought you were a staff member about to catch them trespassing."

"Never thought of that. How much longer is it going to take to get out of this maze?"

"Almost there." I pointed ahead. "There's the freight elevator."

"Good. My wife will be frantic. She's got no one to talk to but me. No one sane. Just who are these people, anyway? The ones having the meeting here at the Inn."

"Ornithologists." Noticing his blank look, I added, "They study birds—specifically owls, in the case of the ones at this conference."

"The things some people get paid to do." From his grumpy look, I gathered he didn't think much of ornithology as a profession. I tried to think of another topic for conversation, but most of the topics that ran through my brain had something to do with the conference, so I was relieved when we reached the elevator and I could see him safely back to the parts of the hotel where guests were supposed to be lurking.

And I reminded myself that I should cut him some slack. He had a reason to be grumpy, given that he and his wife might not make it home to spend Christmas with their family. Never mind that theirs was an utterly predictable plight. How had they ignored the massive media coverage of the approaching storm, complete with stern warnings that if you wanted to be someplace for Christmas you might want to get there by December 20?

As we drew near the freight elevator, he clutched my arm and pointed.

"See that!

"That's the door to the main lobby," I said. "Comes out by the guest elevators."

"No, on the top of the doorframe. It's a doorstop. I didn't see it until just now. This must be where I came in."

Yes, there was a rubber doorstop on top of the doorframe—rather inconspicuously.

"Glad we figured that out," I said as I used my key card to let us into the lobby.

"See you," he said as he trudged across the lobby. I refrained from wishing him a Merry Christmas. No sense rubbing his nose in his plight.

After that, the afternoon wore on at a snail's pace. The afternoon panels ran an hour and a half instead of the mere hour of the morning ones, so I was able to catch the end of a one o'clock panel in which Dr. Hirano, the elderly and distinguished Japanese owl expert, and Dr. Bateman, a grizzled British scientist with a mellifluous voice, gave a joint presentation on the several new owl species they'd recently discovered—Dr. Hirano's finds were in the jungles of the Philippines, while Dr. Bateman and his team had been prowling the deserts of the Arabian

Peninsula. I began to revise my opinion of the ornitholo-gists as bespectacled sedentary souls. They were mostly be-spectacled, actually, but I was beginning to realize why it had been so difficult to convince them that the blizzard was sufficient reason to cancel the midnight owling expedi-tions we'd originally planned. And having dealt with kraits, cobras, and camels in the course of their expeditions, the two adventurous scientists seemed to take Dr. Frogmore's sarcastic comments from the back row in their stride.

At two thirty, Grandfather's latest presentation went well—it was less about science than about effective tech-niques of explaining scientific information to influential nonscientists such as legislators and bureaucrats. And he, too, ignored Dr. Frogmore's sniping with such sublime composure that I started to wonder if perhaps it was time to take him in for a hearing test.

The four o'clock panel, moderated by Dr. Craine, was about reverse sexual dimorphism in owls. Much as I liked Dr. Craine, I decided I could live without spending an hour and a quarter listening to a panel of ornithologists debating their various theories about why female owls tended to be larger than the males. I spent the time going over the banquet plans with Ekaterina instead, which meant that I missed the moment when Dr. Craine told Frogmore that if he interrupted her panelists one more time she'd physically kick him out of the room. Although Rose Noire told me all about it, her voice full of outrage because Ben Green was one of the panelists being inter-rupted. With any luck, given all the cell phones in the room, there would eventually be video.

Technically, there were also roundtable discussions going on in the Lafayette Room during these panels, but by now even the attendees who were supposed to lead these discussions had given up pretending they were going to happen. I wasn't sure whether this indicated that the panels Grandfather had arranged were of such compelling interest that no one wanted to miss one, or whether the community, despite its fussing and fighting, preferred to stay together in a single noisy group. Either way, it was a relief not to see the forlorn faces of neglected discussion leaders peering out of the doorway of the Lafayette Room. I made a note to remind Grandfather of this next year.

Dr. Craine's panel ended at five thirty, giving the attendees half an hour's break before the banquet began. Most of the attendees either headed off to their rooms to change into something fancier or hit the bar to get a head start on the evening's celebration.

Grandfather followed me to the ballroom to inspect the decorations. Thanks to the popularity of the Harry Potter books and movies, a wide variety of owl merchandise was available, so on each of the tables the circle of poinsettias was now crowned with an intricately painted resin replica of Hedwig, Harry's owl. Toy owls and paper owl banners had been added to the existing Christmas decorations without entirely spoiling their effect. I hoped that either the various owls we were displaying were depicted with a reasonable degree of scientific accuracy or the scientists would be too cheerful to complain about any shortcomings. And the huge full-colored posters of various owls had been provided by Grandfather, so I had no worries that they would offend any of the attendees. Although I had given orders to ensure that the barred owl poster had been hung in as inconspicuous a place as possible—in the corner where a giant Christmas tree obscured at least half of it, and completely across the room from the beleaguered spotted owl.

The owls must not have been too bad. Grandfather strolled around the room and nodded with pleasure.

"Yes, I think it looks fine." He was beaming with particular satisfaction at the poster of the great horned owl, which I'd hung as close to his table as possible, since it was his favorite.

"Why am I not at the head table?"

Chapter 10

We turned to find that Dr. Frogmore had picked up a paper I'd left on Grandfather's table, containing a list of people assigned to it.

"There is no head table," Grandfather said. "That's my table. I invited Dr. Hirano to sit with me because we haven't had a chance to talk for a couple of years, and Dr. Arai so he could translate. And the rest of my table's for my family. Most of the tables are open, except for a few groups of people who have asked to be seated together."

"Nonsense," Frogmore complained. "You've got to have a head table for a banquet. And I should be at it." He was patting his pockets as if looking for a pen. If he tried to change the table roster, I'd smack his pen out of his hand.

"Fine—that's the head table." Grandfather pointed to the table next to ours. "Why don't you take charge of it? Invite whomever you like."

"Don't be ridiculous," Frogmore snarled.

"Ekaterina!" Grandfather waved his arms to catch her attention and she joined us, wearing what I thought of as her locked-and-loaded smile—utterly pleasant, but not taking it for granted that pleasant would continue to be relevant.

"That's the head table." Grandfather pointed again. "Dr. Frogmore's sitting there. And whoever else he invites. Make sure they get served first. With the best of everything."

"Of course, Dr. Blake."

"Meg, can you get someone to run off a sign. Two signs. One that says 'head table' and another that says 'Dr. Blake's family table'?"

"No problem." I ostentatiously made an entry in my notebook.

"Hmph." Frogmore frowned at us all and strode away. His expression suggested that he wasn't yet sure if he'd won or if Grandfather was making fun of him.

"Every table will be getting exactly the same excellent food." Ekaterina sounded a little annoyed. "Do you want me to do something special for the new head table? Complementary wine, perhaps?"

"Don't be daft." Grandfather snorted slightly. "Just give Frogmore first crack at what we're all getting. That should shut him up."

"And have your staff treat him with exquisite politeness," I added.

"I will instruct the waitstaff to address him frequently by name," she said. "It will make him feel important. And I'll make sure Raoul is assigned to his table. Raoul can be very deferential."

"Raoul can be downright obsequious," I said. "Frogmore will eat it up."

We smiled at each other and she dashed off.

I checked the guest list for Grandfather's table, to make sure no one had tampered with it. We'd fended off Frogmore, but his minion could still be skulking around, plotting to interfere with Grandfather's plans. No, everything looked fine. DR. J. MONTGOMERY BLAKE. DR. ETSUJI HIRANO. DR. HIRO ARAI. DR. AND MRS. JAMES LANGSLOW. DR. MICHAEL WATERSTON. MS. MEG LANGSLOW. MS. ROSE NOIRE KEENAN.

"If I hold another owl conference anytime soon, I'm going to ban him," Grandfather said. "Gives me indigestion, having to be polite to him."

"So glad you're not trying, then," I murmured.

"What was that?"

"I said no need, just warn me and I'll lose his registration form."

Grandfather nodded and strode off.

Had I taken care of everything? I pulled out my notebook and flipped to the page about the banquet as I went back into the Gathering Area. Rose Noire and Melissa were sitting behind the registration/information table, having what looked to be a lively conversation as they folded something. Aha—the programs. Luckily, according to my notebook, they were the only outstanding banquet item.

"We'll have them all folded in about ten minutes," Rose Noire said as I drew near. "And then we can put them at the tables."

"Any chance one of you could find the wherewithal to make a couple of signs?" Rose Noire nodded, so I explained about the two signs and she dashed off toward the business center.

I sat down and took over her share of the folding.

"I almost didn't come because of him," Melissa said. "Almost backed out of volunteering when I saw his name on the program."

"Frogmore?"

"Yes." She nodded. "I was afraid just seeing him would send me back into the same dark place I was in after Buckthorn rejected me. But you know what? It's been strangely freeing, seeing him here. He's still got power—but not as much as he used to. Not as much as he thinks he has. The world's moving on, and he's not."

"So your feelings toward him are mellowing?"

"Hell, no." She gave a snort of laughter. "I still hate him. But now I realize—everybody hates him. I'm completely normal. That's strangely empowering."

"A relief to know I'm normal, too."

Rose Noire came back with the signs. If I'd been making them, I wouldn't have added flying cartoon owls to the top corners and cute mice scampering along the bottom—especially since, as any of the owl experts would be delighted to explain, the wise owls would be looking at the adorable little mice as hors d'oeuvres. But I try never to complain when people do me a favor, so I thanked her and dashed in to put the signs in place before heading back to the cottage to dress.

As I crossed the President's Garden, I couldn't help thinking how odd it was going to be, dressing up in our elegant finery with the blizzard still raging. Although raging was hardly the right word. The wind had died down—a good thing; we didn't need huge drifts piling up. At any given moment that you looked out the windows, all you saw were snowflakes. Snowflakes so tiny and delicate that you could hardly imagine them causing a problem. But they'd been coming down steadily for a little over twenty-four hours now, and showed no signs of stopping. And I remembered a conversation I'd had once with a friend, Judge Jane Shiffley.

"Big snow, little snow; little snow, big snow," she'd said.

I must have looked puzzled—I certainly was puzzled, since this sounded like nonsense, and Judge Jane's pronouncements usually reflected in equal measure both her keen legal mind and her down-to-earth country woman's common sense.

"Old folk saying," she explained. "If you're getting big wet flakes, it's probably too close to freezing, the snow will melt, and you won't get that much accumulation. But when it's really cold, you're more apt to get small, dry flakes, so watch out! Those tiny, determined little flakes are a lot more likely to add up to a big accumulation."

Determined little flakes, yes. In fact, inexorable, I

thought, as I looked up toward the sky and saw nothing but thousands of them drifting down toward me.

In the cottage, Michael, already in his tuxedo, was sitting on one of the sofas while the boys gave his dress shoes a vigorous polish. A polish that probably wouldn't survive our trip across the icy courtyard, but the boys were having fun.

Horace, now happily released from the warm, wet washcloth therapy, was sitting on the sofa in a set of borrowed sweats, flipping through a pile of DVDs.

"You're welcome to come to the banquet if you like," I told him. "No problem squeezing in another chair. And the black tie is optional—Michael's just wearing it because he's appearing onstage."

"The boys and I have already ordered from room service," he said. "And we're going to wallow in Christmas movies—Ekaterina's got a great selection. *Scrooged, Bad Santa, Die Hard, Elf, Gremlins, A Charlie Brown Christmas, Mr. Magoo's Christmas Carol, The Nightmare Before Christmas, How the Grinch Stole Christmas, Miracle on 34th Street, It's a Wonderful Life, Home Alone . . .*"

"You'll be watching from now until next Christmas," I said. "No *Love Actually*?"

"I didn't think the boys would like it." Horace probably had a point.

"Is it inappropriate?" Josh asked, with keen interest.

"Not that I remember," I said. "You're welcome to watch it if you like, but it's mostly about grown-ups falling in love and proposing to each other. There is a subplot about a kid your age who has a crush on a girl."

"Ick," Josh said, in a perfunctory tone. He and Jamie returned to their polishing.

"If you need us, use this." Michael was handing Horace a walkie-talkie.

I ran into the bedroom and threw on my outfit—a long

black knit dress that draped over my body, rather than clinging to it, a red velvet jacket in case the ballroom got chilly, and a pair of low-heeled shoes that felt dressy to me, although Mother had been known to sigh whenever she saw them. I didn't care. If I was going to be running errands for Grandfather and interference for all the warring ornithologists, I didn't want to be tottering around on heels.

I didn't even want to think about crossing the icy courtyard in heels. Even in my flats, it was nice to be able to hold on to Michael's arm as I did so.

"Cheer up," he said as we stepped into the lobby and shook the snow off ourselves. "Two days down, one to go."

"They won't all leave tomorrow, you know."

"But after the last panel, they'll be mostly Ekaterina's problem, not yours," he countered. "Oh, I know you'll want to help her, but you'll be helping—not in charge."

"I like the way you think."

"Are they going to mistake me for one of their own?" Michael was glancing down at his name tag, which identified him as Dr. Michael Waterston, Caerphilly College.

"You might be too well dressed for an ornithologist. And can you hold your own in a conversation about the conservation status of the barking owl and the chocolate boobook?"

"I'll just nod a lot," he said. "And sip my drink. Assuming I ever get a drink." The pre-banquet cash bar had been set up in the Gathering Area, and the scientists were lining up in droves to patronize it. The hum—no, make that the roar—of conversation almost drowned out the Christmas carols playing over the room's speakers.

Ekaterina appeared.

"The people in owl costumes want me to let them into the ballroom now," she said. "Is that permitted?"

"Yes," I said. "Probably a good idea to let them check out the stage. Reduces the chances that they will fall off of it. Shall I come and shepherd them?"

"That would be most appreciated."

I left Michael explaining to two scientists that no, his Ph.D. was in the dramatic arts, and followed Ekaterina down the corridor to where the group of faux owls was waiting. Or should I call them a parliament?—which, as Dad was so fond of explaining, was the proper name for a group of owls.

There were nine of them: Dad, the five other die-hard SPOOR members who were willing to be snowbound in the hotel for several days to give their performance, and three conference attendees who'd been recruited for either their singing ability or their willingness to get up on stage and demonstrate their lack thereof to the whole conference. All of them were costumed as various species of owl. I only recognized a few, but I'd learned not to ask which species if I didn't have half an hour free to listen to the costume's wearer extoll its incredible accuracy.

Dad, appearing as a great horned owl, was passing out Santa hats, and Rose Noire, the barn owl, was dashing about with safety pins and hairpins, anchoring the hats so they wouldn't fall off during the simple but vigorous choreography that usually accompanied SPOOR's songs.

"Okay," Dad said. "Let's go check out the stage, and then we'll take our places backstage to wait until everyone's seated."

They set off—jingling all the way. Apparently along with the Santa hats, Dad had persuaded them to don anklets studded with sleigh bells. Some of them seemed to be enjoying this, stamping their feet with enthusiasm as they made their way through the ballroom. Others—quite possibly the last-minute recruits—appeared to be regretting the life choices that had brought them to this moment.

I gave them fifteen minutes to familiarize themselves with the stage. Then I shooed them backstage and had the waitstaff open the doors to let in the crowd. I stood near the podium and watched as the more agile of the scientists bounded into the room to claim the best tables for themselves, while the rest followed at a more sensible pace and colonized the remaining tables. Next year—if there was a next year—we'd assign tables beforehand. Though I noticed that nearly all of the attendees were cheerful and cooperative about switching seats so couples and groups could be seated together. Some of the attendees had dressed up for the occasion, with long dresses for the women and suits or even black tie for the men, while others came in the same track suits or jeans and T-shirts they'd worn to the conference—and none of them seemed to care if their tablemates were over- or underdressed.

Our table, of course, was very elegant, with all the men in suits—even, to my astonishment, Grandfather—while Mother, Rose Noire, and I wore long dresses. Granted, Rose Noire's dress was a long gauzy one she also wore for the nicer sort of picnic, but still—we looked festive.

The only trouble spot in the room was the head table, which wasn't filling up very fast. Dr. Frogmore and Dr. Czerny sat there, beaming proudly, until it became obvious that every table other than their own was going to be filled.

"Bloody hell." I glanced over to see Nils Lindquist standing by my side. "Someone's got to sit with the wretched man or he'll be even harder to be around than he already is. Come on, Ben. Ornithology expects every man to do his duty."

"Every person," Dr. Green corrected. He cast a longing glance at Grandfather's table, where Rose Noire was sitting, which had no more empty chairs, then followed

Dr. Lindquist to the head table and ended up serving as a buffer between him and Dr. Frogmore. The rest of the table was finally filled up with latecomers—three young men who didn't seem caught up in the general frenzy of greeting and catching up. Grad students, I thought, attending their first conference, or junior professors who hadn't yet made many friends in the field. From the anxious expressions they all wore you'd have thought that instead of HEAD TABLE Rose Noire had accidentally posted a sign that said PRISONERS WAITING TO BE EXECUTED MAY EAT THEIR LAST MEALS HERE.

Michael took the stage and tapped on the microphone. I'd recruited him to serve as master of ceremonies after Grandfather, presented with the short list of people he should introduce or thank, had said, "Nonsense—just let them read the program."

"Ladies and gentlemen," he said. "While the waiters are serving your salads and beverages, may I present for your entertainment—the song stylings of SPOOR!"

The SPOOR members rushed out on stage in a frenzy of jingling bells and rustling feathers, and launched into their first number:

"I saw three owls come flying in
On Christmas day, on Christmas day,
I saw three owls come flying in
On Christmas day in the morning.

"What did they carry, those ow-ulls three,
On Christmas day, on Christmas day?
A rat, a vole, and a fat mousie
On Christmas day in the morning."

The song went on for several more verses than I remembered there being in the original carol, and the whole time they did their signature dance move—kicking alternately to the left and the right with more enthusiasm than precision. The bells, I decided, had actually been a good decision—they made it harder to notice how rare it was for all nine owls to be singing in precisely the same key.

The crowd loved it anyway. Well, most of the crowd. Dr. Frogmore wore the sort of outraged expression you'd expect to see on the face of the town prude if you tricked her into attending a drag show. And I suspect his mood wasn't much improved by the fact that the SPOORettes nearest him were coming perilously close to brushing the top of his head with their kicks.

They followed their first number with "Deck the Owls" and then, for a sentimental conclusion, "Owl Be Home for Christmas" before prancing offstage to "We Wish You an Owly Christmas."

"Well, that went better than I expected," Michael murmured when they were safely offstage. Indeed, renewed applause greeted the carolers when they reemerged, divested (for the most part) of their costumes and took their seats at various tables.

In fact, the whole banquet went better than expected. Grandfather and Dr. Hirano carried on a lively conversation—through Dr. Arai—that started off on owls but quickly migrated onto the cooking of the Philippines and Vietnam, and professional baseball. To Mother's delight, Dr. Arai also proved knowledgeable about *ikebana*, and he very much seemed to enjoy discussing *wabi-sabi* with Rose Noire.

The only blight on our meal was the voice of Dr. Frogmore at the adjoining table. When not berating the waitstaff for some imagined shortcoming or calling for another glass of wine, he seemed insistent on telling the occupants of his table a lengthy and convoluted story about how he'd shown up someone or other as a fool and an imposter. People at the far end of the room could probably have followed the story if they tried. I managed to relegate his booming, pompous voice to the status of annoying background noise.

The other unfortunates at his table merely chewed glumly and tried to look interested—except for Dr. Lindquist and Dr. Green who, having apparently discovered that they shared a knowledge of American Sign Language, used it for a steady exchange of snarky comments. Well, Lindquist was snarky. Green mostly just agreed with him with a lugubrious expression on his face, as he watched Rose Noire conversing so enthusiastically with Dr. Arai. My ASL wasn't all that good, but I understood enough that I had to struggle not to burst out laughing at times.

Maybe I should have felt sorry for his tablemates, but I found myself feeling even sorrier for Dr. Frogmore himself. In spite of his bluster, he didn't seem to be having a good time. Toward the end of the meal he began rubbing his temples as if his head bothered him, and he snapped at Dr. Czerny to give him an aspirin. Dr. Czerny turned pale when he realized he didn't have any, which led to a general search of pockets until someone at the table—possibly Dr. Green—found him some. I wasn't sure whether to feel guilty that I hadn't rushed over with aspirin as soon as I figured out he needed them or relieved that someone else had taken care of it.

But everyone else was having a great time, and soon it was time for dessert, to be accompanied by Dr. Hirano's keynote speech. The waiters were circulating with platters of crème brûlée and chocolate mousse, and offering the diners their choice of champagne, dessert wine, or sparkling apple juice.

"Let 'em know Hirano's going on next," Grandfather said to Michael.

Michael mounted the small stage, made the next round

of thank-yous—to SPOOR and the hotel kitchen and waitstaff. Then he introduced the two Japanese scientists. But as they stepped forward to their twin microphones, and the audience members began hushing each other, Dr. Frogmore's voice boomed out.

"Oh, great," he said. "This should be rich. He wanders out into the jungle and claims he's found a new owl. I'll believe it when I see it." His face was flushed, as if the many glasses of wine and whiskey were taking effect, and his voice was ever so slightly slurred.

"Now, now," Dr. Green said in a low tone. "He's our guest."

"Not my guest," Dr. Frogmore boomed. "Don't ask me why Blake doesn't ask me to give the keynote, instead of some over-the-hill Jap who never bothered to learn English."

Disapproving murmurs ran through the room. Dr. Hirano looked puzzled. Dr. Arai looked furious.

"But tha's okay," Frogmore went on. "Le's have a toast!" He sprang to his feet. "To all the stupid people at the stupidest conference I've ever seen!" He tossed off the contents of his champagne flute. "I hope you—hope you—!"

His face turned even redder than before and he collapsed, like a puppet whose strings had been cut.

Chapter 11

Dad was already racing to Dr. Frogmore's side.

"Give him some air!" he shouted. And then, over his shoulder to me, "Call Horace. Have him bring my bag." Horace was an EMT as well as a deputy, so that made sense. I pulled out my walkie-talkie.

"Dr. Frogmore! Are you all right?" Dr. Czerny was bending over Frogmore and shaking him.

"Let's stand back so the doctor can take care of him." Dr. Lindquist and Dr. Green dragged Dr. Czerny away so Dad could tend to Frogmore.

As I waited for Horace to respond, I surveyed the room. People weren't rushing over to gawk, thank goodness. Okay, they were all staring, and a few had climbed onto the seats of their chairs to get a better view, but they weren't crowding around and getting into Dad's way. And—

"Meg? What's up?" Horace answered.

"Medical emergency in the ballroom," I said. "Dad said to call for your help. And bring his bag."

"On my way," he said.

Michael had dashed back onto the stage.

"If there are any other medical professionals here who could help Dr. Langslow, please come up to the front of the room," he said. "Everyone else, please keep your seats."

No one stepped forward.

I couldn't see what Dad was doing, but I had a bad feeling when he snapped out an order to Dr. Frogmore's tablemates to help him move the patient to the next room.

Dr. Lindquist and the three late-arriving young men stepped forward, lifted Frogmore easily, and carried him off at a jogging pace with Dad urging them on. Dr. Czerny tagged along with a stricken expression on his face.

Was Dad moving Frogmore to someplace where he could treat him better? Or was he only moving him so the rest of the attendees wouldn't have to watch him die—or stare at his already dead body?

And they'd carried him into the kitchen, I noticed. Horace ran into the ballroom just as they disappeared, and I pointed the way to him. I followed him to the door and paused on the threshold. Part of me wanted to follow. The rest of me thought that was a really stupid idea. So I was still lingering just outside the door when Horace stuck his head out again.

"Your dad says to secure Frogmore's plate and glass."

I nodded.

"I'll do it, at least for now." Michael had come up behind me. Now he strode over to the depleted head table, took up a position behind where Frogmore had been sitting, and surveyed the room. His posture was casual, as if he were standing there because it gave him the best vantage point for seeing what was going on in the room, but when one of the waitstaff approached the table, he was quick to warn her off.

Grandfather mounted the stage, said a few quiet words to Dr. Arai, and then approached the microphone.

"We don't yet know what's wrong with Dr. Frogmore," he said. "We'll tell you when we find out. And for those of you who haven't met him yet, my son, Dr. James Langslow, is an excellent physician, and emergency medicine is one of his special interests. Dr. Frogmore is in good hands."

That was certainly true. Nothing Dad loved better than a nice, dramatic emergency. And there really wasn't any need to mention that he was also the local medical examiner. We could all hope that wouldn't become relevant.

"So if you'll all just take your seats, I'm sure Dr. Hirano and Dr. Arai will do their best to carry on with the keynote speech."

Muted applause. The men who'd carried Dr. Frogmore out reappeared, and seeing that the regular program was getting back underway, they quickly took their seats—although I suspected the three long-suffering juniors were all looking forward to telling their adventures to their friends when the speechifying was over.

Grandfather returned to our table. Before sitting down, he spoke to me in what for him was a fairly quiet tone.

"Find out what's going on and keep me posted."

I nodded and headed for the door through which they'd taken Frogmore—one of the two doors that led to the kitchen. Three of the servers were peering out, wide-eyed.

"Where did they take him?" I asked them in an undertone.

"This way, ma'am," said the oldest, a fortyish woman. "Into the Lafayette Room."

Dr. Hirano said a few words in Japanese.

"Ladies and gentlemen," Dr. Arai translated.

I slipped through the door the server was holding open for me and followed her along the outer fringe of the kitchen. I'd been here a couple of times before during banquets—usually fund-raising events Mother had organized for one or another of the charities she supported. Normally at this point in a banquet, the cooks would be starting to relax while the servers would still be busy with coffee, tea, and water refills. And the dishwashing staff would be frantic. But a hotel security guard stood in front of the dishwashing machine, arms crossed. The coffeepots and pitchers of hot and cold water stood unnoticed on a counter just inside the door. All of the restaurant staff were standing in small clusters, talking.

My guide opened another door and I stepped out of the kitchen into a corner of the Lafayette Room—a corner at the front of the room, just by the podium. Ekaterina was standing with her back to me, but she evidently heard my arrival and moved aside so I could see what was happening. Oliver Frogmore lay on the floor. Dad and Horace knelt on either side of him, with Dad's medical bag close at hand. Frogmore's shirt had been ripped open, and I could see a few bits of medical waste lying on the floor—wrappers, a syringe, a little empty vial of some medicine. Evidently, Dad had injected Frogmore with something in an attempt to save him. But just as evidently, Dad's efforts had been in vain. Dad and Horace were motionless, looking down with glum expressions. Frogmore's face was beet red and contorted, as if he'd died in the middle of a monumental temper tantrum.

Dr. Czerny was sitting on a chair in the middle of the first row of seats with his head in his hands, rocking back and forth like a self-soothing child.

"Time I officially pronounced," Dad said. He glanced at the wrist where his watch would be if he ever bothered to wear it, then looked up at Horace.

"Nine fourteen," Horace said.

I inched a little closer to Frogmore's feet.

"We lost him." Dad looked up at me, his face bleak. "Time of death, nine fourteen."

"If it hadn't been for the snow, maybe we could have gotten him to a hospital," Horace said. "Maybe—"

"I doubt it." Dad shook his head. "It happened too fast."

"Was it mushrooms?" Ekaterina asked.

"What mushrooms?" Dr. Czerny looked up, his face suddenly furious. "You served him mushrooms?"

"No, we didn't serve anyone mushrooms," Ekaterina

said. "But there has been such a fuss about the mush-rooms that I'm sure everyone at the conference knew he was allergic to them. Including anyone who was not fond of him."

"If you fed him mushrooms—" Czerny began.

"This doesn't present anything like an allergic reaction to mushrooms." Dad's voice cut through Czerny's with the commanding note it only held when he was in the middle of a medical emergency.

"You can't know that," Czerny said.

"Actually, I can, to a reasonable degree of certainty," Dad said. "I'm not seeing signs of anaphylaxis. No runny nose or rash, which is usually the first sign. No vomiting or diarrhea. No coughing or wheezing. No signs of swelling in the limbs, the lips, the mouth. He didn't appear to be having trouble breathing before he lost consciousness. We'll be able to tell for sure when we do the autopsy, of course, but I'd be astonished if this was an allergic reaction—to mushrooms or anything else."

"What do you mean, when you do the autopsy?" Czerny said. "I won't allow it! No one's cutting him open until the proper authorities get here."

"Actually, Dad is the proper authority," I said. "He's the local medical examiner."

"And I can't very well do an autopsy here," Dad said. "Not a real autopsy. We don't have the proper facilities."

"But you're not doing anything!" Czerny's voice sounded as if he might be heading toward hysteria. "Why aren't you doing something?"

"I am doing something." Dad's eyes were busy, studying Frogmore. "I can't do a full autopsy, but I can get as much information as possible from an external examination. Horace, we need pictures."

"Roger." A few seconds later Horace was clicking away with his cell phone.

"But you can figure out what happened to him?" Czerny asked.

"Yes." Dad was still studying Dr. Frogmore. "In time."

"And you can figure out who did it," Czerny added. "Someone poisoned him!"

"And possibly who did it." Dad's voice was cautious. "We don't know if it was poison."

"We don't know that it isn't!" Czerny said.

"So we call the chief," Horace said, although he didn't seem to be making a move to do so.

"And treat the ballroom as a crime scene." Dad nodded absently.

"Michael is guarding Dr. Frogmore's place," I said.

"The ballroom and the kitchen." Horace stood.

"About time!" Dr. Czerny looked slightly mollified.

"Meg—perhaps you could try to get through to the chief while I secure the crime scene." Horace held out his police radio. "You know more than I do about the deceased."

"Roger." I took the radio and made sure I knew which buttons to press. "I'll bring it back once I've notified you. You'll be in the ballroom?"

"Eventually," he said. "First I have to improvise a crime scene kit." Horace looked a little overwhelmed at the idea. "Mine's in the trunk of my cruiser. It's only a mile away, but—"

"Going out right now would be suicide," Dad said. "I should have some of what you need in my medical kit. And the hotel has a well-stocked clinic." As Dad well knew, since Ekaterina had given him a free hand in stocking it.

"I will help," Ekaterina said. "You will want gloves, I suppose. We have plenty of brand-new gloves."

"And evidence bags," Horace said.

"Plastic bags? Like food storage bags?"

"No, plastic retains moisture, and that tends to degrade

evidence. Paper bags—any chance you have an unopened package of paper bags—like lunch bags?"

"I think we have something that will serve."

"Before you go," Dad called out. Ekaterina turned. "What's happening in the ballroom now?"

Ekaterina frowned and looked at me.

"Dr. Hirano is making his speech," I said.

"Good." Dad nodded. "When he's finished, can we ask everyone to leave the ballroom so Horace can process it?"

"No problem," I said, and Ekaterina nodded in agreement.

"And we'll need a space in one of your refrigerators," Dad added, looking at Ekaterina. "To preserve the body."

"A refrigerator?" Ekaterina winced, then a stoic expression came over her face. "Of course. But would a freezer not be better?"

"No, no," Dad said. "Freezing would complicate the autopsy."

"I will make the arrangements. And help Horace assemble what he needs."

Clearly helping Horace pull together his crime scene kit was a more congenial occupation. They disappeared together into the kitchen. I knew I should go make the call to the chief, as Horace had asked, but I wasn't sure about leaving Dad to cope solo with Dr. Czerny.

"Do you know if he had any history of heart or circulatory system problems?" Dad looked up at Czerny. "Or—"

"His heart was fine! Don't pretend this is a heart attack! He—"

"The more I know about his medical history the better able I'll be to figure out what killed him," Dad said. "That includes any medications he was taking that might have interacted with whatever he ingested at dinner. So did he have heart problems?"

"No!" Then his face fell and his shoulders slumped. "At

least not that I knew. Then again, what do I know? He would consider that a weakness. He wouldn't want anyone else to know about his weaknesses—not even me. When he had his gallbladder out, he didn't tell anyone, not even me, until he was on his way to the hospital."

I was about to leave them to it when something occurred to me. Two somethings. I sent a quick text to Michael. And then I turned back to Dad and Czerny.

"Dr. Czerny," I said, "the police are going to want to notify Dr. Frogmore's next of kin as soon as possible. Do you know who that would be?"

He blinked and froze, looking stricken.

"I have no idea," he said finally. "I doubt if he's in touch with either of his ex-wives, and he didn't have kids with either of them. I've never actually heard him talk about family."

"I suppose we'll have to call the Buckthorn College human resources department," I said.

"They'd know." His voice was flat. "But they won't be there tonight, and tomorrow's Sunday."

"If Buckthorn College is anything like Caerphilly, a call to the right person would get the HR people scurrying in on a weekend," I said. "Of course, finding that right person's not going to be easy."

Czerny looked at me blankly for a few moments. Then a curiously triumphant smile lit up his face.

"Would the college president do? Because I can give you his number. His home number."

While he pulled out his phone, I grabbed my notebook and pencil.

"Dr. Hosmer Peverel," he pronounced, and rattled off a phone number with a 541 area code. Then suddenly he looked stricken again. "But don't mention my name. Just Dr. Frogmore's. I'm sure once he understands the circumstances he won't mind that I gave out his number, but—"

"But it would save a lot of explaining if we just let him think we found the number in Dr. Frogmore's belongings," I said. "No problem."

"Getting back to Dr. Frogmore's medical history," Dad said. "Apart from the gallbladder surgery, do you remember him mentioning any other medical issues?"

The door from the kitchen opened and the server who'd shown me the way ushered in two of the scientists—Dr. Lindquist and Dr. Green. I'd asked Michael to send them back. They stopped just inside the door and I met them there.

"Whoa," Lindquist said. "Not a false alarm, then."

"The poor man," Dr. Green muttered.

"Dr. Czerny's pretty upset," I said quietly enough that I didn't think Czerny could hear. "Can you figure out who knows him well enough to take care of him right now?"

They looked at each other. Lindquist shrugged. Green winced.

"I think he already lost the only friend he had here at the conference," Green said.

"If not in the world," Lindquist added.

"We'll look after him," Green said.

"See if you can coax him away when Dad's finished talking to him," I said. "Because I don't think having him around will help Dad figure out what happened to Frogmore."

"It wasn't a heart attack?" Green sounded surprised.

"They've got a guard over his place at the table," the more observant Lindquist said. "I figure you're suspecting poison."

"Right now we have no idea," I said. "Dad and Horace have a lot of work to do. So if you can take care of Czerny, it would be a big help."

"You've got it." Lindquist straightened his spine and

headed for where Czerny was sitting. Dr. Green took a few deep breaths before following.

I left the Lafayette Room, crossed the Gathering Area, and closeted myself in the tiny convention office.

And then I froze. I knew how to work the radio. But I had no idea what I was supposed to say on it. What if I didn't use the proper police lingo or—

"Just call," I told myself. "They'll know who you are. You don't have to pretend to be an officer."

Chapter 12

I took a deep breath and pressed what I hoped was the right button to let me talk over Horace's radio.

"Um . . . hello, this is Meg Langslow at the Caerphilly Inn. I'm trying to reach Chief Burke. Chief Burke, can you hear me?"

Static for fifteen seconds or so. Should I have said something to signal that I was done talking? Then the radio crackled into life.

"Meg, this is Debbie Ann. What's the problem? And how did you get a police radio?"

Not surprising that Caerphilly's dedicated dispatcher was monitoring her radio even in the middle of a blizzard.

"I'm on Horace's radio," I said. "Don't worry, he's fine. But we've had a death here at the Inn. A suspicious death. Dad and Horace thought that they should secure the scene at least until Dad can figure out if the guy died of natural causes or was poisoned. So Horace is securing the scene and asked me to get in touch with the chief."

"Oh, dear." Debbie Ann packed a lot of emotion into those two words. "Okay, I'll keep calling the chief. You or Horace should keep the radio nearby, so—"

"I'm here, Debbie Ann. Meg, this is Chief Burke. Are you saying you have a homicide?"

I should pick my words carefully, I realized. Almost anyone could be listening on the police band.

"Dad's not calling it a homicide yet. Suspicious death. But he told me to secure the victim's plate and glasses—

it happened during the banquet. So Michael's guarding them. And for the moment most of your suspects should be still in the ballroom, listening to the keynote speech."

"Ballroom," he groaned. "I bet that means you've got a whole passel of suspects there."

"About two hundred. Three hundred if you count the hotel staff and the handful of guests who aren't part of the convention, but I suspect most of them don't yet know Dr.— Don't know the deceased well enough to want to kill him."

"No way we can keep that many people cooped up until I can get there. It's not as if anyone can travel tonight. The temperature's already down to fifteen, and could drop below zero before morning. And the snow just won't quit. If I can get hold of Randall—"

"I'm here, Chief. Eavesdropping on y'all's conversation. You want me to run you out in the snowmobile as soon as it's safe to try? That probably won't be till morning."

"I'd appreciate it. We're holed up at New Life Baptist. Not that I mind roughing it without power, but it's hard on Minerva, and the kids were excited about having a big snow slumber party at the church and I wanted to be where I could keep my radio charged. And thanks to that generator you lent us, we're eating pretty high on the hog. You bring an appetite, and the ladies will cook you a gourmet breakfast before we set out. Or lunch, or whatever meal it's time for when the storm lets up enough for that snowmobile of yours to make the trip."

"It's a deal."

"Meanwhile," the chief went on, "let's do what we can. Meg, hearing from Randall just now was useful, but if we're going to talk any more about this case, let's do it over satellite phone—if you have one."

"We have several," I said. "I have Grandfather's, and Ekaterina has at least one for the hotel."

We exchanged satellite phone numbers and in another minute we were continuing the conversation by phone.

"Much better," the chief said. "And by the way, I appreciate your discretion on the radio. Now give me the whole story. Who's the deceased?"

"One of our conference attendees," I said. "Dr. Oliver Frogmore, from Buckthorn College in Oregon. We had just finished the banquet, and a distinguished visiting Japanese owl expert was about to give the keynote speech when Frogmore interrupted and started mouthing off— insulting the speaker and the conference generally. Then he got up to make a toast, tossed off the contents of his champagne flute, and collapsed."

"And your dad's sure it's not a heart attack?"

"I don't think he's sure of anything yet. He looks puzzled. And upset. The guy didn't die immediately, but Dad and Horace weren't able to save him. I think if it was a common or garden-variety heart attack, Dad would know it. He's seen enough of those."

"Poison, then? If he collapsed immediately after drinking the champagne?"

"Possibly. At least Dad must think so—as I said, he told me to secure Frogmore's plate and glasses. I assume Horace will bag them when he's free—you heard he was here, right?"

"I did, and was relieved to hear he was safe. We were worried for a while. And useful to have him there, since there's no way I can get there tonight. Does the deceased have family there with him?"

"We're not even sure he has family anywhere." I relayed what little I'd learned from Dr. Czerny, including the Buckthorn College president's name and number.

"I guess it's not too late to call this Dr. Peverel," the chief said. "He'd want to know one of his professors was dead. And it's only nine thirty."

"Which means only six thirty in Oregon, where Dr. Peverel should be," I said. "And Frogmore's not only a professor, he's a department head. And Dad would feel a whole lot better trying to figure out what the man died of if he knew more about his medical history."

"Understood. I'll call him right now, and call you back if he's able to offer any useful information. Meanwhile, tell Horace he's in charge of the investigation, but he should keep in close contact. I want to know exactly what's going on."

"Will do." I could only imagine how frustrating it was for the chief to have the storm cut him off from a murder investigation. Before coming to Caerphilly he'd been a longtime Baltimore homicide detective. Most of the time he was happier living in a small town where serious crime was relatively rare. But as he once admitted himself, the mere suspicion of murder got him revved up like a cat who hears a can opener.

"And a good thing my medical examiner's there on the spot, although I suspect your father won't be able to do a proper autopsy with no facilities."

"Right. I should probably reassure Ekaterina that Dad won't be using any of her food prep tables to cut up one of her guests."

"That would be a kindness," the chief said. "Although we'll need to use one of her refrigerators to preserve the body. I doubt if she'll like that."

"She doesn't, but she's already arranging it."

"Good. Why don't you go find Horace, give him back his radio, and tell him to call me on the satellite phone to brief me on what he's finding as he works the crime scene."

"Can do."

But before I walked out of the tiny office, Dr. Green walked in escorting a dazed-looking Dr. Czerny.

"Can we let Ned sit in here for a bit?" Dr. Green asked. "He's kind of in a state of shock."

"Of course." I stood up and stepped outside, and Dr. Green steered Dr. Czerny into the chair I'd vacated. "Do you think Dad should check him out?"

"When he has time," Dr. Green said. "I don't think it's urgent, and I know Dr. Langslow has a lot to do. But when he has time, yeah. Nils went to get him a drink."

We both studied Dr. Czerny, who sat slumped limply in the chair, staring into space.

"Can you keep an eye on him while I tell Nils where he is?" Dr. Green asked.

I nodded, and he ran off.

"My career is over." Dr. Czerny buried his face in his hands.

"Now, now," I said, and immediately regretted it. At least I'd refrained from patting him on the shoulder. When I was upset about something, few things irritated me more than people patting me on the shoulder and now-nowing me. "I'm sure it's not that bad."

"Actually, it is." He lifted his head and then grabbed both sides of it in what I assumed was a despairing gesture. And he was rocking again. "I'm not going to fool myself. I'm not a genius like he was. I have talents—talents he found useful. Organization. Hard work. And loyalty. He appreciated me. He protected me. But with him gone, they won't want to keep me around."

"But you're tenured, aren't you?"

"Tenured doesn't mean they can't fire you." He glared at me. "It just means it's harder. If they really want to get rid of you, they can find a way. You should know that."

"But it will take them time," I said. "Time you can use to find a way to make them want to keep you around. Time to find some other professor who would appreciate your organizational abilities and hard work." Surely with Frogmore running the department there must be other lazy and disorganized professors he could latch on to, though I couldn't think of a graceful way to say that aloud. And while I thought of adding "Someone who might treat you a little more nicely than Frogmore did," I decided that it was probably too soon to be speaking ill of the dead.

"I suppose they will want to keep me on to finish up his projects." Czerny's flat tone suggested that he wasn't all that sure. "I mean, everyone else has their own projects, right? They won't want to drop their own projects to work on something where they'd have to share the credit with a dead man. A dead man that most of them didn't like anyway. None of them ever really appreciated him." His voice turned angry, and he glared at me as if I was one of the unappreciative Buckthorn College faculty members.

I stifled another "now, now."

"Don't you think they'll feel differently under the circumstances?" I asked instead. "I mean, he was a very strong personality, so it's not surprising that there would be some friction while he was alive, but don't you think now that he's gone they'll start to realize what they've lost?" Actually, I suspected there would be champagne toasts in many circles when the news got out, including some at Buckthorn College—and, no doubt, in the Inn's bar—but this idea seemed to comfort Czerny.

"Yes—they'll be sorry." Not quite the effect I'd been aiming at. His voice had taken on a note of . . . menace? More like peevish satisfaction. "Really, really sorry."

Just then Dr. Lindquist ambled up carrying a glass.

"Whiskey." He handed the glass to Dr. Czerny, who took it mechanically and then looked down at it with a slightly puzzled expression.

"Take a sip," Dr. Lindquist advised. "You've had a shock."

Dr. Czerny obeyed. In fact, what he took was more of a

gulp than a sip. He gasped, coughed, and then took another swallow.

"You know who else will be sorry?" He looked up at me, ignoring Lindquist. "Whoever did this to him. I intend to make sure whoever did this is brought to justice." He fell silent and nodded to himself. "Yes. I'll make sure they pay. Virginia's a death penalty state, isn't it?"

With that he got up and ambled away, glass in hand—clearly lost in thought and with a slightly creepy smile on his face.

"Stay with him," I told Dr. Lindquist. "He's still in a state of shock."

"I liked him better mute," Dr. Lindquist said, but he did as I asked.

"Just what we need," I said to myself. "A vigilante." I figured I should warn Horace, so I set out to look for him. I could start in the Lafayette Room.

As I crossed the Gathering Area, I heard the sound of doors opening down the hallway that led to the ballroom. Followed by voices. I decided it might be a good thing to guard the door to the Lafayette Room.

Which was locked. I knocked, just to see what would happen. The door opened a foot, and Rose Noire stuck her head out.

"It's Meg," she called.

"She can come in," Dad replied.

"If you're going to be in here, maybe I can watch the door from the outside." She grabbed one of the ubiquitous stackable hotel chairs, dragged it just outside the door, and sat with a stern expression on her face. Why was I suddenly reminded of Gandalf, as played by Sir Ian McKellen, shouting "You shall not pass!" to the balrog? Rose Noire looked as if she was ready to challenge a balrog, and quite possibly capable of foiling it. Mere nosy ornithologists didn't stand a chance.

Dad was sitting on another stackable chair, gazing down at Frogmore's body.

The door to the kitchen opened, and I hurried over to fend off the intruders. But it was two kitchen staff members wheeling a long metal cart of some kind, and Dad seemed pleased to see them.

"Just what we need," he said. "Help me lift him onto it."

I decided that was addressed to the hotel employees, although they didn't look any more thrilled at the idea than I was. But they lifted Frogmore without difficulty, and scurried off looking relieved when Dad said he didn't need them anymore.

"Going to keep him here until Ekaterina has the refrigerator ready," he said. "And—oh, good; that must be her."

Actually, it was Horace, but Dad looked happy to see him anyway.

"How goes the processing?" he asked.

"Found something," Horace said. "Maybe it's nothing—or rather, maybe it's completely unrelated. But I found this under the table—the one Dr. Frogmore was sitting at."

He held up one gloved hand and displayed a small red-and-white bottle.

"Oh, my." Dad pushed his glasses up his nose to get a better view of the object. "Is that—?"

Horace nodded. "And nearly empty," he added.

"That could account for it." Dad steepled his fingers and stared into space, as if Horace's find required him to completely rearrange his thinking.

"Give me a clue," I said.

"Sorry." Horace moved his hand so I could see what Dad had. The label on the little bottle read NITROGLYC-ERIN LINGUAL SPRAY.

"That's used for heart problems, right?" I asked. "So does that mean heart attack?"

"Not necessarily," Dad said. "Nitroglycerin's usually

prescribed for angina pectoris—stable angina. If it belongs to Frogmore, it would mean he had some degree of coronary disease—but he could still have been a long way from a heart attack. We need to talk to his physician."

"The chief's working on that," I said.

"And we need to find out what other medicines he'd been taking," Dad said. "Of course, some heart attacks happen without any prior indications that there's a problem, or at least without the patient noticing such clues as there are and seeking medical attention. And it really doesn't present like a heart attack. Still—it would be worth looking for other medications—ACE inhibitors, beta-blockers, digoxin."

"How about if I go find Ekaterina, then, and tell her you want to search Dr. Frogmore's room," I suggested. "And then, if you could use my help—"

"Absolutely," Dad said, and Horace nodded.

"I'll change into something more suitable for snooping," I said.

"While you're there, ask her if she's got that refrigerator ready," Dad said absently. He was, for some reason I decided not to think about, taking off Dr. Frogmore's well-polished dress shoes.

I nodded and left the room. I resisted the temptation to take one last look at Dr. Frogmore's body.

Chapter 13

Out in the Gathering Area, several clumps of people were standing around holding glasses and conversing in low tones. They all looked up and stared at me. Rose Noire was still guarding the door, although she'd abandoned the chair and was sitting cross-legged on the floor with her eyes closed, doubtless performing some kind of meditation. A kind that would permit her to notice and fend off would-be lookie-loos, I hoped.

"Did someone break the news about Frogmore's death?" I asked.

"Michael made a very dignified announcement," she said. "And then we all had a minute of silence. It was quite moving. People still seem . . . subdued."

One of the small groups of attendees burst out laughing, and then quickly hushed themselves, looking around to see if anyone was offended.

"More subdued than last night," Rose Noire added.

"That wouldn't take much," I said. "Last night they were all but dancing on the tables." And I wondered if some of them were repressing the impulse to do so now. "I'm going back to the cottage to change into something more suitable for helping Horace and Dad. I see you've already managed." The long, ethereal, gauzy dress she'd worn to the banquet had been replaced by jeans and an embroidered peasant blouse.

"Your mother spelled me for long enough to change,"

she said. "And then she went off to make sure your grandfather gets his rest."

"Good." If Grandfather was feeling the least bit guilty
about his dislike for Frogmore, rest was the best thing for
him. Although about the most negative thing I recalled
hearing him say about Frogmore personally was that the
field of owl ornithology would be a lot more congenial
with him out of it. Then again, Grandfather wasn't nearly
as prone to guilt as I was. Any dismay he felt might be
largely offset by his relief at the prospect of seeing peace
and harmony restored to the field. If that were the case,
definitely a good thing if he'd gone to bed rather than
hanging about having to pretend a solemnity he didn't
feel. Nothing was more likely to put him in a foul mood.

Just then Dr. Green showed up carrying a tray that held
a teapot and two cups and saucers. To my surprise, he low-
ered his bearlike body into a cross-legged lotus pose beside Rose Noire, with an ease that suggested that he'd put
in some serious hours in yoga class.

"Thank you, Ben," Rose Noire said as Dr. Green handed
her a steaming cup. "Meg, would you like some?"

"I can fetch another cup and saucer," Dr. Green offered.

"Thanks, but I have to run." And even if I didn't have
to, I had detected the familiar unpleasant odor of one of
Rose Noire's famous herbal teas. Dr. Green was sipping
his cup with a look of bliss on his face. Either he was a
consummate actor, he had no taste buds, or he was truly
besotted with her.

"I'll be back," I said, in my best Terminator voice, and
headed for the lobby. I found Ekaterina in her public office, the one behind the reception desk. She seemed to
be tidying up, although, like any other space under her
supervision, the office was already impeccably organized.

"Horace needs a reasonably large space to serve as his
'command post.'" I could tell she liked the term. The of-

fice might just have been permanently rechristened. "I think this will work well."

"He'll be like a pig in clover." I realized as the words came out of my mouth that the idiomatic phrase might not be familiar to the Russian-born Ekaterina, so I went on. "Which is slang for very contented indeed. Any chance you could take Dad and Horace up to search Dr. Frogmore's room?" I'd let them do their own nagging about the refrigerator. It might be some time before I wanted to eat anything that had been in the Inn's refrigerators.

"Of course." She picked up several key cards from the little machine that made them and strode out of the Command Post. I followed her out and headed for the Madison Cottage.

The temperature had plummeted since the last time I'd ventured outside. I only had to be out in it for the few yards that separated the cottages from the main hotel, but my face and fingers were tingling by the time I stepped inside the Madison.

I found Michael and the boys in the living room, swaddled in blankets, watching *Die Hard*. Michael pressed the pause button when he saw me come in, and the boys jumped up to greet me.

"Finally," Josh said. "We have to go to bed early, and we thought you were going to keep us up."

"We want to get up early to get back to our digging," Jamie said.

"Digging?" I echoed.

"We're digging tunnels in the snow," Jamie said. "You want to see?"

They led me over to the French doors that opened out onto a small terrace that ran along the back of the cottage. The last time I'd looked through those doors, I'd seen nothing but snow, drifted some four feet high against the glass. Now I could see that the boys had excavated most of the terrace—an area five by ten feet—to form a cave about two and a half feet high. Along the walls of the cave, tunnels led off in various directions.

"That one goes to Great's cottage." Jamie pointed to the tunnel on the far right. "And from there to Grandpa and Grandma's cottage. That one in the middle goes out some way into the golf course. We meant it to go toward the hotel so we could go by tunnel to feed Percival, but we got turned around."

"So we started another one to go to Percival," Josh said, pointing to the left-hand tunnel. "It should only take us another hour or so to get there in the morning."

"What do you do with the snow you dig out?" I seemed to recall in movies like *The Great Escape* and *Escape from East Berlin* disposing of the dirt was always one of the biggest problems facing tunnel rats.

"We bring it in and put it in the bathtub to melt," Josh explained.

I made a mental note to tip the housekeeping staff more than usual.

"Time for us to get some sleep," Jamie announced. "See you in the morning."

They hurried off to the bathroom, and I heard the sound of toothbrushing.

"I'm not quite sure whether Horace allowed them to do the tunneling or whether they got started after he got called to the crime scene," Michael explained.

"Quite possibly they convinced him that we'd already given permission." I went into the bedroom to shed my finery, and he followed. "Seems reasonably harmless, as long as someone keeps an eye out to make sure they don't stay out too long."

"Which I plan to do if they're still determined to be tunnel rats in the morning," Michael said. "Strangely enough, it's warmer inside their tunnels. And look on the bright side—all that work is burning off an amazing amount of energy that might otherwise make them . . . just a little challenging to share the cottage with."

"Full speed ahead, then. They didn't ask about Frog-more?"

"I filled them in when I got here, and I guess that satisfied their curiosity." He frowned, and his jaw clenched slightly. "When I told them who it was, they said, 'Oh, the mean man.'"

"What did he do to them?" I probably sounded a little fierce, but the idea of Frogmore turning his venom on Josh and Jamie angered me.

"Nothing to them. Apparently they saw him yelling at your grandfather sometime Friday and took an immediate dislike to him."

"Sensible of them," I said. "Well, leave the light on, and expect me and Horace when you see us. Although we'll try not to wake you."

"Don't stay up too late." He gave me a quick kiss. "Solving Frogmore's murder is the chief's job, and you will still have a conference to run tomorrow."

Back in the lobby there were quite a few attendees milling about with drinks in their hands. Was the bar full to overflowing? Or had they figured out that the lobby was the better place to keep an eye on Horace's Command Post and get some clue about what was happening in the investigation

I went into the Command Post. Horace had definitely taken over. He'd improvised a stand for his police radio and had commandeered a satellite phone—not, I hoped, Ekaterina's only one, or she would be cranky. His makeshift forensic kit was arranged neatly on top of the desk. A canvas hotel laundry cart stood in one corner, half full of evidence bags. At least I assumed they were evidence bags. The paper bags Ekaterina had found for him to use were white with the Inn's logo embossed on them in gold—bags the kitchen used when a guest requested a lunch to take with them when on an all-day sightseeing or shopping trip. I wondered what the Crime Lab down in Richmond would make of them.

And there were rather a lot of them, from which I suspected that they'd made at least a preliminary foray into Frogmore's room.

Dad and Horace were engrossed in earnest discussion.

"Of course, it could be completely irrelevant," Dad was saying. "We won't know for sure until the autopsy."

"What could be completely irrelevant?" I asked.

"Everything I've collected, if it turns out he died of natural causes," Horace said. "But we have to keep going. And—"

"Dr. Langslow?"

Chapter 14

Ekaterina came in holding another satellite phone and a slip of paper.

"The chief called," she said. "He has notified Dr. Frogmore's employer, and obtained the name of his primary care doctor. He suggested that perhaps you should talk to the doctor and fill him in on what you learn. The doctor's expecting your call." She handed Dad a paper before disappearing again.

"Dr. Thomas Lanville," Dad said. "And another 541 area code."

Dad put the phone on speaker and dialed.

"Lanville." The voice was deep, gruff, and booming.

"Dr. Lanville, I'm Dr. James Langslow, the local medical examiner here in Caerphilly, Virginia. I have Deputy Horace Hollingsworth with me—he's our forensic expert, and also in charge of our on-site investigation—and my daughter Meg, who's helping us with logistics. Thank you for agreeing to talk to us—did Chief Burke explain the situation?"

"After a fashion. I gather you're snowbound in a five-star hotel, and instead of being able to relax and enjoy yourselves, you have a sudden and suspicious death on your hands, and no real facilities for investigating until the snowplows come to your rescue."

"That's pretty much it," Dad said. "And we understand the deceased was a patient of yours—Dr. Oliver Frogmore."

"Annoying man," Dr. Lanville said. "Sorry; not the

done thing, speaking ill of the dead, but he really was. Complete hypochondriac—the scientific kind. Gets it into his head there's something wrong with him, spends hours looking up symptoms, then storms in demanding treatment for something that it only takes a few simple tests to show is not the problem at all."

"Oh, yes," Dad said. "I know the kind, the ones who have every crackpot pseudo-medical site on the Internet bookmarked."

"Well, to Oliver's credit, he didn't much hold with Internet research," Dr. Lanville said. "If it wasn't the NIH or the Mayo Clinic, he had no time for it. Got himself a whole collection of medical reference books—dozens of them. Maybe hundreds. He used to inspect my bookshelves regularly to see if I had anything new. At least he wasn't a big TV watcher, thank God. I can't stand medical dramas, but my husband loves them. I get him to fill me in on what rare diseases they're featuring each week, so I can have a heads-up on what my hypochondriacs are going to come in with next. Oliver wasn't quite that bad, but still. There was the whole mushroom thing."

"Yes," Dad said. "We understand he was allergic to them."

"Nonsense! He was no more allergic to them than I am. We did three rounds of testing and there was no sign of any sensitivity to mushrooms. Or any of the other hundred or more possible allergens we tested for. What he had was gallbladder disease."

"Gallbladder disease," Dad echoed. "I wouldn't think that would present with symptoms that resembled mushroom allergy."

"No, it most certainly wouldn't," Dr. Lanville agreed. "You know how he came up with the mushroom allergy idea? He had an artery-clogging over-the-top five-course meal in one of Portland's most expensive French restaurants, and between the pâté and the duck confit and who knows what else—well, he made his long-suffering gall-bladder miserable on a truly epic scale. And then decided that the *sauce béchamel aux champignons* was to blame."

"Yes. Easier to give up mushrooms than fatty foods." Dad nodded as if he'd seen it all before.

"He ended up having his gallbladder out last year, and it was all I could do to keep from saying 'I told you so' afterward," Dr. Lanville said. "At least from what I can tell, he'd been doing reasonably well at keeping to a proper post-gallbladder-removal diet. Whining about it, but doing reasonably well. Was doing, rather. Still getting my head around the notion that he's dead."

"Did he have any heart trouble?"

"Not a bit of it," Dr. Lanville said. "Given his age—seventy-two this August—and his relatively sedentary life-style, that's one of the things I check on regularly. But he's fine there. Low cholesterol. Low-normal blood pressure. Passes the stress tests with flying colors. Got the cardio-vascular system of a man twenty years younger. And funny thing—in all his fits of hypochondria, I can't ever remember him convincing himself there was anything wrong with his heart."

"Perhaps because that's such a common ailment for men his age," Dad said. "All too real. And much more fun to imagine you've got something rare and wonderful."

"Much more fun!" Dr. Lanville hooted with laughter. "Yes, that's it exactly. And it would be all too ironic if he died of a heart attack—is that what you're leaning toward?"

"No," Dad said. "We won't know for sure until the autopsy, of course, but I saw what happened—I was sitting at the next table—and it didn't look to me like a heart attack."

"Any idea what it was?"

"Well . . . it's just speculation at this point. I only have what I observed to go on, both when he had his attack and when Horace, our EMT, and I were treating him. But I'm wondering if it could have been an overdose of vasodilators."

"Hmm . . . interesting." Dr. Lanville sounded thoughtful. And I'd have bet anything that if we could see him, his face would be wearing the same slightly puzzled frown that Dad was showing.

Since they showed no signs of explaining anything, I barged in with a question.

"That medicine Horace found under his table—is that a vasodilator?"

"Yes. A nitroglycerin lingual spray," he added over the phone for Lanville. "One that delivers 400 micrograms with each pump."

"He didn't get that from me," Dr. Lanville said. "And I can't imagine why any reputable doctor would prescribe it for someone with absolutely no history of cardiac disease."

"Do people ever use it for recreational purposes?" I asked.

"I don't think there's a chemical out there that some fool hasn't sniffed, smoked, or shot up with for recreational purposes," Lanville said. "I suppose nitro's more plausible than some—the effects for the recreational user are probably similar to poppers."

"Amyl nitrite inhalers," Dad translated. "Which have been very popular recreational drugs for decades."

"And no doubt he could have gotten it on the black market," Lanville went on. "Everything's available on the black market these days. But why would he? Given that amyl nitrite is available legally over the counter. And I've never seen any evidence that he had an interest in recreational substances other than vintage wine and expensive Scotch."

"We don't know for sure it was his," Dad said. "We have to consider the possibility that someone administered it to him without his knowledge."

"Damn. Any idea how much?"

"No, but the spray bottle was nearly empty."

Dr. Lanville whistled in sardonic appreciation.

"And he showed every sign of sudden catastrophic loss of blood pressure," Dad continued.

"He'd be more vulnerable to that than most," Lanville said. "Given his normally low blood pressure. I always kept my eye on that, in case it drifted too low, but it was always rock steady at around ninety over sixty."

"We also found something interesting in his room," Dad said. "Had you prescribed sildenafil for him?"

I frowned at Horace—what was this sildenafil stuff, and why hadn't he mentioned finding something interesting?

"What?" Dr. Lanville sounded very surprised. "Never. He never even asked about it. Are you sure?"

"We found five—no, make that six tablets in an unlabeled plastic pill bottle." Dad held up the little bottle in gloved hands. I was close enough to see the contents—a little cluster of diamond-shaped light blue pills. Nothing I could remember taking—or anyone in my household, for that matter—but they looked vaguely familiar. Annoying that the Internet was out and I couldn't look up sildenafil.

"What is—" I whispered to Horace.

"Viagra," he said. "Sildenafil is Viagra."

"Eww," I said.

Apparently, I said it a little too loudly. Dr. Lanville burst out laughing.

"Eww is right," he said. "And I normally like the silver fox look. But the idea of Oliver . . . well, you never know. There's someone for everyone, they say."

"I just have a hard time imagining any of his someones

would be here at the conference," I said. "He doesn't have a lot of fans in the ornithological community."

"Let's face it—he was easy to dislike," Dr. Lanville said. "Whenever he came in, my nurses would draw straws, and the loser had to do his vitals. But on a serious note—I'm not liking the way this sounds. First nitro and then Viagra."

"Exactly," Dad said. "The two of them in combination—"

"Would be a bad thing?" I asked.

"Nitroglycerin's a vasodilator, as we said." Dad was in full teaching mode. "Which means it causes the blood vessels to relax and dilate. If you're having an angina attack, in which the blood vessels leading to the heart aren't getting enough blood, a vasodilator increases the blood flow, thus providing symptomatic relief. People who are prone to angina sometimes even take it prophylactically when they're about to experience something they know could bring on an attack—like stress, or exercise."

"But you have to be careful with the dosage," Dr. Lanville chimed in. "Because along with increasing the blood flow it also lowers blood pressure. Lower it too much and you're dead."

"And Viagra does much the same thing," Dad continued. "Increases blood flow. Only . . . um . . . in a more localized way."

"And if you combine Viagra with nitroglycerin, it amplifies the risk of a dangerous drop in blood pressure," Dr. Lanville said. "That's the first thing they say on all the warning labels."

"And on the TV commercials," Horace put in.

"And that's one thing about hypochondriacs," Dr. Lanville put in. "They love reading the warning labels. Gives them more scope for working up symptoms. So even if Oliver was taking some kind of medication without telling me, I can't imagine that he'd do so without studying the warning labels."

"The Viagra doesn't have to have been his, does it?" I asked. "Any more than the nitroglycerin spray."

"Viagra's definitely available on the black market," Dr. Lanville said. "And a whole lot more in demand there than nitro. Some idiots use it as a recreational drug. And it's over the counter in England. So just because I never wrote him a prescription for it doesn't mean he couldn't have gotten his hands on it."

"And just because it was found in his room doesn't mean he brought it there," I said. "Say I'm someone who wants to knock off Dr. Frogmore."

"You'd probably have a lot of company," Dr. Lanville said.

"And I'm someone who knows about the danger of combining Viagra and nitroglycerin. I spray a lethal dose of nitroglycerin on something I know he's going to eat, and maybe add in a little ground-up Viagra for good measure. And I discard the spray bottle under the table and hide a few of the pills in his belongings, and hope the police say, 'Oh, well—combining Viagra and heart meds. Sad but not unexpected.' And bingo! Someone gets away with murder."

"I'm glad you don't have it in for me." Dr. Lanville chuckled.

"His face was very flushed when he stood up to make his toast," Dad said.

"Red as a lobster," I said.

"Textbook," Lanville said.

"And when he was insulting Dr. Hirano, he seemed to be squinting and peering, as if having trouble seeing him," Dad added.

"Blurred vision—yes, that would be another symptom." I could hear Lanville turning pages. One of his medical reference books, no doubt. I suspected Dad was itching at being parted from his own collection.

"The slurring and vision problems could have been the alcohol," I pointed out. "He'd had a few drinks."

"Very bad idea to drink when taking either of those medications." Dad shook his head. "And I noticed him taking some kind of medication during the meal. I didn't see what. I was going to check on him after the banquet— see if he was okay. Never got a chance."

"I was sitting closer," I said. "I heard him ask Dr. Czerny if he had anything for a headache. So probably aspirin or acetaminophen."

"So someone gave him pills during the dinner," Horace said. "Could that be how he got the Viagra?"

"I think he'd know the difference," Dr. Lanville said.

"You doctors might," Horace said. "Would he?"

"He might not know what they were," I said. "But if you asked for aspirin and someone handed you a couple of bright-blue diamond-shaped pills, wouldn't you at least ask what the heck they were?"

"Remember, generic sildenafil isn't bright blue or diamond shaped," Dr. Lanville said. "I'm looking at some pictures on the web. Only the ones Pfizer sells under the Viagra trademark come in the blue diamond shape. The generic comes in a variety of shapes, one of which is round and white and not unlike aspirin."

"But the ones Horace found were the classic Viagra," Dad said. "So while that doesn't rule out that someone slipped him something other than aspirin—"

"Point taken," Dr. Lanville said. "And he could very easily have had a headache—it's a classic vasodilator side effect. Of course, we won't know for sure till the autopsy, but I think you've pegged it."

"*We've* pegged it," Dad said graciously. I was sure if they'd been in the same room together they'd be beaming at each other with professional pride.

"If you like, I can do a little digging here," Dr. Lanville

said. "See if I can find any suggestion that he's been two-timing me, professionally speaking."

"That would be very useful," Dad said. "And we need to start talking to some of the people at Dr. Frogmore's table. They were closer than any of us were, and might have seen something that would be useful."

To say nothing of the fact that if either the nitroglycerin or the Viagra tablets turned out to have contributed to Frogmore's death, they'd be prime suspects.

"Do we know who they were?" Dad turned to me.

"Czerny, Green, Lindquist, and three very quiet young men who clearly wished they were at some other table," I said. "I'll see if I can find out their names."

"Dr. Lanville, while I have you, I wanted to ask about one more thing," Dad said. "If you don't mind hanging on until I walk over to where we've put Frogmore's body."

"No problem. So how long have you been a medical examiner?"

"Only the last few years." Dad stood up and slowly strolled out, still talking. From the sound of it I could tell that Dad and Dr. Lanville, having bonded over their theory on how Frogmore had died, were moving into one of those congenial far-ranging medical discussions of their weirdest cases and most brilliant diagnoses.

Chapter 15

I wondered if I should follow Dad or go look for Lindquist and Green, who might have some idea who the other occupants of Frogmore's table had been.

I glanced over to see Horace writing up some kind of form.

"Paperwork for when we submit all this to the Crime Lab," he said, when he saw my gaze. "And I want to make damn sure every bit of it's perfect when I submit those." He nodded at the laundry bin full of gold-embossed lunch bags. "Not that we'll have a chance anytime soon, but it's always a mistake to get too behind on the paperwork. And it's something to do while I'm figuring out what to do next. Or until the chief figures it out."

Ekaterina bustled in.

"Would you mind if I printed out something? Since it is for you, it would be more convenient to do so here."

"Sure." Horace stood up and yielded the desk chair. "You don't have Internet, do you?"

"No," she said. "This is on our internal network. The Internet went out almost with the first flake, as usual. There's another satellite phone if you need one." She pointed to where it sat charging atop a file cabinet.

"Thanks," Horace said, "Dr. Langslow is still talking to Dr. Lanville on the other one."

"What I am printing out is a list of all the guests with their room numbers." She typed a few commands and the printer in the corner began warming up. "Obviously you will want to begin searching all the rooms. Just let me know where you want to begin."

"Unfortunately, we probably have to begin with getting a search warrant," Horace said.

"But I am the manager, and I give you permission." Ekaterina looked slightly offended. "If that is not sufficient, I can contact the owners to get their permission. I can use the satellite phone, so is no problem."

"I appreciate your support," Horace said. "Unfortunately, some courts have decided that when people stay in a hotel room they have a reasonable expectation of privacy. That means we don't dare go in without a search warrant unless we have the occupant's permission. Not if we want the results of the search to be admissible in court."

"That seems silly." She shook her head. "What if you told me what you were looking for and I had my staff search the rooms?"

"Then you'd be acting as agents of the police and the results still wouldn't be admissible," Horace said. "I do want to interview your staff to see if they've noticed anything of interest in the past. But I have to be careful not to even appear to suggest that they go searching for evidence—and you should, too." He had taken the spare satellite phone and was dialing. Planning to bring the chief up to speed, no doubt.

"Curious," Ekaterina said. "I can see the point of giving the bad guys a sporting chance. But this appears to give them the upper hand."

"It's intended to protect the unjustly accused," I said.

"If you say so." She shrugged. "Well, I stand by in readiness to open the rooms once you get your search warrant. Although I suppose that won't happen till the roads are open. There would be no way to deliver a search warrant here tonight."

"We don't have to deliver the search warrant to the

hotel." We all jumped slightly when the chief spoke up over the satellite phone—evidently Horace had reached him and put the phone on speaker. "The warrant just has to exist. Signed by a judge, of course. And Deputy Vern Shiffley is staying out with his aunt, Judge Jane, to help her get through the storm. So if we can figure out grounds for the search that the judge will find acceptable, I can dictate it to Vern over the radio and he can type it up and get her to sign it."

"Of course, first we have to come up with a list of suspects whose rooms we want to search," I said.

"And the grounds for suspecting them," the chief added.

"And there are two hundred of them," Horace moaned.

"We only need to worry about the ones who had some reason for conflict with the deceased," the chief said.

"That cuts it down to a hundred and ninety-nine," I said.

"They can't all have had it in for him," the chief exclaimed.

"You didn't meet him," I said.

"I suppose I should be glad about that," the chief said. "But we have to start somewhere. And I doubt if Judge Jane will issue a blanket warrant for us to search the whole hotel, although I can have Vern ask. So if you had to make a shortlist, who would be on it?"

I sighed. Horace held his pen poised over his notebook.

"Dr. Vera Craine," I said. "Frogmore tried to torpedo her career. She bounced back with Grandfather's help, but she has reason to hate him."

Horace nodded, scribbled, then looked up as if to say "next."

"Melissa McKendrick. Caerphilly graduate student. She blames Frogmore for keeping her out of Buckthorn's graduate school, which was her first choice. Dr. Benjamin

Green. Thinks Frogmore is a heartless savage for wanting to kill thousands of barred owls to protect the endangered spotted owl. Dr. Nils Lindquist. Not sure why he's down on Frogmore, since they're both on the same side when it comes to what to do about the barred owls, but maybe fighting on the same side he's seen more of Frogmore than he can take—I know yesterday he stormed out of Frogmore's panel in a dudgeon. And yeah, we should include Dr. Edward Czerny. Frogmore's minion. On the face of it, the only person who's genuinely upset about Frogmore's death, but who knows—maybe he's secretly resented Frogmore all these years and hopes knocking the old guy off will clear the path for his own plot to take over the department. Stranger things have happened. Of course, those're only the ones I've talked to who had a grudge against him. There could be others with similar motives. They know a lot more about each other than I know about any of them. I bet if you talked to those five, they'd be able to tell you who else to suspect."

"Then let's begin by talking to those five," the chief said. "At least the ones who haven't yet gone to bed. Although if we get a search warrant, we might be waking them up. Meg—since you know them—"

"Not very well," I said.

"I don't even know what they look like," Horace said.

"Meg does." If the chief had been in the room, he'd have been looking over his glasses at me. "So you can find them, right?"

"I can try," I said. "And it's not as if any of them can have gone far in this storm. Which do you want first?"

"Whichever you can find."

I stopped in the doorway and turned back to them. Well, to Horace and the satellite phone.

"Someone on the outside would probably include Grandfather in their suspect list," I said. "Dr. Frogmore has certainly given him a hard time all weekend. But Grandfather wouldn't poison him. He'd just haul off and punch him in the nose."

"We should talk to your grandfather." From his voice I could tell he was smiling. "As conference organizer. Though I tend to agree with your notion of how he'd deal with someone he had a bone to pick with."

I went out into the lobby and looked around. Sami had ventured out into the storm long enough to affix a thermometer outside the wall of glass. If the Weather Channel was looking for new recruits to follow in the footsteps of Jim Cantore and its other demented and intrepid storm chasers, I could certainly recommend him. Several attendees were staring out at the driving snow and exclaiming that the temperature had dropped into single digits, but I didn't see any of the people I was looking for.

The Mount Vernon Grill. I decided to try there. I didn't see any of the three unidentified young men, but I did find two other prime suspects: Dr. Lindquist and Dr. Green. For people on opposite sides of the highly volatile barred owl issue they seemed to be getting along rather well. Was it just my imagination or did Dr. Green seem disappointed not to see Rose Noire following me?

"Come and join us," Dr. Lindquist called, waving a beer mug at me.

"Thanks, but I have a bunch of people to round up for Horace," I said. "People who might be able to give the police more information about Dr. Frogmore. Like you two."

"Suspects," Dr. Lindquist said. "We're suspects." He sounded a lot like Dad, who was never happier than when suspicion lighted on him in a murder case. I wondered if Dr. Lindquist was also an avid reader of mystery books.

"You make this sound like a good thing." Dr. Green clutched his beer with both hands and looked anxious. "Does this mean they've decided he was murdered?"

"That's still undecided," I said. "They may not know for sure until the autopsy. But in the meantime, they want to learn everything they can about what happened during dinner. And about him."

"They want to know who had motive, means, and opportunity." Dr. Lindquist nodded.

"And also whether he'd complained about feeling unwell at any time during the day," I said. "Or whether anyone had been seen messing with his food."

"I'm sure I wouldn't know," Dr. Green said. "I did my best to avoid him. I didn't even like sitting in the same room with him. You could feel the anger coming off him in almost visible waves."

"The police might like to know that," Dr. Lindquist said. "Come, let's go and help them with their inquiries." He gulped the last of his beer and stood.

Dr. Green winced but he followed Dr. Lindquist's example.

"Across the lobby, door marked 'Hotel Office,'" I said. "By the way, have you seen Dr. Craine or Dr. Czerny lately?"

"Vera just left," Dr. Green said. "I assume she was going up to her room."

"Czerny's probably off somewhere performing seppuku," Dr. Lindquist said. "Or would that be suttee?"

"Not really—he's fine." Dr. Green looked disappointed by his colleague's facetiousness. "We were trying to keep him company, but we gathered he really wanted to be by himself."

"Told us to stop pretending we weren't thrilled at Frogmore's death and get lost, actually," Dr. Lindquist elaborated. "Come on, Ben. Let's face the music."

They left the bar, and I watched as they disappeared into the office.

Ekaterina appeared.

"Horace thought you might also find a copy of this

useful," she said, a little stiffly. "The list of our guests, with room numbers. Evidently they will not be able to use it for the search for the time being, but it will still come in handy if you are looking for witnesses to invite to the Command Post."

"Thanks," I said. "It's just what I need. If you see Dr. Czerny—the one who was so upset by Dr. Frogmore's death—could you let Horace and the chief know? Or better yet, just lead him to them."

"Of course." As I expected, the idea of having something to contribute to the investigation seemed to improve her mood.

And I was going to start with the more congenial Dr. Craine. According to the list, she was in room 512. I headed for the elevator.

When I got off on the fifth floor I didn't even need to glance at the direction arrows—by now I'd spent enough time at the Inn that I knew without thinking that room 512 would be to the right. I looked to the left and noted, with satisfaction, the hotel security guard sitting in a folding chair outside 504, which had been Dr. Frogmore's room. Then I headed in the other direction.

The door of 512 was hanging open—rather odd. I hoped that meant Dr. Craine was there—just arriving, maybe, or getting ready to leave. Or filling her ice bucket.

But when I got to the door and peered in, I didn't see her. I saw a slender figure in a gray-and-white uniform rushing about the room—I recognized Serafina, one of the newer members of the housekeeping staff. She seemed to be searching for something—frantically looking in drawers, behind furniture, under stray items, all the while murmuring something under her breath.

"Lost something?" I asked.

"¡Dios mio!" She shrieked, jumped back a foot from the dresser she'd been searching, and began saying something—quite a lot of something—in machine-gun Spanish. My Spanish was good enough—just barely—to help the boys with their homework, but it couldn't even begin to cope with Serafina's monologue.

Someone appeared in the doorway behind me—a very tall someone. I glanced behind me—behind me and up— to find that Chantal, an astonishingly tall African-born member of the housekeeping staff, was also staring at Serafina with a look of astonishment on her elegant brown face.

Serafina finished whatever she was saying, or at least took a long pause, and from her expression and gestures I was pretty sure she was asking—no, pleading for something.

"Did you understand what she just said?" I asked Chantal.

"Not a word of it. I'm from Burundi—we speak French, not Spanish. But I probably know what she was doing."

"Searching Dr. Craine's room, as far as I could see."

"Yes. I heard earlier today that Serafina had lost her key card. She is hoping to find it, because if Ms. Ekaterina finds out she has lost it . . ." Chantal shrugged with graceful eloquence.

Serafina was looking back and forth between the two of us, with hope and anxiety flitting across her face in turns.

I searched my memory and came up with a few useful words.

"¿Tarjeta perdida?"

"Sí." Serafina looked relieved. She also looked annoyed, as if she wanted to say a lot more on the subject, but had by now figured out how unlikely it was that I'd understand a word of it.

"Exactly what would this key card open?" I asked Chantal.

She gave me a curious look.

"Pretty much all the guest rooms in the hotel," she said. "And also all the 'staff only' doors. As you can imagine, a malefactor who had this card could cause a great deal of mischief."

Even stressed as I was, I couldn't help relishing the word "malefactor." I hadn't yet figured out if Ekaterina hired a lot of students who were working their way through Caerphilly College or if she hired smart people and then nagged them until they enrolled. Clearly Chantal was one of her student employees. For all I knew, Serafina would be too in a few months when she'd polished up her English.

"Calm down," I said. "Er . . . *tranquilizate*?" I hoped that meant what I thought it meant. Probably, since Serafina's anxious face showed, just for a second, an expression that clearly said "Easy for you to say."

Using my limited Spanish vocabulary, Chantal's considerable skill at miming, and the calendar on my phone, we managed to learn that Serafina had last had her card sometime Friday evening.

"Which means it's possible that someone has been running around the hotel with it for more than twenty-four hours," I said.

"You think this could have something to do with the man who died?" Chantal asked. "The one they say may have been murdered?"

From the interested expression on Serafina's face, I deduced that she understood more English than she spoke and was eager to hear my answer to the question.

"Maybe," I said. "We should let the police know. Horace, that is. And we should tell Ekaterina that maybe it's not Serafina's fault she doesn't have her card. Maybe it isn't lost. Maybe it's stolen."

Chantal nodded.

"If only I could think of the Spanish word for stolen," I muttered.

"*Robada*," Serafina said. "*Tarjeta robada*."

I made a vow to work harder at my Spanish.

"So let's tell Ekaterina about the *tarjeta robada*," I said. "Ekaterina and Horace."

Serafina seemed much more resigned to telling Ekaterina now that we had defined her card as stolen instead of lost. But she balked at following me down to the Command Post, and I didn't try to force her. I'd let the chief deal with bringing her in for an interview. Or Ekaterina.

It wasn't as if there was anyplace else she could go.

Chapter 16

After wishing Serafina a *Feliz Navidad* and Chantal a *Joyeux Noël*, I texted Ekaterina and asked her to meet us in Horace's Command Post. When I arrived there myself, I found Dr. Green and Dr. Lindquist sitting on the bench just outside the door, with fresh beers.

"Awaiting my turn in the hot seat." Dr. Lindquist said, cheerfully. "Ben's already been through the wringer."

In the office, I found Horace conferring with the chief over the satellite phone—strategizing before they began the next interview. Not surprisingly, neither one of them was thrilled by the news of the stolen card.

"As if things weren't complicated enough already." Horace looked despondent. "If there's someone running around the hotel with a card that gives them access to any place where they might find it useful to plant evidence—someone who's probably our killer . . ." His voice trailed off and he slumped in his chair.

"Do we know precisely which rooms this key card would give someone access to?" the chief asked.

"Not yet." I was hoping Chantal had been exaggerating when she said it could open any guest room. "But when Ekaterina gets here—"

"I have arrived." Ekaterina stood in the doorway. "There is a problem?"

"Someone has stolen Serafina's key card," I said. "We don't know if the killer has it, but even if that's only a possibility, Horace and the chief would like to know what the card would give them access to."

"All guest rooms," Ekaterina said. "Including the cottages. All housekeeping closets. The laundry rooms. The trash rooms. The loading dock. All of the meeting spaces, in case they are called into service to help with speedy turnaround during conferences. All the 'staff only' doors."

"Pretty much anywhere but your office and hotel safe," I said.

"And the kitchen and food storage areas," she added.

"So the housekeepers' key cards aren't restricted to a particular floor?" Horace sounded a little overwhelmed.

"In a much larger hotel, that might be the policy," she said. "But here, it was not feasible. While staff have assigned floors, or sections of floors, we need to be able to reassign them dynamically in case of absences or emergencies. And of course, guests staying at a deluxe hotel like the Inn—especially those in the cottages—often come with greater expectations when it comes to the level of service we provide. Satisfying those expectations is easier when all of the relevant staff are empowered to do so."

"In other words, you need to make sure that when your guests bellow out orders, any staff member within earshot can take care of them. Especially if they're monumentally entitled and demanding cottage guests."

"Not all cottage guests." She smiled. But I noticed she didn't contradict my translation.

"So someone is running around with a key that lets them into a whole lot of places where they could get up to mischief, and we don't know who's doing it and we can't do a thing about it," Horace said. "Like we needed this case to get more complicated."

"I can't tell you who's doing it," Ekaterina said. "But unless you see a reason not to, I can reset the housekeeping-level key codes so they can't do it anymore. Would that be acceptable?"

"Seems like a good idea to me," the chief said. "Horace?"

"Ye-es." Horace sounded hesitant. "Only—could you maybe tell us how the system works?"

"Of course." Ekaterina almost purred. She enjoyed explaining things to people—especially explaining technical things to men. "The card readers on each door are stand-alone, battery-powered units—a good thing, because that means they will still work in the unlikely event of a power outage. And they come with several sets of codes programmed into them—sets of guest codes, housekeeping codes, and master codes. When you check in, the receptionist inserts a blank key card in a little machine connected to the system, and loads the next code for your room onto your card. When you insert the card, the card reader says, 'Aha! New code!' And after that any cards bearing the previous code will no longer work. They also have your checkout date and time encoded in, to help discourage guests from overstaying."

"But I bet the housekeeping and master codes work differently," I said.

"Yes. To change those, I must go around to each card reader with a small machine and tell it that I want it to move on to the next code. And then I must issue new cards to everyone—not just Serafina, in this case, but every member of the staff. That is why I am so stern when they are careless with the keys—changing all those locks and cards is a lot of work."

"But worth it in this case," I said. "Since there is a possibility that a killer is running around with way too much access to rooms we'd rather keep him out of."

"Agreed," said the chief.

"I will begin," she said. "While I am resetting the codes, would you like me to run an audit of the key card readers?"

We all stared at her for a few seconds. At least Horace and I stared, and we heard nothing from the satellite phone.

If neither the chief nor Horace were going to ask . . .

"What would the audit tell us?" I asked.

"Which key cards had accessed that lock at what time."

"Awesome," Horace murmured.

"Of course, it will not tell us who was holding the card," the chief said.

"Alas, no," Ekaterina said. "If we had cameras above all the doors, we could, but I think our guests would find that level of security somewhat intrusive."

"But assuming someone used the stolen card, we can at least figure out where they used it," I said. "And if we compared that to when we know certain people were tied up—appearing on a panel, for example—we could narrow it down."

"Let's not get too excited," the chief said. "We don't know yet that the card's been used. It could just have fallen into a wastebasket or something."

"But perhaps it will tell us everything," Ekaterina said. "I will begin the rekeying and auditing immediately."

She pulled out her key ring, unlocked a small cabinet, and took out a small case with an attached tag that read KEY CARD EQUIPMENT. I was rather hoping she'd open the little case so I could see what the equipment looked like, but she only smiled enigmatically before walking briskly out.

"Well, that could be useful," Horace said.

"Let's hope so," came the chief's voice. "Meg, on your way out, send in Dr. Lindquist."

I took the hint.

Dr. Green looked a little bereft when Dr. Lindquist went into the office.

"And I had such high hopes for this weekend," he said.

"Anything in particular you were hoping for?"

"I thought we had a chance of reaching a more harmonious situation with regard to the position of the barred owl."

"You were hoping to talk Dr. Frogmore out of wanting to kill them all?" Clearly my blunt question made Dr. Green uncomfortable.

"Well, no," he admitted. "I didn't really see much chance of that happening. But I was hoping that a few calm discussions with some of the more reasonable people on the other side of the issue might be fruitful. People like Dr. Lindquist, for example."

"Might such discussions be more fruitful now that Dr. Frogmore is out of the picture?" I asked.

"Are you asking me if I have a motive for murder?" He shuddered. "The idea of taking a life is absolutely abhorrent to me."

"Especially a human life."

"No." He looked thoughtful. "Not especially a human life. That's a very narrow-minded, anthropocentric notion, that a human life is worth more than other lives. We need to start looking beyond that kind of speciesism." He lifted his chin and his face took on the look of noble resignation I was used to seeing on Rose Noire, on those occasions when she felt obliged to utter some New Age pronouncement even though she knew we'd all find it funny or weird.

So if Dr. Green held all lives as equally valuable—even that of a black widow spider—did this mean that he'd willingly sacrifice Frogmore if he thought it would save thousands of innocent barred owls? Or did he hold the equally if not more extreme position that killing any creature for any reason—even, say, to save the entire planet—was morally indefensible? Figuring that out might tell us whether he was a valid suspect or just another witness.

"Is something wrong?" He looked alarmed, and I realized that I'd been studying him as I pondered.

"Sorry," I said. "I was trying to visualize something. And I just realized that you might be able to help me— you were at Frogmore's table at dinner. Do you know the names of those three young men who were sitting there—apart from you, Czerny, and Lindquist?"

"Yes," he said. "And I looked them up in the program to see where they were from. I was going to try to engage them in conversation. Make them feel welcome. Unfortunately, Dr. Frogmore wasn't in the mood to let anyone else get a word in edgewise."

"Can you tell me their names?"

"I already gave them to the detective."

"Who is probably going to ask me to hunt them down when he finishes with Dr. Lindquist. Help me get a head start."

He sighed, pulled out his phone, and began tapping on it. Eventually he nodded—evidently he'd found what he was looking for. "Smith, Whitmore, and Belasco."

I checked them against my lists.

"Belasco's the only one registered at the hotel." I hadn't noticed that when I was taking registrations, and even if I had, I'd merely have assumed they were planning to find a cheaper place to stay. Now . . . "I suspect they're sharing a room with someone."

"Grad students, so I expect so." Dr. Green smiled rather wistfully, as if remembering his own impoverished youth. "Although junior faculty would be almost as poverty-stricken. Nice to have those days behind me," he added quickly.

Was there some reason he'd brought up his greater

financial stability? I reminded myself to delegate checking out Dr. Green to Mother. I'd have my hands full helping Horace. I also made a mental note to give Horace a copy of my conference registration list. I already knew what he'd say. "Not more suspects!"

"I can find Belasco and see if he knows where the other two are," I said aloud. "Thanks."

"Good luck." Dr. Green sighed, got up, and headed for the elevators.

Chapter 17

I wavered outside the Command Post door for a minute or two. It was getting late. Near midnight. Murder or no murder, at some point we'd need to stop knocking on the doors of people, most of whom would turn out to be completely innocent.

But the sooner Horace did his interviews the better. I braced myself for what I assumed would be the inevitable complaints and trudged toward the elevator myself.

No one answered Belasco's door. Or Dr. Craine's. I decided to take a turn through the conference area to see if I spotted any of them. And then, when Horace was finished with Dr. Lindquist—or whoever else I could find for him after Dr. Lindquist—I'd suggest that we knock off till morning. Most of the potential witnesses would turn up for the complimentary continental breakfast—especially any grad students so broke that they were sharing a room—so that would be a good time to nab them.

When I stepped into the conference area I heard sounds of laughter and conversation coming from the Hamilton Room, so I strolled over to see what was going on.

Dr. Craine was perched on the edge of the table at the far end of the room, the one where the panelists would sit if a panel were happening. She was holding a tissue box. A tissue box that had been festively decorated with scraps of red, green, and gold metallic paper but, thanks to the slot at the top, was still recognizably a tissue box.

"Okay—George Voss. You're in, right?"

"Sure." A burly fiftyish redheaded man strode to the front of the room. Dr. Craine held out the box to him and shook it slightly. He stuck his fingers into the slot at the top of the box and pulled them out again, not holding a tissue but a small folded slip of paper.

He opened it up and chuckled.

"No telling!" Dr. Craine warned. "Next. Jeff Whitmore—you in?"

A slight man in oversized glasses with heavy black frames dashed up, pulled a slip of paper out of the box, looked at it, nodded, and went back to his seat. I made a note of where he'd gone—and could that be Smith and Belasco sitting with him?

"And finally—Ethan Zander."

A tousle-haired blond young man whom I recognized as another of Grandfather's student volunteers dashed forward, rummaged in the box for a few moments, and finally emerged with a slip of paper.

Dr. Craine looked up and saw me.

"You're too late," she called.

"Is that a good thing or a bad thing?" I asked. "You're holding a lottery of some kind? You all ganged up to off Dr. Frogmore, like a remake of *Murder on the Orient Express,* and now you're drawing lots to see who's going to take the fall for the rest of you."

The assembled scientists burst into loud and raucous laughter. Mother stepped forward to stand by Dr. Craine's side. What in the world?

"We're doing a Secret Santa," Mother said. "Now remember, everyone—you've got twenty-four hours to come up with a present."

"You can make something, buy something, or create a decorative IOU for something," Dr. Craine said. "The sky's the limit—just do your best to figure out what will please the person whose name you drew. And no telling anyone who you drew! Now go forth and work up some Christmas spirit!"

The scientists—at least ninety of them, which meant nearly half of the attendees—milled about, some of them heading for the door, others forming clumps to chat. Though not, presumably, about whose names they'd drawn.

"Before you go," I called. "The police want to interview everyone who was sitting at Dr. Frogmore's table. Could Daniel Belasco, R. G. Smith, and Jeffrey Whitmore drop by the Command Post—that's the office behind the registration desk—to see Deputy Hollingsworth and make an appointment for your interview."

Quite a few of the assembled crowd turned to stare at Jeff Whitmore and the other two men standing with him, so I deduced that my tentative identification of them as Smith and Belasco was accurate. The three of them looked unhappy but resigned.

Mother favored me with a slightly disapproving frown. I'd spoiled the festive holiday mood she and Dr. Craine had succeeded in creating.

"And don't forget, we'll be having church services by telephone in the ballroom tomorrow morning," Mother called. "Baptist at nine, Episcopalian at eleven."

"And anyone who wants to come to the Hanukkah dinner tomorrow night, sign up at the front desk by noon so the kitchen will know how much food to make," Dr. Craine called out.

"We'll be having brisket, salmon, latkes, matzoh ball soup, and who knows what other delicacies," Mother added.

"Plus Indian food in honor of Diwali," Dr. Craine added.

"Make that Pancha Ganapati," someone called out. "Diwali was in October."

The menu preview had drawn scattered applause from the scientists, but now more of them were drifting out of the room.

"Well, you guys have been busy," I said as I joined Mother and Dr. Craine.

"We thought we should do something for morale," Mother said. "People were already demoralized at being snowbound, and then actually witnessing a murder has really shaken everyone."

"Of course, if we had to have a murder, at least the killer picked someone whose demise wouldn't cause general depression," Dr. Craine said.

"And possibly a little quiet rejoicing," I added.

"The rumor's been going around that the police won't let anyone leave town until they figure out who killed Frogmore," Dr. Craine added. "That doesn't help morale."

"It may not come to that," Mother said. "Are they even sure it was really murder?"

"Dad seems to think so."

"Yes, but you know how he is." Mother frowned slightly. Dr. Craine looked puzzled.

"Dad reads a lot of mystery books," I explained. "Some people think he's just a little too ready to suspect murder."

"I wouldn't want to spoil his fun," Mother went on. "But in this case, he could be inconveniencing rather a lot of other people. I would hate to have it turn out to be a false alarm."

"Horace seems to think there's something in it," I said.

"Oh, dear," Mother said. "Well, then, it's lucky he's here."

"And by the way, Dr. Craine, Horace would like to interview you," I said.

"What stool pigeon sold me out?" Her Edward G. Robinson imitation was actually rather good.

"Me," I said. "I confess, I gave him all the names of

people I knew had a reason to dislike Dr. Frogmore. I expect you and Dr. Green and Dr. Lindquist can fill him in on the motives the other hundred and ninety-odd people have for the murder. If it even turns out to be murder."

"Happy to, actually," she said in her normal voice. "He was a horrible man, but that doesn't give anyone the right to kill him. And I particularly resent that whoever did this didn't seem to care about spoiling Monty's conference."

"Not to mention our holiday season," Mother added.

"Yes." Dr. Craine nodded. "But we'll do what we can to put both right again. Good night. And Merry Christmas."

Mother and I returned the greeting and watched as she pushed through the door to the lobby, looking noticeably less energetic than she had during the Secret Santa drawing.

"You should go to bed, too," Mother said. "I'm going to see if I can find your father and convince him to get some rest. After all, it's not as if whoever killed that poor man will be able to escape tonight. Come on."

We stopped at the front desk to check with Sami, who reported seeing Dad leaving the lobby by the door that led to the President's Garden and the cottages beyond.

"Thank goodness he's being sensible," Mother remarked.

We put on our coats and braced ourselves for the cold—down to six degrees according to Sami's lobby thermometer. Luckily the path from the main hotel to the cottage was short, and partly sheltered from the wind by the buildings around it. When we reached the door of Grandfather's cottage, I was relieved to see that his light was out. Mother wished me good night and headed right toward the Washington Cottage.

I turned left, and was pleased to see that there were still lights on to welcome me to the Madison Cottage.

Of course, I'd been expecting that. Michael wouldn't have forgotten. What I wasn't expecting was to find Dad sitting on one of the sofas, with a pile of books around him.

Immediately after her promotion to manager of the Inn, Ekaterina had hired Mother to improve its decor. The Inn's previous decorator had been a devotee of the practice of filling shelves with fake books bought by the yard for their pretentious leather bindings. Mother thoroughly disapproved of this and had vowed to replace the elegant but empty tomes with real books, albeit attractive ones. She'd recruited Ms. Ellie, the town librarian, to chair the Inn's book selection committee. Anything that went onto the shelves had to be attractive enough to please Mother, obviously. But it also had to be declared worth reading by Ms. Ellie and the committee—a loose conglomeration of library habitués who were willing to drop whatever they were doing and tag along whenever Ms. Ellie heard about a good used book sale going on. Dad was a stalwart, as were Michael, Josh, Jamie, and I, Chief Burke and his wife Minerva, Rose Noire, the Reverend Robyn Smith of Trinity Episcopal, and my grandmother Cordelia when she was in town.

Dad seemed to be looking through a collection of medical reference books. About a dozen of them—part of his contribution to the Inn's bookshelves. Ms. Ellie had been dubious about the need for quite so many, and Michael had wondered if it was really such a good idea to give hypochondriac guests such a lot of fuel for their imaginations. But Dad had promised to distribute them throughout the Inn, so no one bookshelf was overwhelmed, and since they were all beautiful thick tomes with handsome bindings, Mother—the final arbiter—had approved.

I wondered, just for a moment, if he'd envisioned a scenario that anticipated this weekend's events: that he'd be trapped at the Inn during a snowstorm—actually in Virginia a severe hurricane was much more likely—and trying to determine the cause of death for a murder victim. Even for Dad, that seemed a reach. More likely he just thought they'd come in handy somehow, someday. And I was betting he'd remembered just where he'd put each one and hadn't had to spend much time searching.

"Coming up with any new theories?" I asked.

"Alas, no." He stuck a bookmark into the book he'd been perusing—actually, a pale beige tissue folded into bookmark shape. "But I am getting more certain that my hypothesis is correct."

"Death by Viagra?" I asked.

"Nitroglycerin and possibly Viagra," he said. "And the champagne didn't help."

"Maybe you should leave the champagne out of it," I suggested. "Ekaterina wouldn't much like the Inn's Krug being implicated in a homicide."

"I'll just say alcohol, then. I seem to recall that he'd also had quite a lot of wine."

"And whiskey," I said. "If memory serves, he brought a whiskey glass with him to dinner, and went through a lot of wine once he'd finished that."

"And alcohol's also a vasodilator up to a certain level," Dad said. "And the fact that he collapsed just after standing up is also indicative. Postural hypotension. That's what happens sometimes when you stand up suddenly after sitting or lying down for a long time and feel slightly light-headed or dizzy. Could happen to a healthy person who's a little dehydrated, for example, but with no ill effects. For someone whose system is already trying to process an overload of vasodilators . . . well, it wouldn't help. I think we've pinned down the cause of death."

"Now we just need to figure out who did it."

He nodded. He looked down at his book, then lifted his head again, took off his glasses, and rubbed his eyes.

"It's late," I said. "You should be asleep."

"So should Oliver Frogmore," Dad said. "But someone prevented that."

"And Mother just went back to your cottage." I played my ace. "She'll be worried when she doesn't find you there."

"If she calls, tell her I'm on my way." He shut the medical books, tidied the scattered collection into two tall stacks, and headed for the door.

"Good night," I called. "And Merry Christmas."

I turned off the living room lights and tiptoed to bed by the light of my phone's flashlight. No panels until ten, I reminded myself, but I should probably go over earlier to check on the continental breakfast and . . .

Chapter 18

> *Joy to the world, the Lord is come*
> *Let earth receive her King*
> *Let every heart prepare Him room*
> *And Heaven and nature sing*
> *And Heaven and nature sing*
> *And Heaven, and Heaven, and nature sing*

I liked Christmas carols. I really did. And "Joy to the World" was a particularly nice example of the species. But I didn't much like being blasted out of sleep by it in the middle of the night. What time was it, anyway?

I rolled over to peer at my alarm clock. Which wasn't there. Then I remembered that I wasn't at home. I was at the Inn, in the Madison Cottage. Here, the alarm clock was over on Michael's side of the bed.

And it read 9:00 A.M.

And still dark?

Well, no. Probably not still dark outside. The Inn had invested in truly top-notch blackout curtains. Not a ray of light made it past them. Odds were if I could see the light outside it would be dim and gray, assuming the storm was still raging. Still, there would be light, if not for the blackout curtains.

But they couldn't block the joyous strains of song and pipe organ happening outside the bedroom. Apparently in the living room. Why in the world would anyone come caroling at this hour? And how had they managed the organ? And there seemed to be such a lot of them—in fact, it sounded as if the entire New Life Baptist Choir were singing in the room next door.

Of course. The 9:00 A.M. Baptist service by phone. Evidently someone had figured out how to connect a speaker to a satellite phone. Now that I realized what it was, I could detect a certain tinny sound to the music.

I stumbled to the door that led into the living room and peered out. In the living room, the volume was almost deafening. And the room was full of people. Not just family. Along with Mother, Rose Noire, and the boys, I saw at least a dozen assorted ornithologists, all sitting around with cups of coffee and plates of food, basking in the waves of sound. Or maybe bracing against them.

"The music is lovely," I said, when the song was over, and the only thing coming over the speakers was the sound of people rustling their hymn books and coughing. "But wouldn't it be almost as lovely a few hundred decibels lower?"

"Sorry!" Josh leaped to one of the speakers perched on the mantel and dialed down the volume. "We forgot you were still sleeping."

I muttered something that I hoped sounded like "thanks" and stumbled back to bed.

Unfortunately, now I was awake. And likely to stay that way.

And I hadn't seen Horace in the crowd around the speakers. That probably meant he was already up and working on the case.

"Once more unto the breach," I muttered as I crawled out of bed again. A shower might make me feel human enough to tackle whatever was waiting for me back at the conference. A shower and a whole lot of caffeine. I'd seen coffee cups being wielded out there in the living room, hadn't I? And plates of food?

Somewhat heartened, I motivated myself into the shower.

When I emerged from the bedroom, the boys greeted me with cheers—although I quickly realized that the reason for their enthusiasm was that they'd been itching to get back to work on their tunneling project and needed to use the tub in the bathroom for snow disposal. Since the bathroom could only be reached through the bedroom, my sleeping late—by their definition—was holding up progress. The sink in the tiny half bath off the entry wouldn't even hold a single bucket of snow, they informed me with considerable scorn as they donned their outdoor gear.

"I'll be keeping an eye on them," Michael said once they had both disappeared into one of their tunnels. "Might even check out the diggings myself if things stay quiet."

Just then the New Life Baptist Choir launched into a hearty rendition of "Glory to the Lamb," which was a relief, since it meant I didn't have to talk to anyone else before I was awake enough to make sense. I waved at friends, family, and familiar faces, then grabbed a croissant and a cup of coffee before heading over to the main building to see what was happening.

The weather hadn't improved overnight. Snow was still falling and Sami's thermometer registered a balmy seven degrees.

I found Horace in the Command Post, surrounded by paper and looking, as Mother would say, like something the cat wouldn't even bother dragging in.

"Please tell me you didn't stay up all night," I said.

"I knocked off about one," he said. "Couldn't sleep well, though. This is the first time I've ever had this much responsibility for an investigation. And it's not going well."

"It's going as well as you could expect, given the circumstances." I pointed to the vast collection of paper in front of him. "What's all this?"

"Audit records from every key card reader in the hotel. I'm trying to analyze them to see if I can get any useful information about whether anyone used the missing key card." He lifted his coffee cup, found it empty, and set it down with a sigh and looked back at papers in front of him.

I was eager to learn what he'd found, but that could wait.

"You need more coffee," I said. "And have you had breakfast?"

"I had a croissant."

"That's not breakfast, it's an appetizer," I said. "Stay here."

I hurried across the lobby to the Mount Vernon Grill, which was predictably quiet at this time of the morning, given that a continental breakfast was included in Grandfather's conference and there were only a handful of non-attendees in the hotel. Eduardo, back on duty, greeted me, and I put in an order for a full breakfast to be delivered to Horace at the Command Post.

Then I noticed that Dr. Lindquist was in the restaurant, eating a hearty bacon-and-egg breakfast and trying not to get any grease on the book he was reading. He still puzzled me a bit, so I decided to seize the chance to talk to him. I strolled over to his table.

"Not a fan of the continental breakfast buffet, I see."

"Nope." He tore off a piece of toast and began swabbing up the yolk of his over-easy egg with it. "I'm a carnivore. Got to start the day with protein. And I like my breakfast hot."

"I'm with you," I said. "Next time Grandfather throws a conference, I'm going to try to talk him into a full breakfast buffet."

Dr. Lindquist had stuffed the toast chunk in his mouth

and was chewing, but he gave me a thumbs-up with the hand that wasn't busy tearing off another chunk.

"Mind if I ask you something?"

"Fire away," he said, after swallowing.

"Is it fair to say that Dr. Frogmore's demise won't be all that devastating to the campaign for removing the barred owls from the Pacific Northwest?"

Dr. Lindquist burst out laughing and then stopped himself suddenly and looked around as if worried people might be staring. Since the only other people in the restaurant were the depressed-looking Ackleys, who almost certainly hadn't heard of Frogmore and might not even know about his death yet, he didn't really need to worry.

"Sorry," Dr. Lindquist said. "Not funny that the old coot's dead, obviously. It was the way you put it. Yes, fair to say that Frogmore's death won't have any ill effects for our side. Quite the contrary. Without him running around like a jackass, making deliberately inflammatory statements, people might take our side a little more seriously. In fact—" He broke off, stuck another small egg-dipped chunk of toast in his mouth and chewed thoughtfully. "Hindsight's twenty-twenty," he went on, eventually. "And I admit that I'm not a Frogmore fan. Never have been. But—you know that movie they always show this time of year? *It's a Wonderful Life?*"

"Love it," I said. "I watch it with the family every Christmas."

"That whole thing about seeing what the world would be like if someone had never been in it. Be interesting if you could do that with Frogmore. You ask me, the whole battle over the spotted owl's habitat back in the eighties would have been a lot less . . . toxic if he hadn't been in it. Frogmore had a positive genius for riling people up and getting them to dig in their feet on issues where it should have been possible to reach a compromise. I can think of two, maybe three examples that I witnessed myself in West Coast ornithology and conservation circles, and I've done my best over the years to stay away from anything he's involved in."

"A genius for riling people up," I repeated. "Sounds a little like my grandfather."

"Nope," he said through a mouthful of home fries. "Blake riles people up, yeah, but he usually does it for a reason. And he's a realist. Knows when he has the ammo to stand his ground and when he needs to compromise. And he's a sharp dealmaker when he has to be. Frogmore—if he was trying to cut a deal and got ninety-nine percent of what he wanted, he'd let the deal die over that one percent."

"So not someone you'd want on your side when you're fighting for an important issue."

"Not anyone you'd want anywhere near the battle. Too many people got hurt by friendly fire when Frogmore was around, if you don't mind my running the military metaphor into the ground. If it really was friendly fire. A lot of people suspected Frogmore's motives. Me included, frankly."

"His motives for what?" I asked.

"You have to wonder—could he really have been as misguided and off base as he seemed?" Lindquist had stabbed a couple of small home fries and was gesticulating with the fork. "Back in the nineties some people weren't sure where his loyalties really lay. He had this positive gift for taking an environmentally sound position and then exaggerating it until it sounded like some kind of wildly impractical scheme dreamed up by a bunch of superannuated brain-damaged hippies. You had to wonder—was he really that crazy? Or was he actually on the other side? In the spotted owl issue, for example, that would mean on the side of the lumber industries."

He popped the home fries into his mouth and chewed slowly.

"Wait—people actually suspected he was on the lumber industry's side in the spotted owl issue?"

"Not just on their side—in their pay. He lived pretty comfortably—always had. More comfortably than you'd expect on a professor's salary. Me, I figure he probably had family money. But there are people who'd swear up and down that the lumber companies bought him off."

I digested this for a while as I watched Dr. Lindquist methodically apply butter and strawberry jam to another slice of toast.

"So it's not just his personality that made him . . . less than popular at gatherings like this."

"If you're looking for someone with a motive to knock him off, there's a whole lot of us," Lindquist said. "Some of us hold grudges over stuff he'd pulled in the past. Some of us think he was up to no good now. And when you add in all the academic backstabbing he's done over the years . . . well, it's a good thing we bird brains are generally a mild-mannered bunch."

"That's a relief," I said. "I think. So you know this crowd. If you had to bet on who knocked off Frogmore, who would you pick?"

"Interesting question." He took a bite of toast and chewed it thoughtfully, as if giving due consideration. "A very interesting question. As I said, a whole lot of people with a motive, but now that I think about it, not a lot of them actually here at the conference. Maybe it's the East Coast location. Or maybe people found out Frogmore was coming and canceled out."

"We did have rather a lot of cancellations at the last minute," I said. "I thought it was people freaking because of the weather."

"That could be. But if it happened right after you sent

out the lists of panels and presentations—hell, I kicked the wall a couple of times when I saw Frogmore's name on it. And then I said 'what the hell' and came anyway. But I bet I could name some people who bailed."

"Under ordinary circumstances, the police would probably be checking on them anyway," I said. "In case any of them came here in disguise to knock him off. But I think someone would have noticed if someone with a known grudge against Frogmore came skiing in during the storm. So, of the people who are here, who do you like for it?"

"Good question." He grinned. "If you ask me, given the interviews the police have been doing, you've already got the likely candidates pegged. Me, Ben Green, Vera Craine, and that black grad student, Melissa something."

"McKendrick," I said.

"Right. And I suppose you have to include Czerny, of course, but I don't figure that's very likely unless it happened on the spur of the moment. I can see him losing his temper and lashing out, but in the cold hard light of day, he knows better than to kill the goose laying his golden eggs. He won't last long at Buckthorn without Frogmore's protection. And I don't see Vera doing it, either. Pretty sure she's into living well as the best revenge. She's going to miss seeing Frogmore squirm whenever someone rubs his nose in her vastly superior curriculum vitae."

"And the rest of you?"

"Probably not Melissa," he said. "She has a pretty low opinion of him, but it's not like he's the only entitled over-the-hill white jerk who's ever tried to hold her back. She made a good impression here—asked some intelligent questions in a couple of panels. She's on track. And she's sharp enough to realize that Frogmore accidentally did her the biggest possible favor—I mean, would you have wanted to work with him or with Dr. Blake? Strong women don't bother Blake, and he's the closest thing to color-blind I've ever seen, which is all the more unusual, given his age. No, Melissa's in a good situation now, and I don't see her spoiling it, risking everything she's earned by murdering an old fart who doesn't have any power over her anymore."

"And Dr. Green?"

"Ben doesn't hate Frogmore." Lindquist shook his head with vigor and chuckled slightly. "He's deeply, deeply disappointed in Frogmore. And under the delusion that if he had just kept the communications channels open, got a dialogue going, eventually he could have resolved their differences. And besides, he's completely opposed to violence of any kind. Wouldn't hurt a spider."

Interesting. Most people would have said "wouldn't hurt a fly."

Chapter 19

I filed away Dr. Lindquist's curious turn of phrase to think about later. And to share with Horace and the chief.

"That covers all the suspects," I said aloud. "So . . . wait. There's still you."

"I was hoping you'd forget about me." He laughed. "Well, I know I didn't do it, but I can't expect you to take my word for it. And I won't even pretend that his death isn't going to make things a whole lot easier, not just for me, but for everyone on both sides of the barred owl issue."

I waited while he seemed to be thinking over what to say.

"I was this close to getting him." He held up his thumb and forefinger less than an inch apart. "I've been nosing around, trying to get proof of my theory that he was in bed with the lumber industry back in the eighties. And that he's not all that hostile to them now. I wanted to see him publicly humiliated—revealed as the slimy, backstabbing crook that he is. That he was." His face fell. "What's the use now? He won't pay for what he's done. If I made public what I've found out, I'd be trashing the reputation of a guy who's not around to defend himself anymore. At best, Buckthorn College would go 'Eek! If we'd known that we'd have fired him!' And then turn around and take another big donation from some conglomerate that needs a tame biology department to do its dirty work. Nothing would change."

"So not you, either?" I said. "If none of his enemies would have done him in, why isn't he still running up and down the halls bellowing insults at everyone?"

"Beats me. You got any lumberjacks staying here? I hear they don't like him much. Maybe one of them did him in."

"No lumberjacks," I said. "And I thought you said he was on their side."

"Lumberjacks wouldn't know he was in the pay of the timber barons. They'd just blame him if they'd ever been laid off. And the timber barons might knock him off if they were afraid he'd spill the beans about some of the dirty tricks they were up to, but I doubt if they're here, either. Both of his ex-wives would probably knock him off in a heartbeat, but if either of them is here she's well disguised. Not a lot of women here I don't know as colleagues or colleague's wives. Maybe he offed himself to drive us crazy. Do they know what he died of? Some kind of poison, I assume."

"They don't really know yet." It wasn't really a lie. No matter how confident I was that Dad and Horace had it figured out. "They won't know for sure until they can do the autopsy. And a tox screen."

"So meanwhile we're in limbo."

I nodded.

"Ah, well. Make sure the police don't lose sight of the suicide angle."

"You really think he would?"

"Not under ordinary circumstances. But what if he just found out he's got something terminal, and decides to off himself while casting suspicion on a whole bunch of people he hated."

"Revenge by suicide?"

"You never know."

I deduced from his expression that we'd pretty much exhausted his interest in Dr. Frogmore's death, and that he wouldn't protest if I let him get back to the book he'd started glancing down at: *Moult, Ageing and Sexing of Finnish Owls*. With text, I could see, in both English and Finnish.

"I'll let you get back to your book." I'd noticed Eduardo leaving the restaurant with a loaded tray. Probably a good thing to make sure Horace actually ate the breakfast I'd sent, instead of losing himself in that mountain of paper.

"No problem." He looked down at his book and then back up at me.

"They don't really think it's Dr. Blake, do they?" he asked.

"Why would they think that?"

"Rumor has it that they talked to him more than twice as long as they did to anyone else," he said. "And he quarreled with Frogmore yesterday. Pretty badly."

"If Grandfather bumped off everyone he ever had a shouting match with he'd have run out of family, friends, and colleagues by now," I said. "Don't worry about it."

"If you say so." Lindquist went back to his book, but his face suggested that he was still worried.

Maybe I should ask around to find out exactly what the rumor mill was saying.

As I crossed the lobby, the familiar choral version of "I Heard the Bells on Christmas Day" was nearing its conclusion. Next would be the equally familiar instrumental rendition of "We Three Kings." Followed, as always, by an overly lush vocal version of "O Holy Night" that I hadn't even liked the first time I'd heard it. And I could only imagine how Sami and the other employees felt about the Inn's carefully selected but all-too-limited Christmas carol playlist.

Not the moment to tackle Ekaterina about the issue,

though. We had other, more important problems. But later . . .

"Thanks," Horace said through a mouthful of something when I reentered the Command Post. "I should have thought of this."

"You've had other things on your mind," I said. "What have you discovered?"

"I looked through all the audits to find all the times the stolen card was used," he said. "And it was only used four times."

He pointed to a five-by-eight index card he'd taped up on the wall above the desk. It contained four lines:

506-Green-Friday, 8:11 p.m.
Door to loading dock and freight elevator-Saturday, 1:15 a.m.
524-Lindquist-Saturday, 5:39 p.m.
Jefferson Cottage-Dr. Blake-Saturday 5:47 p.m.

"Curious," I said. "No sign that it was used on Dr. Frogmore's room?"

"Which would be 504, and no." He frowned at the list, clearly finding it as unsatisfactory as I did. "Which means it couldn't have been used to plant the Viagra in Frogmore's room."

"Where did you find the Viagra, anyway?"

"In the drawer of one of the bedside tables. Only thing in the drawer, apart from the hotel-issued Bible."

"So it could have been there for a while without being noticed," I mused.

"If you're suggesting that some previous guest left it behind and the staff never noticed—"

"No, that's pretty unlikely. The housekeepers are really thorough about their post-checkout cleanup. They know Ekaterina does a lot of random inspections. But I was thinking that if someone planted the Viagra, they could have done so at any time between when he checked in on Thursday and when you searched his room."

"But not with the stolen key card." Horace looked glum. "So who knows if the key card has anything to do with the murder?"

"What's the story on the three stray sheep?" Seeing Horace's puzzled look, I elaborated. "The three guys who had the bad luck to sit at Frogmore's table and ended up with a front-row seat for his demise. Remember, I sent them in last night."

"They don't seem to have any connection to Frogmore," Horace said. "All from the East Coast. Only knew him by reputation before coming to the conference. Didn't seem to enjoy being at his table. Oh, and they confirmed what you said about Frogmore taking something for a head-ache near the end of the meal. Not that we doubted you, but they gave us a lot more detail." He glanced down at his notebook, flipped a couple of pages, and continued. "Frogmore asked Czerny if he had anything for a head-ache. Czerny didn't, so Frogmore made the request again to the whole table. Lindquist said he had some Tylenol in his pocket, but Green intervened and started what sounded as if it was going to be a long lecture on the dan-gers of combining acetaminophen and alcohol."

"Dad will be pleased," I said. "To know that someone else is looking out for the endangered livers of the world."

"So then Lindquist interrupted to say, 'Just give him an aspirin, then, if you have one,'" Horace went on. "And Dr. Green did, and Dr. Frogmore took it and went back to his monologue. Without even thanking Dr. Green accord-ing to more than one witness."

"Are we sure it was aspirin?"

"Not yet." Horace sighed. "They were in one of those little individual-dose sealed packets that are easy to slip in your pocket. Dr. Green originally had two on him. I confiscated the one he had left, and I bagged the empty packet as evidence. Odds are it will be only aspirin. I suppose you could make an authentic-looking fake aspirin packet with poison in it, and carry it around in your pocket on the chance that someone you want to kill will come down with a headache at the right moment, but it seems a little far-fetched."

"Yes." I nodded my agreement. "Of course, if you wanted to kill someone with something that could be mistaken for aspirin, you could carry it around in your pocket, along with a legitimate individual-dose sealed packet from which you'd already removed the aspirin—"

"I hate you sometimes," Horace said, in a tone free of any real animosity.

"But I think that's equally far-fetched," I went on. "And I can't really see Dr. Green doing something that sneaky. Or that organized. I've been wondering if whatever college he teaches in assigns him a keeper."

"He struck me that way, too," Horace said. "So who stole the key card? That's what I'm trying to figure out. Along with, what were they up to in those four places, and does it have anything to do with the murder?"

"Why use it on the Jefferson Cottage at all?" I wondered aloud. "Grandfather was making it available to attendees who wanted to hold small meetings or prep for their sessions, which means that anyone at the conference could probably find an excuse for traipsing through there sometime on Saturday."

"So now I'm trying to see if I can eliminate anyone," Horace said. "For example, Dr. Czerny used his own key card to go into his room at five forty p.m. Saturday night. He's in room B212."

"Oooh," I said. "He didn't rate one of the nicer rooms in the South Wing, then." Actually, even the worst rooms at the Inn were pretty darn nice, but Ekaterina liked to reserve the larger rooms in the South Wing for her most distinguished guests—which was why most of the more prominent ornithologists at the conference were all along the same corridor. "And I see what you mean," I went on aloud. "No way he could make it from Lindquist's room on the fifth floor to his own room in one minute."

"So that eliminates him," Horace said.

"Not necessarily," I said. "What if he and, say, Melissa McKendrick were in cahoots? He could have used it Friday night to hit Green's room and the freight elevator, and then given it to her to enter Lindquist's room and the cottage."

"Did I mention that I hate you sometimes?" He looked crestfallen. "I should have thought of that. Yes, it could be two people in cahoots."

"Or maybe whoever used it Friday night lost it or threw it away after doing whatever they wanted to do," I said. "And someone else found it, figured out what it was, and used it for their own purposes."

He nodded.

"Sorry," I said. "Back to the drawing board?"

"Not really. So far I was just noting instances where someone was using their card at about the same time as the stolen card was being used someplace else. I hadn't gotten around to eliminating people altogether because I haven't yet timed the distances involved. And as far as why anyone would want to break into those four places, your guess is as good as mine. Possibly better—you know these people better than I do."

Maybe now was the right moment to bring up the odd thing Dr. Lindquist had said—that Dr. Green wouldn't hurt a spider.

"Look—this may having nothing to do with the stolen

key card," I said. "But did you hear about the black widow spider Dr. Green found in his room Saturday morning?"

"I heard about it." Horace's tone was careful. "Your grandfather told us all about it last night when we questioned him, but neither he nor your father thought it could account for Frogmore's symptoms, so I'm not sure what it could possibly have to do with the murder."

"Maybe nothing," I said. "But what if it has something to do with the stolen key card? I was talking to Dr. Lindquist just now—asking him what he thought of some of the suspects. He said that Ben Green wouldn't hurt a spider."

"Instead of 'wouldn't hurt a fly,' you mean." He glanced at the index card. "You think he put the spider in Green's room?"

"It's possible. They seem to be friends, in a weird *Odd Couple* kind of way. Lindquist appears to enjoy teasing Green, who doesn't seem to mind."

"I'm not sure he even notices," Horace said. "He's very . . . earnest. And literal. And considering it's me saying that, he's pretty bad."

I nodded. Yes, if you were describing Horace, earnest and literal might be two of your adjectives. I'd have gone with doggedly precise, myself, and I could think of worse things to call a forensic specialist.

"So he sneaks the black widow spider into Green's room as a prank," I said aloud.

"Knowing that his friend could get bitten? Sounds more like attempted murder than a prank."

"Not really—their bites are not as dangerous as the popular myths make it seem," I said. "I mean, yeah, it's serious, but it's unlikely to kill a guy Green's size. You should know that, as often as Grandfather has lectured us on how black widow spiders get a bad rap."

"Your grandfather also thinks crocodiles, wolverines, and rattlesnakes get a bad rap," Horace replied.

"And besides," I went on, "Green's a biologist—Lindquist might have reason to assume he'd recognize a black widow spider and know how to deal with it."

"So maybe just a prank, but also maybe he had it in for Green," Horace said. "You're thinking the Friday evening access to Green's room is when someone—possibly Lindquist—put the black widow in the bathroom?"

"The timing fits. The spider arrives Friday night, but Green doesn't find it until he's using the bathroom when he's wide awake on Saturday morning."

"Okay, weird idea," Horace said. "But could someone have been trying to put the spider in Frogmore's room? It's right next door. I'll have to check, but I think the common wall between the two is where the bathroom is. Maybe Frogmore was in his room, so they didn't want to go in, but they took the spider into the bathroom and turned it loose right next to where the pipes go through the wall."

"Seems farfetched," I said. "They'd have no way of being sure the spider would go where they wanted it to go. Better just to come back later and put it right where they want it."

"You're right. Stupid idea."

"Of course, if the spider was meant for Frogmore, it could still have ended up in Green's room. What if the bringer of spiders got the room number wrong? The most distinguished guests are all there in a row on the fifth floor, where the fanciest rooms are."

"I like that theory." He looked cheerful again. "I should call the chief and brief him."

Something struck me.

"Good grief," I said. "Dr. Green was right between Dr. Frogmore and the Vosses. Ekaterina had her staff spray all three rooms with whatever the hotel uses to kill and repel spiders. What if that poisoned him?"

"And had no effect on Dr. Green and Dr. and Mrs. Voss?"

"Maybe it affected them to a lesser degree."

"And doesn't the Inn brag about how they only use the most environmentally friendly cleaning products?" Horace asked.

"Environmentally friendly doesn't necessary mean Frogmore friendly," I said. "What if whatever the Inn uses is something he's allergic to? Or maybe it affected Frogmore only because it combined with something he drank or ate. I don't know. Even if it's a completely stupid theory, if I can think of it, so can the defense attorney who's representing whoever you eventually arrest for this."

"So I'll need to find out what's in the spray the hotel uses," Horace said. "And find out—"

Someone knocked on the door. Horace and I looked up to see the door open, revealing Dr. Czerny.

Chapter 20

"Can I talk to you?" Czerny's posture seemed to have improved a little—I supposed he no longer had to crouch to appease Dr. Frogmore.

"Of course," Horace said. "What can I do for you . . ."

It occurred to me that Horace was trying, unsuccessfully, to remember our visitor's name. Not surprising—he'd interviewed a lot of people in the last twelve hours.

"How are you doing, Dr. Czerny," I said. "I know you've had a terrible shock."

"I have confidential information." Dr. Czerny glared at me, doubtless to suggest that his information was for Horace's ears only.

"I see." Horace slid a chair over toward Dr. Czerny. "Meg, why don't you shut the door so no one can eavesdrop. And take your notes in shorthand. More confidential," he added, beaming at Dr. Czerny. "Meg's the mayor's executive assistant—we were lucky to have her available to provide administrative support for our investigation."

I deduced that, for whatever reason, Horace wanted company for his talk with Czerny. I sat down, took out my notebook and pencil, and tried to look official.

Our visitor didn't look happy, but he didn't protest.

"I have a lead for you." He ignored me and focused on Horace.

"Want to tell me about it?" You probably had to know Horace pretty well to figure out that he was thinking, "Please, no; not another wannabe sleuth."

Dr. Czerny leaned forward and fixed his eyes on Horace's.

"Those three strange men who were at Dr. Frogmore's table." Having said that, he sat up and looked triumphant.

"Ye-es?" Horace said, in an encouraging tone.

"They're the ones?"

"All three of them?"

"Quite possibly. Or one of them."

Horace glanced at me. I shrugged almost invisibly, to indicate that no, I didn't get it, either.

"Who are these men?" Horace asked. "And—"

"Exactly!" Dr. Czerny exclaimed. "I don't know them. Dr. Frogmore didn't know them. If Drs. Green or Lindquist know them they're not admitting to it. Who are they?"

"Two of them are grad students," I said. "Smith and Whitmore, if memory serves. And the third, Belasco, is an assistant professor—I can't remember where. Northwestern maybe? Or University of Chicago. Someplace in Illinois, anyway. But Horace already interviewed them, so I'm sure he has everything about them in his notes."

Horace nodded.

"And what were two graduate students and a very junior professor doing at the head table—at Dr. Frogmore's table? Can you answer that?"

I could, obviously, but I wasn't sure Dr. Czerny would like the answer.

Horace spoke up.

"They all said there was no place else to sit. They came in late, and Dr. Frogmore's table was the only one that still had seats."

"Ridiculous!" Dr. Czerny glared at us.

"I think the problem was that most of the other attendees were too intimidated to sit with Dr. Frogmore," I said. "After all, it was the head table! And you have to admit that Dr. Frogmore is—was—pretty imposing."

"I suppose that's true," he said. "But I still don't buy it. They engineered it. They must have chased everyone else away somehow. Told them the seats were taken, I suppose. But it was all part of their plot to insinuate themselves into Dr. Frogmore's presence so they could assassinate him!"

Horace and I exchanged a glance.

"Do you have any idea why they would want to, er, do away with Dr. Frogmore?" Horace asked.

"How do I know? That's your job, isn't it? They were at the table, and they shouldn't have been. Isn't that enough? Although if you want more—they've been behaving very strangely. Acting nervous and edgy. Easily startled. Constantly trying to sneak away. I've been keeping my eye on them, and I can assure you—they're definitely behaving strangely."

Behaving strangely? What Czerny had just described sounded like exactly how I'd behave if I noticed that he was following me around the conference and glaring accusingly at me.

I scribbled madly in my notebook, mainly so I'd have a reason not to keep looking at Czerny's face, with its fierce, predatory expression.

Horace glanced over to see what I was writing and almost lost it when he saw that I was writing, over and over again, "I must not tell Dr. Czerny what an idiot he is. I must not tell Dr. Czerny what an idiot he is." He turned away suddenly, overtaken by a sudden coughing fit, and didn't turn around again until he had his face back under control. And then his mouth twitched again and he looked at me for help.

"Thank you for bringing this to our attention, Dr. Czerny," I said, in the most solemn tone I could muster. "I can assure you that these three men are very definitely on Horace's suspect list." Horace nodded, and emitted a few more gentle coughs. "We can't say any more than that about the progress of an ongoing investigation, you understand."

I reached into my purse, pulled out a box of cough lozenges I'd tucked in there in case any of the speakers needed them, and handed one to Horace.

"Well." Dr. Czerny stood. He still didn't look entirely content. "As long as you're taking this seriously."

"Very seriously," I said. "And before you go—be careful. We're aware of these men now. Don't put yourself at risk. Remember, we're looking for someone who committed a brutal, cold-blooded murder. Don't follow these men, or keep watch on them, or give them any reason to suspect that you're on to them. In fact, you should probably avoid them entirely. Right, Horace?"

Horace, sucking ostentatiously on the cough lozenge, nodded briskly. Then he opened his mouth and, after a brief introductory cough, croaked out the words, "Stay safe!"

Dr. Czerny nodded, and turned to leave in what I'm sure he thought was a dignified manner. He paused in the doorway and turned back to us.

"And I don't believe the rumors going around about Dr. Blake," he said. "I can't imagine him doing anything like that. I'm sure he's completely gotten over his disappointment about the medal."

"Medal?" Horace asked.

"The Frogmore Medal for Excellence in Ornithology." Dr. Czerny's tone suggested that next to this the Nobel Prize was small potatoes. "Named after Dr. Frogmore, of course, who was its first recipient. I'm sure they'll get around to honoring Dr. Blake sooner or later."

As he turned to go, I could tell from his smile that he thought he'd handed us the solution to the case.

I followed him to the door and shut it carefully behind him.

"Oh, Lord," Horace said, his voice normal, though interspersed with chuckles. "Those poor guys. Sorry to drag you into it, but I'd already noticed that the guy's a little unbalanced over losing his boss—I didn't want to talk to him without backup."

"No problem."

"And what he had to say explains a lot. I'll have to tell the chief."

"Explains what?" Surely Horace wasn't taking the Frogmore medal thing seriously.

"I interviewed all three of them this morning," he said. "With the chief on the radio. And all three of them came across as . . . well . . . twitchy."

"I'd be twitchy, too, if Dr. Czerny were following me around."

"Exactly. Just talking to him makes me twitchy," Horace grumbled. "And what is this about a medal that Dr. Blake is supposed to be put out about not getting?"

"Beats me," I said. "I never heard of it. And do you really think Grandfather would care that much about a medal named after Dr. Frogmore?"

"Good point," he said. "Enough of Dr. Czerny. Any chance you could bring Dr. Lindquist here? I'm going to brief the chief—about all this, including the bug spray theory—and then we can tackle Lindquist about the key card."

"Can do," I said.

I stepped outside and looked around to make sure no one was nearby. Then I called Ekaterina.

"How is the investigation going?" she asked.

"I think they're making progress," I said. "Horace needs something. Can you bring him a container of whatever you had sprayed to kill the spiders?"

There was a pause.

"Meg, that spray is environmentally correct! Because

we have no desire to poison guests! Is made with essential oils and—"

"I assumed it would be." In fact, I knew she'd consulted several environmentalists, including Grandfather, about her choice of cleaning supplies and pesticides. "And I can't imagine that the bug spray had any effect on him—but we need Horace and Dad to examine the spray and confirm that. So if anyone tries to start a nasty rumor and blame the hotel, we can all say that no, our forensic and medical experts say that was not a factor."

"That would be helpful," she said. "I will bring samples of the spray to the Command Post." With that, she hung up. I headed for the restaurant to look for Dr. Lindquist. Who had finished his breakfast fifteen minutes earlier, according to Eduardo. I found him in the Gathering Area, talking with two other scientists.

Actually, when I got closer I realized he was telling them owl jokes.

"I give up," an angular woman in jeans was saying. "Why did the owl invite all his friends over?"

"He didn't want to be owl by himself!" Dr. Lindquist roared with laughter. The other two scientists' appreciation was more subdued.

"Okay, here's another," Lindquist said. "What kind of books do owls like to read?"

"Hoo-dunnets," I said.

"You already heard it?" Dr. Lindquist looked crushed.

"From my middle-school twin boys," I said.

Dr. Lindquist's audience seemed to find this funnier than the joke.

"Dr. Lindquist, Deputy Hollingsworth wants to pick your brain about something," I said. "Could you drop by and see him sometime soon—whenever you're free."

"I'm free now." He looked at his watch. "And I'd just

as soon get it over before the first panel starts. Catch you later," he said to the other two.

He strode toward the door to the lobby and I followed along behind, in the hope that Horace would let me kibitz on his interview. After all, I was the one who brought the possibility of Dr. Lindquist as the card thief to his attention.

When I entered the office, I heard Horace talking— presumably to the chief.

"Oh, good," he said. "Meg just brought in Dr. Lindquist. I expect he can help us with this."

Dr. Lindquist took one of the guest chairs. I sat in the corner and tried to look official, while not making any noise, in case the chief hadn't intended for me to stay.

"Dr. Lindquist. Thank you for dropping by." The chief's voice sounded very genial. He was probably trying to lull Lindquist into a sense of complacency. I tried to make my expression neutral and reassuring.

"Meg said you had a few more questions? Happy to help."

He didn't look anxious. Did that mean he wasn't guilty of killing Frogmore? Or only that he was confident that he'd gotten away with it?

"Yes, there is one thing we'd like to clear up. On Saturday morning, Dr. Benjamin Green found a black widow spider in the bathroom of his hotel room."

The grin that crossed Lindquist's face convinced me that yes, he was the one who'd planted the spider.

"That must have been quite a shock for him," he said.

"Yes." The chief paused for a moment. "So would you like to tell us how you obtained the housekeeping key card you used to plant the spider? And also what else you did with the key card while you had it?"

Lindquist's grin vanished.

"How do you—? Wait a minute. I didn't do anything else. What are you accusing me of?"

"Why don't you tell us precisely what happened?"

Lindquist nodded and glanced at me and Horace before continuing.

"Okay, so Ben and I like to play pranks on each other. Well, it's mostly me playing pranks on him, but he seems to get a kick out of it."

Maybe he did. Green was definitely an odd bird. Of course, so was Lindquist.

"The night before I took off to come here, I found the spider in my carport, and I thought it would be a great gag to plant it somewhere and let Ben find it. See how sincere he was about the whole deal of respecting even the smallest of life-forms? I figured I could find someone on the housekeeping staff to let me into his room to put it there—I hadn't decided whether to pretend it was my room or say I had a surprise gift for him. And as it turned out, I didn't need to. I was so busy Friday that I didn't even get away from the conference until after dinner, and halfway up to my room I realized that the housekeeping staff would almost certainly have gone home. Or gone to wherever in the hotel they were staying, I guess, given the weather. But I remembered seeing this room at the end of the hall where they stash the cleaning carts when they go off duty. I stuck my head in, just in case one of the housekeeping staff might be hanging out there, and saw one of them had left her key card lying on top of her cart." He sat back as if he'd just explained everything.

"So you stole it." The chief's stern tone seemed to rattle Lindquist.

"No, I only borrowed it," he protested, "For maybe ten minutes. The spider was in my room, just down the hall, so I grabbed it, took it to Ben's room, and let it loose under the sink. Then I took the card right back and left it just where I'd found it."

"On the housekeeper's cart."

Lindquist nodded.

"That would be a yes," Horace said for the chief's benefit.

"Did anyone spot you?" I asked.

"The staff had gone off duty."

"Any other guests passing by?" Horace asked.

"Not that I remember. But I'm not sure I even noticed, so there could have been." Dr. Lindquist seemed to find that thought reassuring. "Anyone else could have done the same thing. And someone else must have if any mischief was done with it."

"About what time was it when you stole the card?" the chief asked.

"I didn't— I don't know precisely when I *borrowed* the card. It was during Dr. Blake's after-dinner party Friday night. I noticed that he and Ben were deep in conversation about something, so I figured it was a good time to plant the spider. The party ran from eight to nine, and this would have been closer to the beginning than the end. Maybe eight fifteen. No later than eight thirty."

Horace nodded and glanced at something he was holding—the list of times when the key card was used, which he'd remembered to take off the wall before Lindquist had come in.

"And you didn't borrow the card again later that evening?" the chief asked. "Or at any time on Saturday?"

Lindquist shook his head and then belatedly said, "No."

"Horace? Any other points you want to ask about?"

"No, Chief."

"That will be all for now, Dr. Lindquist."

The emphasis he put on "now" was very subtle, but it didn't escape Lindquist's ear.

Chapter 21

Dr. Lindquist stood and hesitated for a moment.

"But don't leave town without telling you, right?" he said sardonically.

When the chief didn't say anything, Lindquist stood, nodded to Horace and me, and left. Horace and I stayed silent until thirty seconds after the door closed behind him.

"I don't like it," Horace said. "There's no proof he returned the card. We have only his word."

"There's also no proof he ever stole it," I pointed out. "The chief bluffed him into admitting it."

"Should hold up in court if it comes to that," Horace said.

"But would he have so readily admitted it in the first place if he'd hung on to it longer and done something else less innocent with it?" I asked.

"A good point," the chief said. "And there's also the fact that we haven't figured out what, if anything, the illicit access to the freight elevator, Dr. Blake's cottage, and Dr. Lindquist's own room have to do with Dr. Frogmore's murder."

"That's true." Horace slumped slightly and blew out a frustrated breath. "I forgot that. He'd have no reason to use the stolen card to open his own door."

"No reason," I said. "But the two times the card was used on Saturday were during the half hour break between the end of the last panel and the start of dinner, right?"

"That's right," Horace said. "Five thirty-nine p.m. and five forty-seven p.m."

"So if he went up to his room before dinner, he'd have been in a hurry," I said. "He could have pulled out the stolen card by accident, thinking he was grabbing his own."

"Quite possible," the chief said. "And let's not forget that just because the stolen card wasn't used on Dr. Frogmore's room doesn't mean no one accessed it without his knowing. Horace, have you made arrangements with Ekaterina for us to interview the housekeeping staff who handle that floor?"

"To see if any of them got any requests from guests to let them into Dr. Frogmore's room," Horace explained to me.

"Or any other rooms, for that matter," the chief added.

"The first few should be here anytime now," Horace said. "I have to say, hunting down witnesses and suspects is a lot easier with nobody able to skip out on us. By the way, Meg, thanks for telling Ekaterina to bring us the bug spray."

He pointed to a corner of the long desk where half a dozen different spray containers rested. There were several different kinds, all with either "eco" or "natural" in their names. And all boasted in large letters that they were nontoxic to children and pets.

"Smart lady," the chief said. "Apparently she brought us all the containers that were not sealed. If necessary, we could have them all tested to make sure they only contain what's on the label."

I heard something outside, so I got up and peered out the door.

"I think your first few interviewees are here." Serafina, Chantal, and a male housekeeping staff member whose name I didn't remember were all sitting on the bench outside the Command Post. None of them looked very pleased to be there, and I was willing to bet that none of them would admit to letting anyone into anyplace. Still, Horace had to try. "I'll leave you to it."

I stepped out into the lobby and looked around. About the usual number of people were watching the snow, debating how many inches had fallen, and gasping over whatever ghastly new low temperature the thermometer revealed. Mother, Mrs. Ackley, and another woman were sitting together by the fire. Mother waved to me, and although a casual observer would never have noticed, I picked up a certain frantic note to her manner. I strolled over to see what was up.

"Meg, dear." Mother gave me a kiss that almost landed on my cheek instead of the air. "This is Mrs. Voss—her husband's attending your grandfather's conference. And this is Mrs. Ackley—she and her husband came to visit Caerphilly and didn't manage to get out before the storm began."

Mrs. Voss was a pleasant fiftyish woman who was doing an intricate crewelwork picture of an owl. She nodded and smiled at me before going back to squinting at her work. Mrs. Ackley was a little older—in her sixties, I'd have guessed, and seemed nice enough, if a little anxious.

"That's lovely," I said to Mrs. Voss.

"Thanks." She smiled briefly. "Wish my husband thought so. Apparently whoever designed the pattern took liberties with the owl's plumage. Or as George puts it, 'there is no such owl.' They can be so literal."

"Tell him it's a new species Dr. Hirano hasn't yet published about."

She burst out in chuckles at the thought and plied her needle with a happier expression.

"My daughter Meg is helping her grandfather organize the conference," Mother was saying to Mrs. Ackley.

"That must be very interesting for you, dear." Mrs. Ackley

turned to me. "And what a nice opportunity—there must be a few young, single scientists here, I suppose."

"There probably are," I said. "But I haven't seen any nearly as handsome as my husband, so I think I'll stick with him."

"Oh, silly me," she said. "You hardly look old enough to be married."

I could get to like this woman.

"Then again, ever since we moved to Florida, I hardly ever get to see anyone under retirement age," she said. "I try not to let Jim know, because I know he meant well, but I really wish we hadn't moved. We had a couple of acres at our old house, and this new one doesn't have a yard to speak of. And in our old house we'd have had plenty of room for the kids and grandkids—in Florida they're staying in a hotel. It just won't feel like Christmas. If we even get there. We could be stuck here. And even if we do get out, there won't be time to cook. And there's a lot of cooking. Jim insists on prime rib, and the kids want ham, because we used to have Christmas with my parents and that's what their grandmother always served, and of course, as soon as they went to college, hardly a holiday went by without one or another deciding to be a vegetarian just in time for the holidays. So I always make a big dish of macaroni and cheese. The children have settled down, thank goodness, but I know it's only a matter of time before the grandchildren start going through vegetarian phases."

Mrs. Ackley went on at great length about the particular way she had to make the macaroni and cheese, although if there was anything special about her recipe it must have been a subtlety that escaped me. She also had much to say about the preparation of the vegetables and the need to make what sounded like a different pie for every member of the family. Mrs. Voss looked up and rolled her eyes from time to time. Mother was gazing at Mrs. Ackley with an expression of rapt attention on her face, but I knew her well enough to suspect that she wasn't listening to a word.

Was there some reason we were sitting here listening? Granted, Mrs. Ackley looked happier than she had before. But if Mother didn't have things to do, I certainly did.

I could pretend to spot someone across the room who needed to talk to me. Yes. A good plan.

I was about to put it into practice when Mrs. Ackley suddenly did exactly what I'd been planning to do. Although a quick glance across the lobby showed that she wasn't feigning. Her husband had arrived.

"There's Jim." Mrs. Ackley stood, and dithered a bit, as if unsure whether to stay and continue talking or leave. "My husband, Jim. He seems to be looking for me. I should go. It was so nice talking to all of you. We must do it again soon!"

With that she tripped across the lobby.

"Not if I can help it," I muttered.

"Amen." Mrs. Voss glanced over at where the Ackleys were talking. "No offense, but I'm leaving before she decides to come back."

She gathered up her canvas and her threads and beat a hasty retreat to the elevators.

"Well, I hope it was at least useful," Mother said.

"Useful?" Was this some form of unusually subtle sarcasm that completely escaped me?

"For the case, dear." Mother was patience itself. "I know you're doing your best to help Horace and your father. I thought if we got her talking, you might notice a clue that would help you solve the case."

"Getting her talking doesn't seem to be a problem," I pointed out. "Shutting her up, maybe."

"Yes, she could talk the hind leg off a donkey."

"She could talk all the legs off a whole herd of centipedes, and I can't imagine she'd drop any useful clues."

"Isn't her husband a suspect?" Mother asked. "I thought all the scientists were suspects."

"Her husband isn't a scientist," I said. "Retired businessman. They're two of the precisely three hotel guests who have no connection whatsoever with the conference. Mrs. Voss's husband is a scientist, so feel free to take another crack at her."

"I would have, if Mrs. Ackley had given me half a chance." Mother closed her eyes and sighed heavily. I resisted the urge to apologize or feel guilty. Had I suggested that she interrogate Mrs. Ackley? "The time I wasted on that tiresome woman."

Mrs. Ackley, heading for the restaurant in her husband's wake, waved at us in passing. Mother waved back with a smile that didn't get anywhere near her eyes.

"Well, I'm going up to the spa," she said. "I assume except for that third unconnected guest, the other people there will be either scientists or partners of scientists."

"Definitely," I said. "And actually, our conversation with Mrs. Ackley wasn't completely wasted. Ekaterina has a project." I explained about the need to find out what everyone was expecting in the way of Christmas food.

Mother, as I had hoped, was charmed by the idea.

"Splendid! Ekaterina's right—that will go a long way toward building Christmas spirit. I'll start immediately in the spa. Just one thing—do you happen to remember what the Ackley's Christmas meal was like? I confess, I'd rather tuned her out by that time. I was thinking of chintz and passementerie—that always improves my mood."

"Prime rib, ham, mac and cheese for any transient vegetarians, green bean casserole, mashed potatoes, clover-leaf rolls, and four kinds of pie."

"Lovely." Mother took out her pocket notebook—a far cry from my bulging, utilitarian notebook-that-tells-me-when-to-breathe. It was tiny and elegant, and had a little loop to hold the minuscule gold-colored pen. She quickly scribbled down the list I'd rattled off, then returned it to her purse.

"You can tackle that, then?" I asked. "Given that I'll be pretty busy, between the conference and the investigation."

"Leave it to me, dear."

"And one more thing," I added. "Have you noticed that Dr. Green—"

"Seems rather taken with Rose Noire," she said. "And we don't really know much about him, do we? So I'm having him checked out."

"Don't interrogate him too harshly," I said. "He's already pretty shook up at being a murder suspect."

"Don't worry, dear. I borrowed a satellite phone and asked Kevin to see what he could find out." I nodded with approval. Information my nephew Kevin couldn't find online probably didn't exist. "So I can concentrate on finding out what everyone eats for Christmas."

She sailed off toward the elevators with a look of cheerful determination on her face. Woe betide the hotel guest who tried to withhold information about his family's customary holiday menu.

During our conversation with Mrs. Ackley, two of the three hotel staff members had, in their turn, entered the Command Post and eventually departed looking relieved. I watched as the third entered and glanced around. Shouldn't there be more arriving for their turn?

Ekaterina's problem, not mine.

I was about to return to the conference area when I spotted two figures sitting in front of the huge glass wall of the lobby—in fact, they appeared to have turned their chairs, the better to watch the falling snow outside, although they were also engaged in a lively conversation. Melissa McKendrick and the Australian scientist. I decided to see what they were up to.

Chapter 22

Both Melissa and the Australian ornithologist said a quick hello when I neared them, although they continued on with their conversation. I took a surreptitious peek at the man's badge: Dr. Lachlan Pearce from Sidney.

"But the most amazing thing about the tawny frog-mouth is its ability to camouflage itself." It sounded rather dashing in Pearce's Aussie accent. "The brown, gray, and white plumage is perfect for blending in with tree branches. They're nocturnal, like owls, and after hunting all night they spend most of their day perched in a tree, camouflaged to look like part of it. In fact, they often sit on a broken branch and then twist themselves into a posture that makes them look like a continuation of the branch." He contorted himself into a weird posture. He didn't look much like a tree branch, but then he didn't look much like an edible bird, either. Maybe if he had the tawny frog-mouth's feathers to help, his tree impersonation would be a lot more believable. "It's brilliant."

"You have them in Sydney?" Melissa asked. Was she interested in the bird, the bloke, or only hearing more of the bloke's charming accent?

"All over. They're amazing for pest control—almost everything they eat is either a household pest or a garden threat. I rescued one a month or so back—he'd hopped into a wheelie bin for a sticky and couldn't get back out."

"A wheelie bin's what my Australian nieces and nephews

call a garbage can," I translated, seeing Melissa's puzzled look. "And I guess a sticky's a foraging expedition?"

"Close enough. Anyway, the frogmouth was so fierce-looking, the bin's owners were scared to stick their hands in, so they called the ornithology department and I went out to save the day." He basked in the memory for a few moments. Then he seemed to notice the snowy window again. "Damn, the snow's slowed down a bit, but it's not exactly stopping, is it? How long has it been now?"

"Closing in on thirty-six hours," I said. "But you're right—it's not coming down as heavily as it was. Tapering off, thank goodness."

"I suppose it's time, but I've had a blast watching it. We don't get much snow in Sydney. In fact, we don't get any," Lachlan said.

"Much the same for Atlanta, where I grew up," Melissa said. "We had a white Christmas in 2010, but before that we literally hadn't had one in a century."

"This could be my first white Christmas ever," Lachlan proclaimed. "Unless it's all going to go away over the next few days."

"The high temperature won't get out of the twenties for the next few days," I said. "So if you're sticking around, the snow will be, too."

"I warned the family that I might miss the usual festivities," he said. "And they promised they'd do it all over again when I got home, even if I didn't show up till Anzac Day."

"If there's anything that would make the holiday feel more festive, let Ekaterina know," I said. "Especially when it comes to meals. What foods will you miss most if you're stuck here?"

"Cold prawns for Christmas lunch," he said readily. "Cold seafood generally. And a pav for dessert. Of course, we usually go for the cold foods for Christmas because it's damned hot in December—in the twenties. Celsius. I think that's the seventies in Fahrenheit. So most of us are running around in boardies and thongs."

I wondered if my jaw had dropped quite as noticeably as Melissa's. Not that the thought of the lean, muscular Lachlan in skimpy underwear was off-putting—quite the contrary. But still . . .

"Although I think here you'd say swimming trunks and flip-flops," he went on. From the twinkle in his eye, I suspected this wasn't the first time he'd had fun confounding Americans in this way.

"I suspect Ekaterina might manage the prawns," I said. "Or at least some kind of cold seafood. Your thongs might be a little harder."

"Not sure I'd want them in this weather," he said with a chuckle. "There's also the traditional game of backyard cricket, but even if we had the gear, I doubt if anyone would be up for it in the snow. And if I'm still stuck over here after Christmas Day, I hope I can find some channel that's showing the Boxing Day Test Match—big five-day cricket match. Sometimes I think Boxing Day's the best part of the holidays—plenty of leftovers that you're not yet tired of, all the rellos have gone home, and you can just lie on the couch with a Carlton's and a sanger and watch the test match."

He looked almost dreamy eyed at the prospect, and I got the feeling he was just a little homesick. I made a mental note to ask Ekaterina about the prawns. I was about to ask what pav, Carlton's, and sanger were when Grandfather's voice rang out from across the lobby.

"Pearce!"

We all looked up to see Grandfather waving at us. Mostly at Pearce, I suspected.

"I should go see what the good doctor wants," he said. "Talk to you later."

He loped across the lobby at a good pace and disappeared into Mount Vernon Grill with Grandfather.

"Nice guy," I said.

"Not my type," Melissa said with a grin. "But there's nothing wrong with window shopping. Besides, it's a nice change to talk with someone who knows very little and cares even less about the barred and spotted owls."

"I hear you."

She looked away from the snowy window and stared for a few minutes at the roaring fire that filled the hearth. She shivered slightly.

"Warmer near the fire," I said.

"I'm not really cold," she said. "Just a little creeped out. I've never seen someone die before. Dead bodies at funerals, yeah, but not someone actually dying. And I wish they'd figure out who did it. I was really enjoying the conference until Frogmore bought it. Now, every time I talk to someone, I can't help but wonder if he did it. Especially—"

She stopped herself and stared back out at the snow again.

I got the feeling she needed to talk, so I just stared out at the snow with her.

"I've been wondering if I should tell the chief something." She stopped and looked down at her feet.

"Something you saw?" I asked, finally.

"Something I overheard." She looked up, seemed to come to a decision, and words began tumbling out. "I was sitting in the conference office yesterday afternoon and I overheard Dr. Green talking to Dr. Lindquist. He was really mad—Dr. Lindquist, I mean—and Dr. Green was trying to calm him down."

"Mad about what?"

"Dr. Frogmore. He was really going on about it. What a buffoon he was, how badly he treated anyone he didn't think was important enough to suck up to, how incompetent he was. How he was making the whole barred owl issue a laughingstock, no matter which side you were on. And he kept saying . . ." She paused and took a deep breath before going on. "He kept saying they had to get him. Dr. Frogmore. 'We've got to get him,' he said. 'No matter what it takes. We can't let him go on like this. We've got to get him.'"

"That's kind of creepy," I said. "He wasn't more specific—about how they were going to get him?"

"No." She shook her head slowly. "At the time, I thought they meant—you know, professionally. I mean, most people have figured out that Frogmore isn't—wasn't—the Einstein of ornithology or anything. He had a lot of power, for some reason, but he hadn't really done that much in the field. I thought Dr. Lindquist was talking about showing him up. Like . . . I don't know. Taking some of this papers apart and demonstrating how useless or even downright wrong they were. That kind of thing. But now . . ."

Her voice trailed off, and she stared out at the snow again.

What she said didn't clash with what Dr. Lindquist had told Horace and the chief. Or what he'd said to me. Maybe he had been talking about exposing Frogmore. Discrediting him. But what if that wasn't all he and Dr. Green had been talking about?

"Are you thinking now that maybe he decided to knock Frogmore off?"

"That doesn't sound like him," she protested. "And what I overheard—I got the idea he was really angry at something Dr. Frogmore had just done. Maybe he was just blowing off steam. Making empty threats. Dr. Green's pretty good at calming people down."

"Yeah," I said. "But what if they weren't empty threats,

and what if even Dr. Green couldn't calm him down this time?"

"You think I should tell the police, then?"

I nodded.

"Even if it gets Dr. Lindquist in trouble? And maybe even Dr. Green for not reporting it already?"

"How do you know Dr. Green didn't?" I asked. "He seems like the kind of earnest guy who would. For that matter, I bet he confessed any hostile, negative thoughts he'd had himself about Frogmore."

"That sounds just like him." She giggled slightly. "Yeah. They'll keep it secret, won't they? The police, I mean. That I'm the one who reported the conversation?"

"If you ask them to, they will for the time being," I said. "If it goes to trial and what you overheard turns out to be an important part of the case, they'll need you to testify."

"But they'd need to have a lot more evidence for that, right? Because, damn it, I like Dr. Lindquist. And he's kind of a bigwig. If it turns out it's not him after all—"

"I like him, too, and I hope it turns out to be someone else," I said. "And remember, if they arrest everyone who's ever said a bad word about Dr. Frogmore, we'll all find it very crowded in the jail."

She smiled briefly and sat for a few moments, nodding. Then she stood up rather abruptly.

"I should get it over with." She squared her shoulders and marched toward the Command Post.

Chapter 23

I watched as Melissa knocked and was admitted to Horace's lair. I wasn't sure whether to be pleased that I was sending another potentially useful bit of evidence his way or depressed that the evidence seemed to implicate one of the nicer scientists.

Just then I became conscious of something my subconscious had been trying to get me to notice for a while now. The music had changed. Oh, it was still Christmas music. But someone had added new material to the playlist. It took me a few seconds to realize that the speakers were now playing a lush orchestral version of "I Saw Mommy Kissing Santa Claus." I had to chuckle. And then the next number began, and I muttered "Yes!" under my breath. One of my favorites—Wendy and Carnie Wilson's version of "Hark! The Herald Angels Sing." I closed my eyes and listened, appreciating anew the close harmony and the slow, stately arrangement. I needed to find out who had been tinkering with the Inn's Christmas music playlists. Later. For now, I just needed to listen.

"Meg?"

I waved whoever it was into silence until the last strains of the carol had died out. Then I opened my eyes to find Dad standing in front of me, a slightly worried frown on his face.

"Are you all right?"

"I'm fine," I said. "I was listening to the carol—it's one of my favorites, you know. What's up?"

"Good catch on the bug spray!" He sat in the chair Melissa had just vacated. "Of course it's unlikely to have anything to do with Frogmore's death."

"But not impossible?"

"All of the sprays Ekaterina is using are composed chiefly of essential oils," Dad said. "Which contain chemicals that are either harmless or actually beneficial to humans but that repel or even kill bugs. Cinnamon oil, tea tree oil, lavender, orange, peppermint—things like that. They'll mess with a bug's neural system, but ours works differently."

"And while I've heard a lot of insults aimed at Dr. Frogmore, I don't recall anyone accusing him of being an invertebrate."

"Precisely. So good thinking!" Dad beamed at me. "Of course, we'll have to test the contents of all those bottles to make sure no one doctored them. And we need to do some research on whether any of the sprays' ingredients have shown toxic properties, either if used to excess or in combination with any other substances Dr. Frogmore has been exposed to. Lanville's going to start working on that until I have access to my library and the Internet." Dad looked a little disappointed at not being able to start the quest himself.

"Don't fret," I said. "The snow's almost stopped. The county can start digging out—in fact, I wouldn't be surprised if Randall has gotten them started already." Of course, it could still be days before the digging reached the Inn, but seeing how his face lit up, I decided not to mention that.

"Really?" Dad glanced at the wall of glass, which still looked pretty solid white. But now you could see the mounds of snow-covered trees and shrubs, not falling flakes. "Fabulous! I've got to run. Conference call with Lanville."

He raced off, although he stopped to say hello to Mrs. Voss, who appeared to be looking for a quiet corner. She headed my way.

"Mind if I take this chair?" She gestured to the chair Dad had just vacated.

"As long as you don't feel insulted by the fact that I'm going to race off in a minute or so," I said. "I'm just waiting for someone."

"Don't worry about me," she said. "I have plenty to keep me busy."

She unfurled her crewelwork owl, and I leaned over to see it.

"Looks as if you're almost finished," I said. "Of course, I realize it's incredibly meticulous work, so I suppose 'almost finished' to me could mean you have another year or two ahead of you."

"Nothing like that." She laughed, and stretched her neck as if easing out a bit of stiffness. "A few more hours to go. And my husband's champing at the bit. Can't wait for me to finish."

"Wait—I thought your husband hated your owl for not being accurate."

"Oh, he does. But a few minutes ago—you see, he drew Dr. Czerny in the Secret Santa. He's been driving me crazy all day, badgering me to help him think of a suitable present. I finally suggested giving Czerny this." She held up the canvas. "Kills two birds with one stone. George doesn't have to look at my horribly inaccurate owl—and he gives Dr. Czerny what looks like a thoughtful and appropriate present."

"Only the inaccuracy will actually drive Dr. Czerny crazy."

"You know, we're not sure," she said. "The inaccuracy might bother him, but I don't think he'd ever be so rude as to say so. Not to the wife of someone important enough to help him out as he scrambles to rebuild his career. Not that George has any use for him, but Dr. Czerny probably doesn't realize that. No, if he notices, he'll probably hang it up anyway and brag about how kind it was of the Vosses to give it to him—a piece of Mrs. Voss's own handiwork! And if he doesn't notice, I'm sure someone will be rude enough to point it out sooner or later. Probably at the most inopportune moment. You know, I can't help feeling sorry for the poor man."

"Dr. Czerny?" I hoped I didn't sound too surprised.

"Yes. Whoever killed Dr. Frogmore might as well have put Dr. Czerny out of his misery at the same time. It would have been the humane thing to do. You know, I wonder if the police have thought of that."

"Euthanizing Dr. Czerny? Probably not legal."

"Alas, no." She paused and I looked away—strange how it bothered me to see her needle inserted in the embroidered owl's left eye. "What I mean is—they're busy figuring out who disliked Dr. Frogmore. And yes, that's a long list. But I wonder if they've given any thought to who has it in for Dr. Czerny. Because if you wanted to hurt Dr. Czerny, I can't think of a better way than to take away his lifeline. Maybe you'll think it's a silly idea."

I turned the idea around in my mind. It wasn't a bad idea at all. And Mrs. Voss knew the people involved rather better than I did. Did she have something here?

"Nothing silly about it," I said. "I'll mention it to Horace. He might want to talk to you about it."

"He's welcome to, as long as he doesn't make me put down my needle on the home stretch."

"I'll warn him. And there he is now—I should run; I want to catch him."

Melissa was leaving the Command Post, looking a lot less worried than when she'd gone in. And Horace followed her out and strolled over to where Sami was standing behind the reception desk.

"It's all Melissa's doing," Sami was saying as I drew near enough to hear what they were saying.

"Really?"

"What's all Melissa's doing?" I tried not to sound suspicious.

"The new music," Sami said. "Maybe our pretty limited Christmas playlist doesn't bother the guests."

"Yes, it does," Horace and I said in unison.

"Melissa brought in a flash drive with a whole bunch of new Christmas music and figured out how to load it into the system. I like carols as much as the next guy, but if I had to listen one more time to Mannheim Steamroller doing 'Deck the Halls'—"

"I kind of like that one," Horace said.

"So did I three weeks ago," Sami countered.

"Ah," Horace said. "Anyway, I have good news. I think." He didn't actually sound like someone delivering good news. "Judge Jane finally signed the search warrant." He opened up his notebook. "For Lindquist, Green, Craine, McKendrick, Czerny, Smith, Belasco, Whitmore, and Blake."

"Oh, you're doing Grandfather?" I said. "Dad will be overcome with jealousy."

"Well, the judge said it was also okay to search anyone else who actually volunteered for it, so we can search your dad if he really wants us to," Horace said. "But he got so little sleep that maybe he'll be just as happy to skip it this time, and I can't imagine that anyone else would really want me poking through all their stuff."

"You never know," I said. "Some people might want to be searched so they can prove their innocence."

"Searching won't do that," Horace grumbled. "If we do

find something, that will be useful, but not finding anything could just mean that they were smart enough to figure out how to get rid of anything incriminating while we were twiddling our thumbs waiting for the search warrant. Anyway—you seen Ekaterina? I need her to open up the rooms for me."

"I'll page her." Sami picked up his walkie-talkie and took a few steps away, no doubt to avoid interrupting Horace.

"By the way," I said. "Mrs. Voss—the lady over there embroidering—wonders if you've considered that whoever killed Frogmore might have had it in for Dr. Czerny."

"And administered the poison to Frogmore by mistake?"

"And killed Frogmore because without him Czerny probably has no career. Czerny said as much to me, but I just assumed he was panicking. If Mrs. Voss, who seems like a very sensible woman, says the same thing . . ."

"Duly noted." He pulled out his notebook and scribbled in it. "Not that we need more complications, mind you."

"Incidentally, why is Dad so short on sleep?" I asked. "I could have sworn I sent him back to the cottage before midnight."

"He borrowed your grandfather's satellite phone and spent a couple of hours talking to that doctor in Oregon."

"Dr. Lanville?"

"That's the one. Apparently Lanville's an insomniac, so he loved having someone to talk to in the middle of the night. Not sure if he's a mystery buff like your dad or if he's just taking it really personally that someone knocked off one of his patients, but he's fired up do any legwork your dad wants to suggest."

"So when do you start? The search, I mean." I came close to asking "when do we start?" but changed it at the last minute. Horace wasn't as touchy as the chief would be about my kibitzing on his investigation, but even he had his limits.

"Soon, I hope."

"You hope? If you have the search warrants, what are you waiting for?"

"This." A broad smile lit Horace's face and he strode toward the front door, where two well-bundled, snow-covered figures were just coming through, giving the impression that two yetis had stumbled into the Inn. "Chief's here!" he called back over his shoulder. "Randall brought him on the snowmobile."

Chapter 24

Sami rushed over, and he and Horace began helping the new arrivals with their wraps. Several layers of wraps. They were both so bundled up that you couldn't have told them apart if not for their dramatically different shapes. The tall lanky yeti had to be Randall—Shiffleys were almost invariably gifted not only with height but also the enviable ability to eat anything they wanted and still resemble beanpoles. The shorter, rounder yeti would be the chief.

"That was quite possibly the most miserable trip I've ever taken in this county," the chief said, when he'd removed two scarves, a pair of goggles, a thick woolly ski mask, and a down coat. "No offense, Randall; I can't tell you how much I appreciate you bringing me out here, but good Lord, what a journey!"

"What're you complaining about?" Randall said, with a laugh. "Some people fly to resorts and pay good money to run around on snowmobiles."

"Welcome, Chief. And Mr. Mayor." Ekaterina arrived, carrying two hot coffees and followed by several staff members who took over the complicated process of extricating the travelers from their remaining wraps, and then hauled all the wet clothes off to be dried.

"Don't take mine too far," Randall called after them. "I'm only staying to thaw out a bit," he went on, turning back to us. "Then I need to get back to town. Now that the snow's finally ending, we're organizing a shovel brigade. Got a lot to do. First we dig out the snowplows, then while

Osgood and Beau get to work, we're going to start digging our way to people's houses that might need checking on. And then there's the hospital parking lot, and rounding up a chainsaw crew for all the fallen trees. Chief, if you finish up here and decide you need to come back to town, just radio me."

"Thanks," the chief said. "I'll do just that. Depends on how things go here. Horace, where are we?"

"I was just about to notify the folks whose rooms we're going to search," Horace said. "Meg, can you help me track them all down?"

I pulled out my phone and checked the time.

"They should all be going to lunch in a couple of minutes," I said. "I'll lead the way. Randall, why don't you stay long enough to have a hot meal before you head back."

"I won't say no," Randall said. Few people ever did to a meal at the Inn.

"And we need to rekey those rooms now," the chief said. "Before anyone hears that we're searching their rooms. Not that they haven't had plenty of time to dispose of anything incriminating in the last twelve hours, but you never know."

"If you give me a list of the rooms concerned, I will run new keys for them now and send a staff member around to activate them," Sami said. "And then I can hold the new keys and release them to the occupants only when you give the okay."

"Perfect," the chief said.

"Shall we go find your suspects?" I asked.

"Persons of interest," he corrected. "Yes, please."

We made quite an impression when we entered, since the chief's arrival doubled the number of uniformed law enforcement officers on site. And Randall's bearing, along with the fact that he'd walked in shoulder to shoulder with the chief, would probably give rise to rumors that he was with the FBI or something. I sent Randall through the buffet line while I scouted out where the various persons of interest were sitting.

Smith, Belasco, and Whitmore, the three young men who'd had the bad luck to be sitting at Frogmore's table, were sitting together. Had they arrived at the conference friends, or was their friendship a relatively new one, forged by their sufferings here—enduring Frogmore, witnessing his death, being stalked by Dr. Czerny, and finally having to undergo a police interrogation? I'd be curious to find out. Horace went to notify them, while I led the chief over to the table where Grandfather was sitting with several other persons of interest.

"A visitor from the outside world! Welcome!" Grandfather exclaimed when he saw the chief. "This is Chief Burke," he said, turning to the rest of the table. "Chief, that's Dr. Vera Craine."

"Nice to put a face to the voice." Dr. Craine offered her hand.

Grandfather proceeded to introduce Dr. Green and Dr. Lindquist, and then looked up at the chief with a twinkle in his eye.

"So, are you here to interrogate us in person?"

"First things first," the chief said. "We have a warrant to search some of your rooms. Doctors Craine, Blake, Green, and Lindquist. I don't have a physical copy of the warrant with me, but I can read you the text if you like, and I can provide you or your attorney with a written copy as soon as the weather permits. You'll be notified when we're finished, and at that time you'll need to pick up a new key at the front desk."

Grandfather and Dr. Craine nodded matter-of-factly. Dr. Green muttered, "Oh, dear," and wiped his palms on his trouser leg. Dr. Lindquist beamed as if this were one of the more entertaining occurrences of the weekend. I was relieved that none of them asked for a formal reading of the search warrant, since I doubted it would be either a short document or an entertaining one.

"You'll tell us what you find, I assume?" Grandfather said.

"If we take any items into custody as possible evidence, we'll give you a search warrant return, which is basically an itemized receipt."

No one had any other questions, so I led the chief over to where Melissa McKendrick was sitting. She, like the crew at Grandfather's table, took it calmly.

Horace had finished notifying the three lost lambs, as I called them, and had moved on to Dr. Czerny. Who didn't seem at all calm about the prospect of being searched. But you couldn't exactly say that he was resisting the idea—more that it appeared to have triggered an anxiety attack. We hurried over to rescue Horace.

"You'll notice we're searching the rooms of everyone who was at Dr. Frogmore's table," the chief pointed out. "Purely a matter of procedure in some cases, of course." Eventually he managed to calm Czerny down. We headed back to the Command Post to arrange the logistics for our search.

Actually, their search, I reminded myself. While my help had saved them time on what I assumed amounted to serving the search warrants, they could probably do just fine without me during the search itself.

Ekaterina was waiting for us in the Command Post, with a fresh laundry cart and a carton of gold-embossed lunch bags.

"Did Michael tell you what he and your sons are doing?" she asked.

"Nothing too destructive, I hope," I said, warily.

"Nothing of the kind!" she exclaimed. "They are helping the staff with snow removal. That is most helpful. Now that it has stopped snowing, some of our guests will be eager to leave, and I wish to ensure that when the roads are ready, they will find no impediment on the grounds of the Inn."

"Amen," I said.

I was about to head back to the conference when Horace spoke up.

"Chief," he asked. "Since there's only the two of us— can we bring someone along to help with the logistics?"

Which was how I ended up pushing the laundry cart and toting a clipboard that held a supply of blank search warrant return forms.

We started out on the fifth floor. Ekaterina walked briskly up to each door, knocked, and then opened the door with her master key card. Then she and I watched with interest as Horace and the chief quickly and methodically searched each room.

I rather enjoyed watching them search Dr. Green's room. He had at least a dozen crystals of various sizes and shapes strewn about in what appeared to be a random fashion, although I suspected they had been carefully placed according to the principles of feng shui, *vastu shastra,* or some idiosyncratic energy flow system of Green's own invention. A collection of reeds in a hotel water glass made an improvised stick diffuser, and the air positively reeked of lavender. A yoga mat was unrolled on the floor between the bed and the window, and a bamboo flute lay on the dresser.

"It's as if he and Rose Noire were twins separated at birth," I murmured to Ekaterina.

And had he really brought along all of this new age paraphernalia to the conference or had Rose Noire supplied some of it? I could easily imagine her taking pity on a kindred spirit, stranded on the wrong coast without an adequate supply of crystals and essential oils. And had

Rose Noire lent him her treasured unicorn-shaped incense burner or did he own an identical one? Food for thought in either case.

The only feature of interest to the chief and Horace, though, was the bathroom where—in addition to marveling at the large number of vitamins, supplements, and both alternative and conventional over-the-counter medicines—they studied the spot where the black widow spider had been found. They eventually decided that it was theoretically possible for her to have traveled through the opening around the sink's drain pipe into the wall. And Dr. Frogmore's bathroom was on the other side of the wall, so it was remotely possible that the spider could have traveled from one to the other. But not all that probable.

"And Dr. Langslow doesn't think there's any chance he died of a spider bite," the chief added. "So it's not all that relevant anyway."

Since I was the one tasked with writing out the search warrant return forms for Horace's signature, I was relieved that they only confiscated a few items from Dr. Green's vast health arsenal—although I could already foresee that he'd declare some or all of the missing items vital to his continued survival and pitch a fit. And unfortunately for Horace, the chief wanted a list of any and all medicines found during their search. Dr. Green took up three pages.

Dr. Craine's room wasn't nearly as interesting. Only a modest collection of medicines, to Horace's relief, and none of them of sufficient interest to be taken as evidence. We moved on to Dr. Lindquist's room.

Ekaterina and I were watching from the doorway with diminished interest, since the first two rooms had produced nothing of interest. And at first it looked as if the search of Lindquist's room would be similarly uneventful.

Then while the chief was finishing up a methodical examination of the contents of the suitcase, Horace, who had been inspecting the contents of Lindquist's conference tote bag, said something under his breath. Then he held up an object in one gloved hand and called out to the chief.

"Check this out."

Ekaterina and I forgot about trying to be nonchalant as we peered into the room, trying to see what he'd found.

A wadded-up piece of paper?

I took out my phone and surreptitiously used its camera's zoom function to get a closer look. Definitely paper, but not wadded up—folded up.

Horace unfolded it slightly and showed it to the chief, who nodded solemnly. Horace looked up, saw Ekaterina and me gawking, and couldn't repress a quick smile.

"Is that what I think it is?" the chief asked Horace.

Chapter 25

"It appears to be the product information insert from a package of sublingual nitroglycerin spray," Horace said, no doubt as much for our benefit as the chief's. "I'll check it against the bottle we found in the ballroom, but I'm pretty sure it's a match."

"Meg," the chief said. "Unless I'm mistaken, I saw several tote bags just like this down in the ballroom."

"Every conference attendee got one," I said. "We put the conference program in it, and their badges, and a few other goodies Grandfather convinced various organizations to donate—coupons and flyers from places like the Audubon Society, the American Bird Conservancy, the National Wildlife Federation. A copy of the Cornell Ornithology Lab's bird-watching calendar for the coming year. Some of them carry it around and use it to stash handouts and water bottles, and whatever other gear they might not want to run back to their rooms for. Others just leave it in their rooms once they check in."

"And idea which camp Lindquist would have fallen into?"

"No idea—you might be able to tell from the contents."

Horace picked up the bag's contents from the table where he'd placed them and began sorting through them.

"Here's the calendar Meg mentioned," he said. "Discount on Audubon membership—wouldn't they all already belong? National Wildlife Federation pamphlet. Caerphilly Inn notepad and pen."

"May I take a look?" I asked. "I know exactly what we packed in those bags."

Horace brought over the tote bag's contents and showed them to me, item by item.

"Original contents," I said when he'd finished. "Nothing added, nothing missing."

"Except for this." Horace held up the package insert.

"In other words," the chief said, "while Dr. Lindquist will almost certainly claim that someone else planted the insert in his tote bag, it appears that he brought the bag to his room and left it here untouched."

"Of course, he hasn't done anything to personalize his bag," I pointed out. "There's a slot on one side that could hold a business card—do you think any of them ever use it? No, they all run around picking up each other's identical bags."

"So even though it's almost certainly his, his lawyer will try to cast all kinds of doubt on it." The chief sighed. "We'll keep looking."

"Maybe it will have fingerprints." Horace tucked the folded paper into an evidence bag.

"Let's finish inventorying his medicines and move on," the chief said.

The next search was uneventful. It turned out that the three lost lambs were sharing a room—only Belasco, the junior professor, was registered, but Smith's and Whitmore's gear was definitely there. I wasn't sure how Ekaterina would take this. She'd never have thrown them out in the storm and probably wouldn't even have charged Belasco any extra fees, but still . . .

"Wasn't it nice of Dr. Belasco to take those poor students in when they figured out they were going to get stranded here?" I said. "And I do hope they were able to get their deposit back from the bed-and-breakfast they'd originally planned to stay in."

I was relieved to see that she took the discovery of the two stowaways calmly. It probably helped that she'd have been hard pressed to find another room for them. And the search of their room was unproductive. Later, perhaps, I'd suggest to the lambs the wisdom of being seen spending money freely in the Mount Vernon Grill. And point out to Ekaterina what while Smith and Whitmore might be stowaways, at least they didn't appear to be homicidal ones.

The search of Dr. Czerny's room was also unproductive. And a little depressing. The entire top of the dresser was taken up with stacks of handouts for Dr. Frogmore's presentations and bundles of Dr. Frogmore's academic papers and reprints from professional journals, only a couple of them including Czerny himself as a junior author. On the desk were the galleys of a lengthy and highly technical article—again by Dr. Frogmore, although it looked as if Dr. Czerny had been doing the Herculean task of proofreading it. Apart from a few items of clothing hung in the closet and a handful of toiletries on the counter in the bathroom, he didn't seem to have unpacked—his suitcase was still half full of socks, underwear, and whatever else he'd brought.

We locked the laundry cart in the Command Post before searching the cottages, though I was still allowed to come along, in case they needed help carrying the evidence bags.

Apparently my parents had taken in Melissa McKendrick, who was sharing the study in the Washington Cottage with Rose Noire. I had a feeling Melissa had packed in a hurry when she'd realized she was likely to be snowbound. Everything she'd brought fit neatly in one drawer. Although I doubted she and Rose Noire had had quite as much fun with the Murphy beds as the boys, they'd clearly taken advantage of the library. Melissa appeared to be in the middle of *A Wrinkle in Time*.

And while we found a lot of really interesting things at Grandfather's cottage—a large collection of owl pellets and a taxidermied wombat for starters—none of them appeared related to the case. Which was a good thing, actually—so many people had been coming and going from the cottage that tying anything found there to any one of the chief's suspects would have been next to impossible.

When we'd finished with the cottage, the chief thanked me and Ekaterina for our assistance and he and Horace headed back to the Command Post. Ekaterina dashed off to see about preparations for the upcoming Hanukkah dinner. I had long since regretted having nothing to eat since the croissant that had constituted my breakfast. I was hovering between dashing off to see if there was anything left from the buffet and retreating to our own cottage to see if there was anything in the refrigerator there when my walkie-talkie sputtered to life.

"Meg?" Grandfather's voice. "Meg? I need you to do something."

Of course. I glanced at my phone. Well, the buffet was probably out anyway. The lunch hour was past, and we were ten minutes into the next panel session. I hoped whatever Grandfather had in mind could wait until after I'd grabbed a bite of lunch.

"What do you need?" I asked.

"Percival. We're canceling the pesticide panel—it was Frogmore's show anyway. I'm substituting a session with Percival. I'm not quite as knowledgeable as Clarence, but I think with your dad's help I can give a pretty good presentation on his case. We need someone to bring him to the conference area. I'm filling in on a panel now, or I'd do it."

And that someone would probably have to be me, I realized with a sigh. The attitude of the hotel staff toward Percival ranged from wary to downright terrified, and be-

sides, Grandfather took a dim view of allowing just anyone to take charge of his owl. And knowing Grandfather,
I'd be better off fetching the owl and then eating. He
wouldn't leave me in peace until Percival was at his side.

"Remember, I don't do mice," I said.

"That's fine," he said. "I'll want to feed him during the
presentation, so skip the crickets, too."

If Michael and the boys were available—but no, they
were shoveling snow.

Never mind. I could do this. I'd taken him down there,
hadn't I? His cage was huge and bulky, but not heavy,
and I'd managed to get it onto the dolly before with no
problem.

I made sure I had the right key card in my pocket and
began the long trek down to the storage room.

Percival seemed moderately glad to see me, probably
because he was expecting more crickets.

"Sorry, pal." I was putting on the heavy leather gloves
we kept there for anyone who might be putting their digits within reach of the owl's formidable beak and talons,
as I'd have to do when I lifted the cage onto the dolly.

But Percival remained well-behaved—probably because
before tackling his cage I'd stashed the mice and crickets
on the front end of the dolly, thus galvanizing his attention on them. I rolled the dolly over to one end of the
cage and heaved that end up until it was resting on the
edge of the dolly's platform.

Percival ruffled his feathers slightly and fixed his attention on me rather than the mice, making me glad I had
the gloves. He looked annoyed, but then he always did. It
occurred to me that "resting owl face" would make a nice
gender-neutral replacement for "resting bitch face." Or
would I be accused of speciesism for suggesting it? I filed
away the thought as I lifted up the other end of the cage
and gently shoved it onto the dolly.

"Hope you're ready for your star turn," I told Percival.

I set my tote on top of the mice and cricket cages and began turning the dolly so I could pull it out the door. The otherwise narrow corridor widened into a little antechamber that gave just enough room to get the dolly out and turn it so you could steer it down the hallway. I propped the storeroom door open and began pulling it out into the corridor. Percival gave a harsh shriek and flapped his wings as we got going.

And then something swooped down, cutting out the light and wrapping my arms. I struggled, but my arms were completely enveloped in whatever had fallen on me.

Make that whatever someone had thrown over me. I could feel someone fishing in my pockets, removing everything in them—my phone. My key card. A used tissue that I hoped the sneak thief would find sufficiently disgusting. Then he pulled me away from the dolly, opened a door, and shoved me through it. I heard the door slam closed behind me.

I was outside. In the snow. With no coat.

Chapter 26

I struggled to my feet and disentangled myself from whatever had been trapping me. A quilted moving blanket. There had been a small stack of them in the corner of the antechamber. I wrapped it around me for warmth.

I tried the door, but it was locked, of course. My key card would have opened it, but my assailant had taken that. Odds were that I couldn't have texted for help even if I had my phone—the wireless didn't seem to extend to the storage area. But if I'd clipped the walkie-talkie or the satellite phone to my jeans, instead of leaving them both in the tote bag—

"Enough," I said aloud. Never mind how I got here. I had to get inside before frostbite set in. Or worse, before I froze to death.

"People rarely freeze to death." I could hear Dad's voice, in one of his wide-ranging dinner table conversations. "They're much more apt to die of hypothermia. And it doesn't even need to be freezing to cause that—just colder than 98.6."

"But how long does it take when it's this cold?" I wanted to ask. How long did I have? I remembered Sami saying that in weather like this it could take as little as ten minutes to get frostbite. Wasn't that bad enough? I had no desire to lose fingers or toes.

I could take off walking along the edge of the hotel. Of course, it wouldn't exactly be walking—it would be floundering through drifts four, sometimes five feet high. I wasn't at all sure I could make it in time.

Maybe staying near the door was smart. Grandfather would probably send someone to fetch Percival if I hadn't yet shown up by the time his panel drew near. I could keep banging on the door and hope they came in time. Not an optimal plan. It could be an hour before anyone got here, and what if they were so focused on fetching Percival that they ignored the banging?

Just then I noticed something. There were only a couple of inches of snow right outside the door. Someone had cleared the area. And I saw a small depression in the snow near the edge of the cleared area.

I waded over to the depression and started scooping snow out.

"Yes!" I exclaimed.

I'd found the start of Josh and Jamie's tunnel.

I wriggled my way in, sternly repressing my claustrophobia, which kept urging me to wriggle out again and run away. It was a tight squeeze—I had to take off the quilted blanket to do it—but at least I fit. A few years ago, before the boys' growth spurt had sent them shooting up to nearly my height, I wouldn't have.

I began crawling along the tunnel, pushing the blanket ahead of me, in case I needed it for warmth later.

I hoped they'd found a pretty direct route from our cottage to the wing the storage room was in.

And what if they'd started a new tunnel at the door I'd been locked out of, a tunnel that hadn't yet met up with the one that led away from the cottage? What if I came to a dead end that marked the limit of their excavations before they'd gone off to shovel snow at the front of the hotel?

"Then I'll stand up and get my bearings," I muttered.

There couldn't be more than a foot or two of snow overhead. I could dig through that, couldn't I?

I noticed that it seemed warmer inside the tunnel than it had outside. Was that possible? Or was I just getting used to the cold? That wasn't a comforting thought. Wasn't getting used to the cold a step along the journey to frostbite?

And what if whoever had shoved me outside came back to look for me. To check on me, or more likely finish me off?

"Then you're no worse off here than you would be back there," I told myself. I crawled on.

I realized that the tunnel had been sloping up for some time. Well, that made sense. The short route from the cottage to the storage room led down a flight of stairs at the end of the terraced gardens that surrounded the cottages and overlooked the golf course. The long way was to make a detour into the golf course where the land sloped down more gently. I'd been rather hoping the boys' tunnel had led to the stairs. Okay, evidently we were going through the golf course. I just needed to keep crawling.

I had to choke back tears of relief when I spotted a literal light at the end of the tunnel. I started crawling faster, and in another couple of minutes I found myself in the cave right outside the French doors of the Madison Cottage.

I tried the door handle with trembling hands and breathed a sigh of relief. It was open.

I stepped inside, closed the door behind me, and shut my eyes for just a moment, savoring the warmth. Then my eyes flew open again.

"No time for that," I muttered. I raced out the front door, across the courtyard, and through the lobby. When I burst through the door of the Command Post, the chief and Horace looked up in surprise.

"I think someone just tried to kill me," I blurted out.

"What?" The chief rose to his feet.

Michael appeared in the Command Post doorway, with the boys pressing in behind him.

"Meg, are you all right?" he asked. "We saw you running through the lobby."

"Someone threw this blanket over my head, stole my phone and my key card, and shoved me out in the snow when I was fetching Percival," I said. "I might have frozen to death if I hadn't been able to use the boys' tunnels to get back to the cottage."

"Awesome!" "Go, Mom!" the boys exclaimed.

"Who is Percival, and what are these tunnels?" the chief demanded.

"Percival is an owl that we've been keeping in a storage room at the far end of the hotel," I said. "Grandfather needs him for his panel in—yikes! Fifteen minutes. I should go get him."

"I'll get Percival." Michael gently pushed me back into a nearby chair. "Josh, can you fetch your grandfather so he can make sure Mom is okay? And Jamie, please tell Great that Percival might be a little late."

"Michael, while you're fetching Percival, you can show Horace where all this occurred," the chief said. "And meanwhile Meg can give me a more complete account of what happened."

Everyone but the chief and I dashed out.

"Okay, tell me about it," the chief said.

I gave him the blow-by-blow account. When I'd finished, he looked thoughtful.

"You seriously think the person who did this was trying to kill you?"

I took a deep breath and considered the question.

"Good point," I said. "If their goal was to kill me, they

could have just hit me over the head. More accurate to say that whoever did it didn't care if I lived or died. So what was their goal? Not birdnapping, I expect. Percival's an interesting specimen, but I can't imagine why anyone would steal him."

Actually, I could imagine a scenario in which someone wanted to steal Percival—what if they'd needed to hide something small and valuable? They could get Percival to swallow it—maybe by taping it to a mouse they were feeding him—and then retrieve it when Percival puked it up in a pellet that would also contain the indigestible parts of the mouse. In which case, seeing me about to haul Percival away and not knowing where I was taking him, they might well want to stop me and preserve their access to Percival, at least until the sought-after pellet appeared.

But just because I could imagine such a scenario didn't mean I believed in it. I suspected even Dad, if faced with such a sequence of events in one of his beloved mystery books, would—well, not toss it across the room. Not his style. But he would gently suggest to anyone who asked him what he thought of the book in question that he'd found the plot a trifle far-fetched.

"We'll find out in a few minutes if the owl is safe," the chief said.

"And it's more likely they were after something I was carrying," I said. "Maybe my phone. More likely my key card. Ekaterina gave me one with pretty broad access privileges."

"That seems more likely," the chief said. "It's also possible that whoever did this wanted to prevent you from seeing him there in the storage area. It would be interesting to find out why—when Horace calls in, I'll tell him to start a search. Did you notice anything about your assailant?"

"Not really." I closed my eyes and replayed the incident

in my mind—what there was of it. It had happened so fast. "Except that whoever did it wasn't tiny. He wasn't reaching up to throw the blanket over me. He was more or less my height. And strong enough that he didn't have too much trouble shoving me out the door. I was too surprised to fight much but still, I'm no lightweight. And I'm saying he, but I can't remember anything to disprove the idea that it was a tall woman."

"We should go and check to see who's been safely ensconced in a panel for the last hour." The chief glanced at his watch, and then at a copy of the conference program that I'd given Horace. "And then—"

"Chief?" Horace opened the door and peered in.

"What's up?"

"The owl's fine. Dr. Blake has him now. And I have Meg's phone and her tote bag." He stepped into the Command Post and handed them to me. "I came back to get my kit—I figured I should process the scene. Could be attempted murder."

"Assault and battery, at the very least," the chief said. "And reckless endangerment. So yes; process the scene, and then I'll come help you search the area. What if Meg interrupted something the perpetrator didn't want anyone to see?"

Horace nodded and went to pick up his kit.

Someone else knocked on the door.

"It never rains," the chief murmured. "Come in!" he called, more loudly.

Dr. Craine opened the door and stood in the doorway for a moment. Then she strode in and took the vacant chair that I'd come to think of as the hot seat, since it was where Horace and the chief tended to put the people they were interviewing.

"Chief Burke." She fixed a steely gaze on him.

"You remember Dr. Vera Craine," I said. Apart from

their brief meeting when the chief was notifying his persons of interest, all their interaction had been over the phone, so I wasn't positive he'd remember who she was.

"Of course," the chief said. "What can we do for you?"

"I came to face the music," Dr. Craine said.

Chapter 27

Face the music?

Dr. Craine sat with her feet planted on the floor, arms resting on the arms of the chair, leaning forward in what came across as an ever-so-slightly tense and anxious posture, only moving her head as she shifted her gaze from the chief, to Horace, to me, and then back to the chief again.

"Face what music?" the chief asked.

"To come clean. I knocked off Frogmore. I can't let Monty take the fall for something I did."

Face the music. Come clean. Knock off. Take the fall. What was it about a murder investigation that compelled people to pepper their speech with clichés out of a thirties gangster movie?

Her confession didn't completely surprise me—after all, she'd been on the list of suspects I'd pointed out to the chief. But still, I wasn't sure I believed her. Or maybe I just didn't want to.

The chief studied her for a few moments. Was he running over what he remembered from her interview? Sizing up the probability that she'd thrown the quilted blanket over my head? She was tall enough.

"Why don't you tell us all about it?" he said finally.

"Glad to." She leaned back, crossed her legs, and launched into an account of how Frogmore had tried to ruin her career.

A lengthy account. In much more detail than she'd

given me Saturday morning in the bar. She'd told me Frogmore had accused her of falsifying her research—now she gave chapter and verse of every accusation, every refutation. After twenty minutes she'd only just begun to touch on the charges of plagiarism. Horace was scribbling in his notebook as fast as he could but the chief just sat and listened. I knew he often liked to let his witnesses talk freely—give them enough rope to hang themselves, if they were guilty. But I was a little puzzled that he hadn't made at least some attempt to move her along from motive to means and opportunity.

Or maybe he'd decided she was talking so fast that he didn't fancy his chances of getting a word in edgewise. Eventually she unscrewed the top of the water bottle she was carrying and took a long pull. The chief used that brief pause to take back the conversation.

"I think we can understand your motive, Dr. Craine," he said. "And I'm sure your defense attorney will be able to make constructive use of this information. But perhaps we could move forward to the actual crime. As I'm sure you're aware, due to the extreme weather conditions, we haven't yet been able to pursue our investigations in quite the way we usually would. Limited technical capabilities. But perhaps you can help us out—just how did you kill Dr. Frogmore?"

"I poisoned him, of course."

She beamed at us as if very pleased with herself.

"Yes. Precisely what did you use?"

She frowned.

"You mean you haven't figured that out yet?"

"We haven't yet been able to get any samples off the grounds of the Inn," the chief said. "Much less down to Richmond for toxicology testing. And to be perfectly frank, those tests cost an arm and a leg—and we're a very small county. If we can tell them what to look for and they just have to confirm it, the bill will be a lot lower than if they have to test for every poison in creation."

Odd. I'd never heard the chief say that before. Of course, we were in the last few weeks of the budget year, but still . . .

"Dr. Langslow hasn't figured it out yet?" Dr. Craine said.

"He's still working on his theories. So you could help us out here. . . ."

Now I knew the chief was up to something.

"I'm not sure I should say any more," Dr. Craine said. "I don't want to get anyone else in trouble."

"So you had an accomplice?" the chief asked.

"No! I did it all myself. But I don't want to get anyone else in trouble for unwittingly helping me."

"And I don't suppose you're going to tell me what you put this unknown poison in."

She paused as if considering, then shook her head.

The chief was silent for a few moments. Then he chuckled slightly.

"Dr. Craine, I'm perfectly willing to believe you have the strongest possible motive for killing Dr. Frogmore. But unless you can tell me how you did it, you're not going to convince me that you killed him."

She frowned at him.

"Ironic," she said finally. "I bet if I were denying that I'd done it you'd be trying to prove I did. But now . . ."

She shrugged, sat back in her chair, and took another swig from her water bottle.

Horace looked completely puzzled. Anyone who knew him would think the chief's face was impassive. I could tell he was slight puzzled and more than slightly annoyed—probably because he shared my suspicion that Dr. Craine's confession was taking time from more urgent things.

"Dr. Craine was telling me about all this yesterday." I kept my eyes on her. "About how Dr. Frogmore did his best to ruin her career. She also told me about how Grandfather saved it. Dr. Craine, would it ease your mind at all to know that the chief doesn't seriously suspect Grandfather?"

She frowned and appeared to be choosing her words carefully.

"That would be good to know," she said finally. "I had heard rumors. Including one that incriminating evidence had been found in his room. Which I knew was nonsense, of course, since I did it. The murder, I mean. If incriminating evidence was found in Monty's cottage, someone else must have planted it."

"And anyone could have done it." Horace had obviously picked up on what I was suggesting. "The SPOOR members were rehearsing there, Dr. Blake let a whole bunch of people use it for meetings if they couldn't find a room someplace else. Finding something in his room would be about as incriminating as finding it in the lobby."

"Dr. Craine, where were you for the last forty-five minutes?"

"In a panel. Appearing on it, I should say. The panel started at one."

"And you were in it all the time?"

She frowned, then nodded.

"Who else was with you?"

"Ben Green and George Voss. And Ned Czerny, of course, but Monty sort of added him in as a sop, since he'd canceled the panel he and Dr. Frogmore were going to give at two thirty."

"Were you together the whole time?" the chief asked.

"Hard to give a panel from separate rooms," she said.

"I meant, did any of you come in late, leave early, or skip out in the middle for any reason?"

"Oh, I see. No. Even Ned Czerny stuck it out till the bitter end, even though it was clear the poor man was out of his depth."

The chief nodded.

"Dr. Craine," he said. "If you want to continue confessing, you're welcome to, but unless you're prepared to give a few more specific details about how you did in Dr. Frogmore, it's a little hard to take you seriously."

"Okay," she said. "It was a stupid idea, anyway. I was worried about Monty—Dr. Blake. I'm sure all this has taken it out of him, and the idea that he might end up in jail, even temporarily . . ."

"You heard rumors," I said. "Exactly what were they?"

"Word around the conference is that they'd had a knock-down-drag-out quarrel about something Frogmore did that made Monty completely lose it," she said. "And that Chief Burke snowmobiled over specially to arrest Monty. And worst of all, that when you searched his cottage you'd found the package from whatever poison was used to kill Frogmore. I heard that part from George Voss. No idea where he got it."

The chief nodded thoughtfully. Horace was frowning. So was I. The rumor wasn't entirely accurate—we'd found the package insert, not the package, in Dr. Lindquist's room, not Grandfather's. But still, how had anyone known?

"I'll stop interfering with your work, then." Dr. Craine rose.

She opened the door just as Dr. Lindquist was about to knock on it.

"You missed a good panel," Dr. Craine said to him on her way out.

"So I heard." Lindquist looked perfectly cheerful. "With any luck I can catch most of the next panel—after the chief asks me whatever he wants to ask?" He didn't look worried. But he did look a little sweaty and disheveled.

He raised an eyebrow and stood in the doorway as if expecting he could answer a quick question and then catch up with Dr. Craine and rejoin the conference.

"Come in, Dr. Lindquist. Horace, if you wouldn't mind getting started on that new search. Meg, you look as if you could use a rest."

In other words, the chief wanted to be alone with Dr. Lindquist.

Horace picked up his forensic kit and left. I grabbed my tote bag and followed him out.

I went straight to the Mount Vernon Grill and begged Eduardo to put a rush on a chicken Caesar salad.

"Are you sure?" he said. "Because the combination Hanukkah, winter solstice, end of the conference dinner is going to be fabulous. You don't want to spoil your appetite for that."

"I haven't eaten since breakfast," I said. "Which consisted of a single croissant. If I have to wait until six to eat, I will probably die of starvation."

"Give me five minutes."

I took a seat at a table just inside the restaurant entrance, where I'd be able to see anyone who went into or came out of the Command Post.

Dad came rushing up.

"Let me see your fingers!" he said. "And was there any sign of numbness in your toes? Let's check them out."

"I'm fine," I said. "No sign of numbness."

But Dad insisted, so I let him check me for signs of frostbite. It would pass the time until my salad arrived. And as I watched him tugging off my shoes and socks, it occurred to me that he could help me catch up on whatever had happened while I'd been gone.

"Did I miss any excitement?" I asked. "While I was helping with the search and crawling through the snow tunnels?"

"Well . . . Ned Czerny had kind of a breakdown during lunch," he said. "Some people at the table next to him were laughing over something—nothing to do with Dr. Frogmore, but he suddenly got up and yelled something about how heartless everyone was and ran out."

"Sounds dramatic," I said.

"Rose Noire and Ben Green ran after him, and I guess they calmed him down. He showed up for the one o'clock panel, at any rate, and seemed calm and composed, although come to think of it, he didn't say a word. And I was a little worried when your grandfather rather took him to task—came right out and told him to grow a backbone and find a new boss who wasn't a jackass like Frogmore, but Czerny actually took it pretty well. And Nils Lindquist disappeared for quite a while—we might not have noticed except that we thought maybe Czerny wouldn't be up for the one o'clock panel and we might want Nils to sub."

"But Dr. Czerny showed up and all was well."

"Ye-es—except by then we were a little worried about Nils. I mean, we'd had one person poisoned already. And he wasn't anywhere to be found and didn't answer his room phone or come to his door when they knocked on it. And then when the chief said he wanted to interview him again—well, that got us really worried. But then he showed up just as the one o'clock panel was ending, and it turned out he'd felt a migraine coming on and had to lie down for a bit to let his meds work."

Eduardo showed up with my salad, and I dug in. Dad waited until Eduardo had left before continuing.

"And then just as the panel was breaking up, I heard a rumor that your search had found something incriminating." He looked at me with a faint air of disappointment, no doubt because he'd had to hear the rumor from someone else, instead of the straight scoop from me. Since this was the first time I'd seen him since the end of the search, I resisted the urge to apologize.

"What did the rumor say?" I asked instead.

"You should know," he protested. "You were there."

"And I'll tell you what we found. First, tell me what the rumor was."

"I heard two versions. Both involved finding incriminating evidence in your grandfather's cottage. Which wouldn't be all that incriminating, of course, since anyone at the conference could waltz in there anytime during the day."

"As the chief well knows. What did the rumor say they found?"

"One version was that it was the package from the poison used to kill Dr. Frogmore."

I nodded. That was the version Dr. Craine had heard.

"The other was that they found . . . well . . . more Viagra tablets in his bedside drawer. Minus the proper packaging. Which doesn't seem very plausible."

"I wonder if Grandfather would find that statement insulting or a vote of confidence." I found it amusing that Dad seemed mildly embarrassed—normally he'd have had no qualms about discussing erectile dysfunction medications. "No, they didn't find any more Viagra. They did find a folded-up paper that appears to be the product information insert from a package of nitroglycerin lingual spray."

"Oh, my."

"Horace thinks it's the same brand and dosage as the almost empty spray bottle he found under Frogmore's table. It's on his to-do list to check with you to make sure, but with only the two of them—"

"I understand. And someone planted it in your grandfather's cottage?"

"No. We found it in Lindquist's room."

Dad's eyes widened and I could see him putting pieces together.

"Oh, dear," he said finally. "I do hope it's not him. I rather like him. As does your grandfather. And I know he was very angry with Dr. Frogmore but that doesn't automatically mean . . ."

His voice trailed off.

"He's in with the chief now," I said. "And—"

I broke off when I saw the door to the Command Post open. Dr. Lindquist stumbled out looking anxious and disoriented. The chief followed him. They exchanged a few words. Then Dr. Lindquist stumbled off. Not toward the conference. Toward the elevators.

The chief saw the two of us peering out of the restaurant and walked over.

"Are you arresting Dr. Lindquist?" Dad asked.

"Not yet," the chief said. "But I've told him I don't want him leaving town just yet, even assuming that might become possible sometime soon. We don't have a full case yet—we don't even officially know what Frogmore died of—but it's not looking good for Dr. Lindquist."

"Grandfather thinks the world of him," I said.

Dad nodded and looked worried, no doubt at the thought of how Grandfather would react. The chief merely nodded. I wondered if the bits of evidence I knew about—the stolen key and the package insert—were enough to convince him of Lindquist's guilt or if there were other factors. Since Lindquist was from Washington State—well west of the storm—the chief could have used his satellite phone to check up on Lindquist. What had he found?

Maybe I should put in my own call to my nephew Kevin.

"Does Lindquist have an alibi for the time when I was getting shoved out in the cold?" I asked.

"No." The chief frowned. "He says he started feeling a

migraine coming on about the time we were starting to search people's rooms, and since he couldn't lie down in his own room, he put a towel over his face and lay down on the floor of one of the ice- and vending-machine rooms until his medicine took effect. Doesn't sound all that plausible. Peculiar thing to do."

"Not if you get migraines," Dad said. "If you're lucky enough that you get warning of an oncoming migraine—and lucky enough to have found a medication that will stave it off—you'll do anything that works. Lying down in whatever place you can find is pretty normal. I had a patient who swore that he could short-circuit a migraine by drinking a slushy really fast—brings on a sphenopalatine ganglioneuralgia—"

"In English, that's a brain freeze," I put in.

"—and when that goes away, so does his migraine," Dad continued.

"Point taken," the chief said. "Although it would help if we could find anyone who actually saw Dr. Lindquist lying on the ice- and vending-machine room floor—we're checking with the staff who handle that floor. Because right now we have only his word for it that he was getting a migraine—and I hope you won't consider me insensitive to the pain of the migraine sufferer if I point out that it would be a pretty easy thing to fake if you needed an excuse for not being someplace you're expected to be."

"Agreed," Dad said. "Although he does appear to be a migraine sufferer."

"Really?" The chief looked slightly surprised. "You can tell by looking at him?"

"No, I can tell from his medications," Dad explained. "Horace shared the list of those you found in the rooms you searched—in case any of them might be substances that could have contributed to Dr. Frogmore's condition. Dr. Lindquist had Imitrex in his bathroom. Which is one of the medicines that can help avert a migraine if you feel it coming on. And it's not something doctors hand out just because someone complains of headaches—there's a whole diagnostic procedure."

"So Dr. Lindquist probably is a migraine sufferer," the chief said. "It still doesn't prove he was having one today."

"No." Dad shook his head.

"I'm off to help Horace process our latest crime scene," the chief said. "You've got the number of my satellite phone in case anything comes up."

Dad and I both nodded, and the chief headed off toward the elevators.

"And the last panel should be starting any minute now," Dad said. "Let's go."

He hurried off toward the door that led to the conference area. I finished the last forkful of salad and followed. I wasn't sure I would find the contents of the last panel interesting. But I definitely wanted to see it. Because it would be the last panel of the conference.

Chapter 28

The last panel. Finally.

Not the last event—we still had the Hanukkah dinner to look forward to—although it had now expanded into a Hanukkah, winter solstice, end-of-the-conference, thank-heaven-the-snowplows-are-coming dinner. After that would be the group caroling session in the lobby and the exchange of Secret Santa presents. An undetermined number of attendees would be staying around for an as-yet-unpredictable amount of time, and they were all making plans to occupy themselves Monday with improvised panels, informal discussions, ad hoc debates, impromptu strategic planning sessions, and maybe even field trips into the woods to do a bit of owling, weather permitting. But this was the last official panel.

Which Grandfather had described, rather vaguely, as a time for "wrapping up the conference and looking forward at issues facing us." He'd originally invited Vera Craine, Ben Green, George Voss, and Nils Lindquist to join him on the panel—not being expert in the field, I wasn't quite sure if they were the most distinguished ornithologists in attendance or merely the ones Grandfather found most entertaining. Alas, Dr. Lindquist's seat was conspicuously empty. I wasn't sure if the chief had told him he couldn't attend or if he preferred not to. Maybe his migraine had come back. Or maybe becoming a prime suspect had brought one on for real.

As people filed in and took their seats, I found Dr. Czerny standing near the back, gazing at the panel with a lugubrious expression.

"If only Dr. Frogmore could be here to take part," he said when he noticed me looking at him.

"If only," I agreed. Not that Frogmore would add much to the panel if he were here—or that Grandfather necessarily would have invited him to be one of the participants. But life would be so much less complicated if Frogmore were still alive. And if Czerny was under the erroneous impression that we'd left the fifth seat behind the head table vacant in Frogmore's honor, and not in the hope that Dr. Lindquist would eventually show up, I wasn't going to disillusion him.

And to give Czerny credit, he didn't seem to resent not being tapped to carry the Frogmorian banner on the panel. He just looked melancholy. He took a seat in the back, as far as possible from the rest of the participants—no doubt so he could more easily maintain his position as the one person still dutifully grieving his fallen hero.

Grandfather took his seat at one end of the panel, to general applause.

"I'm not going to introduce myself or the other panelists," he said. "If you don't know us by now, you haven't been paying attention."

More applause, and a few cheers.

"I'm thinking of holding this shindig again next year," Grandfather went on.

Enthusiastic applause greeted this announcement.

"So if any of you have any suggestions about how we could improve things for Owl Fest 2020, don't be shy about speaking up. Not that most of you ever are." Laughter rippled through the room. "And before you all bring it up, if we hold it next year, we'll have it a little earlier. September, October—even November would be an improvement.

Not close to Thanksgiving, though, or Rosh Hashanah or Yom Kippur, and well before the weather gets really bad around here. Meg will help me figure out the best date."

More applause and a few people turned to smile and wave at me.

"Now that we've got that out of the way, any suggestions?"

"Bring back the Owlettes!" someone called, to much laughter and scattered applause. Apparently SPOOR had been a hit.

"I have a suggestion." Melissa McKendrick stood. "Next year, can we select the sacrificial victim by popular vote?" Clearly this was a little edgy for some—Dr. Czerny looked thunderous—but still, most of the crowd laughed. "Not that I'm complaining about this year's selection, you understand, but if we're going to make this a regular feature of the conference, I think it would be good to get all the attendees involved in the decision. More democratic."

"I'm sure we can all think of a few candidates," Grandfather said. "And I bet I'd be on a few people's lists."

Many shouts of "No!"

"I have an idea." Dr. Craine leaned forward to her microphone.

I noticed someone moving forward from the back of the room. I initially assumed it was someone coming to the front to make a suggestion—real or humorous. Then I realized it was Mr. Ackley. What was he even doing in the panel, much less making suggestions? I started to follow him, out of some instinct that maybe whatever he was up to would be something we'd want to fend off.

He strode forward until he was standing right beside Grandfather, reaching into his jacket for something. Then he turned and I could see that he was holding a gun. He pointed it at Grandfather's head.

"Everybody stay in your seats!" he shouted. "Don't cause trouble and no one will get hurt."

Everybody followed orders. The entire crowd seemed frozen, except for Grandfather.

"What the hell do you want?" he growled.

"I want to make a public statement," Mr. Ackley said. "I want you all to listen to it. And I want the media to cover it."

"The media?" Grandfather sounded puzzled.

"The media," Ackley repeated. "TV. Radio. Newspapers. And all those bloggers and tweakers. I want them all here."

I'd edged my way forward to the front row of chairs, though there was still a six-foot gap between me and the table behind which Grandfather and the other panelists were sitting—and Ackley was standing. Since no one else was speaking up, I decided to.

"The media can't get here yet," I said. "There's more than three feet of snow out there. The county snowplows are still stuck in it. That's the reason most of these people are still here at the hotel instead of being halfway home by now. They can't get out, so how do you expect the media to get in?"

"Then how did the police get here?" Ackley asked.

"Chief Burke came in a friend's snowmobile," I said. "And I heard it was a pretty miserable trip. It could be hours before anyone from the media gets through. Maybe days."

"Fine. We'll just wait, then." The entitled Ackley was back, the one completely unable to grasp that he couldn't summon a taxi to take him to the airport in mid-blizzard.

"Fine." Grandfather crossed his arms and leaned back in his chair. "Sooner or later you'll fall asleep, and then we'll take your silly gun away."

The audience, who had variously been whispering, shifting uneasily, looking around, whimpering, or peering hopefully at the exit doors, all gradually settled down, in apparent solidarity, into an imitation of Grandfather's posture—arms crossed, feet firmly planted on the ground, frowns and eyes locked on Ackley.

"I want the media here or I'll start shooting people!" Ackley shouted.

"Look, there's no way the conventional media can get here," I said. "But who needs them in these days of social media? Who here has a cell phone?"

Most of the audience raised their hands. Craine, and Green followed suit. Even Grandfather grudgingly lifted one hand for a few seconds.

"We can all take video," I said. "And then once we get the Wi-Fi working again, we can all upload the video to the Internet. It'll go viral."

"Go viral." Ackley frowned. "I never know what people mean when they say that."

"Potentially bigger audiences than TV and newspapers combined." I had no idea if that was true, but it sounded good. Although I couldn't imagine what Ackley could possibly do or say that really would go viral, and I hoped I never found out.

"Everybody—get out your smart phones!" I said aloud.

Those who already had their phones in hand held them up higher, while the rest of the crew dug into purses and pockets. I hoped none of them were armed and under the delusion that starting a gun battle with Ackley would be the smart or heroic thing to do.

Ackley frowned nervously and held the gun closer to Grandfather's temple. I could see Grandfather watching him out of the corner of his eye. I had to admire his sangfroid, but I hoped he wouldn't do anything stupid and heroic, either, like trying to wrestle the gun from Ackley's hand.

Within a minute or two, nearly all of the almost two hundred people in the audience were holding up their phones. It reminded me of concerts from my youth, when at some point in the evening it always seemed mandatory to hold up a lighter and wave it around. Several of my non-smoking friends had routinely carried lighters just for such occasions. Of course, it had been a while since I'd been to a concert, and I'd heard that these days cell phones had replaced lighters in this time-honored ceremony.

Ackley gazed out over the sea of iPhones and Galaxies. He looked puzzled, but not entirely unhappy.

"Are you ready, Mr. Ackley?" I asked.

He nodded.

"Everybody! Three . . . two . . . one . . . action. Take it away, Mr. Ackley."

"My name is James Renfield Ackley."

If he was expecting a dramatic reaction to this announcement he was disappointed. I saw nothing but blank looks. Blank looks and phones.

"My brother and I used to own a company called Ackley and Sons. A company our grandfather founded. We were the third generation of Ackleys to run it."

Still blank looks on all the faces except Grandfather's. Grandfather's face was screwed up as if he were trying to remember something.

"We'd still be running it, and planning for the day when we'd pass it along to our children if it wasn't for you miserable owl lovers!"

"Ackwood Lumber." Grandfather nodded as if to confirm that he'd figured something out.

"Yes!" Ackley shouted. "Ackwood Lumber was our largest subsidiary. We were one of the biggest, most successful lumber companies in the Pacific Northwest. We manufactured millions of board feet every year!"

Out of the corner of my eye I saw the door that led to the kitchen opening at a rate that would make an elderly snail look speedy. When it was open about six inches or so, an eye peered out. Horace. He seemed to be staring at Ackley's gun. Or Grandfather's head. They were so close he could hardly help seeing the one when he looked at the other.

Just for a moment I found myself wishing that we were snowbound with Deputy Vern Shiffley instead of Horace. I felt guilty almost immediately. After all, Vern wouldn't have been nearly as useful for the chief to have on site handling the murder case over the past two days. But now, I suspected, they'd be thinking about how to take down Ackley before he hurt anyone. And you couldn't argue with the fact that if a situation called for the skilled use of firearms, Vern was the officer you wanted to have around. Vern regularly brought home trophies from a variety of marksmanship competitions. Horace always passed his annual firearms qualification, but he also always sweated it beforehand. If someone was going to try shooting Ackley without hurting Grandfather . . .

I silently apologized to Horace.

"And Oliver Frogmore was the worst of all!" I'd almost completely tuned out Ackley's rant, but hearing him roar out the murder victim's name snapped me back to attention.

"Did you kill him?" someone called out.

A look of malicious triumph crossed Ackley's face.

"He was the worst of you," he said. "You all deserve to die, but him most of all."

He went on ranting about how horrible Dr. Frogmore had been—what a jerk, what a liar. Actually, he might have had most of the crowd shouting out "Amen!" and "Sing it, brother!" if it hadn't been for the gun he kept firmly pressed against Grandfather's head.

Although any burgeoning feeling of solidarity vanished

pretty quickly when Ackley moved on from vilifying Frog-more to asserting his God-given right to clear-cut every single tree in the Pacific Northwest if he wanted to, with a side order of pro-pesticide sentiment.

At the kitchen door, Horace's eye had been replaced by the chief's eye. I found myself wondering if he was a better shot than Horace. I assumed he'd have to pass the same annual firearms qualification, but I'd never heard how he scored. Of course, the chief himself would know, if it came down to choosing between himself and Horace. And the chief would be very good at hostage negotiations, assuming Ackley would ever shut up enough to be negoti-ated with.

I suddenly noticed that Grandfather appeared to be trying to catch my eye. He was doing something with his fingers. Very slight movements that I had to watch a couple of times to understand. Pointing to his own chest. Pointing down. Pointing up. And then at me.

I deduced he was suggesting that he was going to dive for the floor, at which point I should rush Ackley. I shook my head slightly. He frowned and repeated the sequence.

Great. Grandfather wasn't just going to do something stupid and heroic. He was going to make me help him.

Better to help him than let him act alone.

I glanced over at Ben Green, who was sitting next to Grandfather. Maybe it was time to test my admittedly fee-ble ASL skills. I managed to catch his eye and sign out what I hoped was "It's time."

He frowned, and signed back "Time for what?" At least I think that's what he said.

I signed back "Three, two, one, help Grandfather." I was pretty sure I had the numbers right, and I saw him glance over at Grandfather when I'd finished.

I repeated the numbers, this time just holding up three fingers, two fingers, and one finger. Green nodded.

I wasn't at all sure what he planned to do, but if Grandfather was going to start something, the more of us joining in the better. It would be better still if I could coordinate whatever Grandfather had planned with some action from the chief and Horace, but neither of them seemed to be peering through the doorway to the kitchen at the moment.

I looked back at Grandfather, who was scowling openly at me.

Mr. Ackley had segued off into a denunciation of global climate change, which was bound to enrage the assembled scientists. And his frenzy seemed to be reaching some sort of crescendo. I was afraid any minute now he'd decide the time had come to finish it. Or maybe he'd just get so angry he'd pull the trigger by accident.

I nodded to Grandfather and held up three fingers.

He nodded back and I could see him tensing.

I changed my finger sign to two.

Ben Green looked as if he might throw up.

I held out only one finger. Then I lunged toward Ackley. Grandfather hurled himself to the floor, and Green lunged sideways, throwing his considerable bulk on top of Grandfather—and thus between Grandfather and Ackley's gun.

Ackley froze in mid-sentence when I started moving, and I was able to grab his gun hand and knock him to the floor. The gun didn't fire. And mercifully he fell silent—probably because one of my knees had landed on his stomach, knocking the wind out of him.

Almost immediately other people joined the fray, rolling me off Ackley and pinning him down.

"Dammit, Ben, I'm grateful, but you weigh a ton," Grandfather was shouting. "Get up!"

"Stand back, everyone." The chief. "And leave the gun to me."

"Meg, are you all right?" Dr. Craine was looking down at me, offering me a hand up.

When I was on my feet, I found myself face-to-face with the chief.

Chapter 29

I braced myself for the tongue-lashing to come. I'd endangered myself and others. Why hadn't I waited for him to handle the situation? Did I realize how lucky I was to be alive?

"Good job," he said.

"Good job?" I echoed. "I was expecting 'are you crazy, tackling someone with a loaded gun?'"

"I assumed you also realized that the gun's safety was on," he said. "Which doesn't make it safe—it would only take a second to flick it off—but given the circumstances it does rather suggest that he was unaware of this himself, making it much less dangerous to tackle him."

"I wish I'd known that," I said. "I only tackled him because if I didn't, Grandfather was going to try doing it all by himself."

"Well, I knew it," Grandfather said. "Or I wouldn't have suggested you tackle him."

Had he really known? Or was he merely pretending, to avoid looking stupid and foolhardy?

I sat down in the nearest chair before my knees gave way. Being the brave, stupid person wasn't how I wanted to see myself. The chief led Mr. Ackley to the back of the room.

"You're under arrest," I heard him begin.

"Ladies and gentlemen." Horace was standing at the front of the room, trying to get the crowd's attention. "Ladies and gentlemen! May I have your attention!"

"Someone go find Lindquist and tell him he's off the hook," Grandfather called.

". . . anything you say can and will be used against you . . . ," the chief was saying.

"Could I ask those of you who took video of today's events to please email it to me?" Horace was asking. "The email is . . ."

". . . if you cannot afford an attorney . . ."

"Shut up and do what Horace says," Grandfather shouted. "The sooner we do that, the sooner we can get back to the panel."

". . . Do you understand the rights I have just read to you? . . ."

"That's Hollingsworth: H-O-L-L-I-N-G . . ."

Eventually, the chief led Mr. Ackley away. After the third time Horace had spelled out his email address, Grandfather finally wrote it on the room's whiteboard. The flurry of emailing died down, and the panel got underway again.

"Before we get too deep in the topic at hand," Grandfather said, "I understand there might be three or four of you who forgot to sign up for the dinner tonight. I'm told you can probably still get in if you grovel a little bit at the door. And you might want to. Everyone else will be there."

When I thought my legs would hold me up again, I decided to sneak out to see how the dinner preparations were going.

In case it ever happens again, I should find out what you're supposed to do when you're trying to be unobtrusive and a whole roomful of people give you a standing ovation.

Out in the hallway, I could see the chief and Horace standing on either side of Mr. Ackley, with an excited-looking security guard lurking helpfully nearby. Mr. Ackley appeared to have regained his former belligerence.

"You're damned right I'm exercising my right to remain silent," Ackley was shouting. "I'm not talking! You won't get a word out of me! But you know what? You might want to be careful what you eat around here. Or drink. Me, I wouldn't put anything into my mouth that didn't come out of a can or bottle. That I'd opened myself. That's all I'm saying."

Then he folded his arms and not only shut his mouth but clenched his jaw so hard it was painful to see.

I hoped not too many of the scientists had heard him back in the Hamilton Room, or it would cast rather a pall over the gala dinner. The chief waited a minute or so to make sure Ackley really had begun his policy of non-talking, then walked over to where Ekaterina was standing nearby.

"Do you have someplace where I can lock him up securely?" he asked her. "Someplace you can spare until whenever I'm able to get him to town and lock him up in the jail?"

"There is a small storage room across the hall from my office," she said. "I will arrange to clear it out as soon as possible."

"Perfect," the chief said. "And then I'd like it if you could let Horace and me in to search Mr. Ackley's room."

"You might want to talk to Mrs. Ackley first," I said as I joined them. "If she's the sweet little old lady she appears to be, she'll be frightened to death if you go barging into their room unannounced, and on the off chance she's as big a fruitcake as her husband, you might want to know where she is and what she's up to."

"There's a wife?" Evidently the chief didn't find this good news.

"Yes," I said. "And speak of the devil, here she comes."

I had spotted Mrs. Ackley trotting down the hall. Mother was following her, more slowly.

"Horace!" the chief called.

Horace left Mr. Ackley, now safely handcuffed and being watched by the security guard. He hurried over to us.

"What's up, Chief?"

"Gunman's wife coming down the corridor," he said in an undertone. "In the pink dress, I assume," he added to me—though without taking his eyes from Mrs. Ackley.

"Yes, that's her," I said.

"Thanks. Could you two stand between her and the prisoner?" the chief asked me and Ekaterina. "It can be very distressing to see a loved one in handcuffs."

We arranged ourselves to block as much of Mrs. Ackley's view as possible.

As Mrs. Ackley drew near, the chief approached her—warily, I noted. After all, we didn't know for sure that she wasn't involved. Though from the way her face lit up when she spotted him, I decided she probably wasn't. I doubted that people involved in poisonings and hostage takings usually displayed such enthusiasm at the sight of a police uniform. She hurried up to him.

"What's wrong? Is Jim hurt? My husband? They haven't murdered him, too, have they?"

"Your husband is fine, ma'am," the chief said. "But I'm afraid I'll be taking him into custody."

"Well, isn't this just typical." She crossed her arms and looked belligerent. "You might want to take a look at the locals, instead of arresting someone just because he isn't from around here."

From his expression, I deduced the chief was counting to ten before answering her, so I spoke up.

"Actually we have a whole hotel full of people who aren't from around here to suspect," I said. "Your husband is the only one who's been holding a bunch of his fellow guests at gunpoint."

"I don't believe it," she exclaimed. "He wouldn't."

"We have witnesses, ma'am," the chief said.

"And video," I added.

She looked from the chief to me. Then her shoulders sagged and she sighed deeply.

"Oh, dear," she said. "This always happens when he stops taking his meds."

The chief blinked and stared at her for a few seconds.

"Do you mean he's done this before?" he asked. "Taken hostages at gunpoint in an attempt to get publicity for his, um, demands?"

"Oh, no!" The idea seemed to shock her. "I can't imagine why he'd ever do that—he just does crazy things, like yelling at the poor cashiers in the McDonald's drive-through, as if it was their fault the company discontinued the hot mustard sauce, and having arguments about politics with perfectly nice people we've known for years and always got along with in spite of them being a little too liberal for his taste, and then the whole idea of moving to Florida."

She said all of that in one long burst. And she didn't sound as if she planned on stopping anytime soon, but luckily Mother stepped forward, took her by the arm, and began to lead her away.

"You've had a shock, dear," she murmured as she gently tugged Mrs. Ackley back in the direction they'd come from. "Let's go have some tea."

"We were perfectly happy in Sonoma," Mrs. Ackley was continuing as they started back down the hallway. "Well, I was perfectly happy, and he was no more unhappy than he was anywhere else we've lived. But he stopped taking his meds for a while and the next thing I knew we were living in this gated community with no trees to speak of, and while I suppose it's very nice, I miss our little house in the woods. And what nonsense, blaming these perfectly nice scientists for Ackley and Sons going out of business—as if his father hadn't already run it into the ground long before the hoot owls showed up. And I'll tell you one thing I like about owls—they don't come around during the daytime, not like the birds in Florida. The size of some of them! I can't tell you how many times I've looked out the back to see a huge bird with a bill as long as I am tall, stabbing the fish—gives me the creeps just to think about it—and of course I had to give up the idea of a koi pond. Egrets and flamingos and herons . . ."

Her voice had gradually faded in the distance. I made mental note to thank Mother later for taking one for the team.

The chief was watching them go with a look of annoyance and disbelief on his face.

"We got an address yet on Mr. Ackley?" he asked Horace.

"Yes, I've checked his wallet," Horace said. "Town called Port Charlotte, Florida. You want the street address?"

"Write it down for me, will you?" The chief was studying their prisoner. "I think I'll get in touch with the Port Charlotte police to see if verbally abusing the McDonald's employees is all Mr. Ackley's gotten up to down there." He turned to Ekaterina. "Might I ask you to rekey the Ackleys' room and let me have the new key? We'll need to search it. And is there any way you can find a new room for Mrs. Ackley? We don't want her underfoot while we're searching, and I think it will be better for everyone if we relocate her altogether."

"Of course." Ekaterina strode off toward the lobby.

"When you've got him locked up, why don't you and Horace join us for dinner," I said to the chief. "I realize you still have a lot of work to do, wrapping up the case—"

"But at least we can celebrate what we've accomplished so far," the chief said. "Since there's only so much more we can do while snowbound. I'll take you up on that. Breakfast was a good long time ago."

A good long time ago, yes. It felt like several years. Luckily I'd had lunch—and rather late—but everybody else was probably counting the minutes till dinner. I glanced at the sign-up sheets on the information table. Grandfather was right. There might be three or four people who hadn't signed up, but that was all.

I should go make sure everything was ready.

Chapter 30

Down the hall, in the ballroom, things were chaotic. Tables and steam tables were set up, and dishes were emerging from the kitchen to fill them, but instead of putting them in place the waitstaff appeared to be running around with them in random directions. Had the drama next door unnerved them?

After making a few inquiries, I figured out that half the staff had been instructed by Ekaterina to put all the special Hanukkah dishes in one section and the various nostalgic Christmas foods in another, while the other half were following Mother's orders to arrange the meal by course and content—meat dishes together in one section, fish in another, vegetables in another, and so on. One poor busboy had been carrying a bowl of horseradish back and forth for fifteen minutes. I hunted down Mother and Ekaterina, explained the problem to them, and then sat down in a corner to watch them sort it out. They soon came to an agreement, and the buffet took shape.

Not only was there a Hanukkah section, there were also sections with Indian food and Japanese delicacies. And everything was neatly labeled, so anyone who wanted to avoid anything—meat, milk, pork, beef, seafood, onions, garlic, gluten, mushrooms, and who knows what else— could safely navigate the buffet.

"I think we're ready," Ekaterina said finally. And just in time. We heard a loud burst of cheering and applause from the Hamilton Room next door—apparently the last panel was over.

"I'll open the doors," Mother said.

The first few people to enter the ballroom halted just inside and stood gazing at the buffet in amazement. Then they hurried to grab plates and another batch of awe-struck diners took their place.

First in line was the Hanukkah table, all a-glitter with blue and silver tinsel and featuring a huge antique Art Deco menorah in sterling silver. There were platters of smoked salmon, trays of rugelach, babkas, and sufganiyot, and on small nearby steam tables, dishes of brisket and of latkes. The main table also held a large collection of side dishes or trimmings—cream cheese, applesauce, onions, pickles, horseradish, tomatoes, capers, and such—and was strewn with Hanukkah gelt and chocolate-marshmallow dreidels on pretzel sticks. I'd had the Inn's brisket before, and planned to hit that table before it ran out if I had to trample a few scientists to do it.

Next up came Indian food: samosas, pakoras, dal, naan, poori, paratha, chicken tikka masala, butter chicken, tan-doori chicken, rogan josh, lamb vindaloo, malai kofta, matar paneer, and biryani. Since Indian was one of my favorite cuisines, I was planning a stop there, too.

The soup kettles included oyster stew, chili, matzoh ball soup, tomato soup, vegetable beef soup, hot and sour soup, and miso soup. The main dish table featured tur-key, Virginia ham, prime rib, standing rib roast, pork roast, roast goose, Peking duck, lasagna, pizza, burritos, tamales, macaroni and cheese, and, in direct defiance of Grandfather's orders, grilled portobello mushrooms in red wine sauce.

Anyone who had an inch of space left on their plate by this time would have to choose between mashed potatoes, candied sweet potatoes, collards, grits, black-eyed peas, okra, glazed carrots, green bean casserole, corn pudding, baked beans, stewed tomatoes, cranberry relish, cranberry gelatin mold . . . and I was probably overlooking a few things.

I planned to hit the four or five kinds of salad heavily and do what I could to ignore the dozen kinds of bread and rolls. But no power on earth could keep me away from the dessert table, though I hoped I could keep my foraging there to a crème brûlée cup or two and a chocolate chip cookie. Okay, Mother had conned someone into making *the* family pumpkin pie, so add that in. And there were blueberry, pecan, cherry, apple, and key lime pies. Chocolate, yellow, angel food, and carrot cake. Brownies, sugar cookies, M&M cookies, and more gingerbread people. Chocolate mousse. Plum pudding.

Beyond the desserts was a section I wasn't sure I wanted to visit—though I was curious to see how Dr. Hirano and Dr. Arai would react to it. The two Japanese scientists were moving methodically down the buffet line, taking tiny samples of each dish on offer. Their politely smiling faces didn't quite convince me that they were delighted with all this. More likely, they were taking detailed mental notes of the kind that would be useful when they got back home and wanted to regale their friends and family with stories about the peculiar foodstuffs the Americans tried to feed them.

But I kept my eyes on them, and even though their backs were to me I could tell the second they hit the part of the buffet Ekaterina had arranged with them in mind. I had no idea what dishes were there—a passing glance had revealed that the ingredients included rather more tentacles and seaweed than I wanted to think about, much less eat. But clearly Dr. Hirano and Dr. Arai were delighted. They took generous portions of everything in that section and hastened back to their table to dive in. I suspected they wouldn't be disappointed. The Inn hosted enough Japanese tourists that Ekaterina had seen the wisdom of hiring a chef whose training had included a stint at the Tsuji Culinary Institute.

I took my seat with Michael and the boys, who had worked up enormous appetites while shoveling snow. I was delighted to see that the boys' heavily laden plates included a wide variety of foods—including some of the seaweed and tentacle concoctions intended to delight the Japanese scientists.

"This is great, Mom," Jamie exclaimed, through a mouth full of prime rib. "We should eat like this more often."

Josh was too busy consuming some tentacles to comment, although he gave his brother's suggestion a thumbs-up.

"We can have any of these foods whenever you like," Michael said. "Just don't expect all of them at once, since we don't have a dozen staff members to cook them for us."

Grandfather either hadn't noticed the presence of mushrooms on the buffet or was taking a mellow holiday attitude toward them. I worried a little when I saw Dr. Czerny bustle up to him holding a conference tote bag full of . . . something. A whole lot of paper, by the look of it. But to my relief, it seemed to be something Grandfather wanted, or at least wasn't entirely displeased at receiving. Not that Grandfather wasn't perfectly capable of telling Dr. Czerny to go to hell if the occasion warranted. But it had been a long and tiring weekend and I wanted to spare him stress. I felt slightly easier when I saw that Dr. Czerny had only stayed long enough to drop off whatever it was. He then filled a plate at the buffet and slipped out. And I cheered up even more when, a few minutes later, Grandfather handed over the tote bag and his key card to Rose Noire, who dashed off with them. Good.

Whatever Dr. Czerny had been entrusting to Grandfather, it was out of his hands—and, I hoped, off his mind.

He seemed to be having a wonderful time, sitting with the two Japanese scientists on one side of him and Dr. Craine on the other, with Dr. Green and Rose Noire nearby. Although I did notice that whenever the door opened for another attendee to enter, most of them looked up. And when Dr. Lindquist arrived, a little later than most, he got a round of applause and cheers. He still looked slightly shaky—was it the close call with jail or the aftermath of his migraine? But he also looked happy as he took his seat at Grandfather's table.

When the traffic at the buffet had died down a bit, I noticed that the staff were taking turns slipping out of the kitchen and filling plates at the buffet—although they went down the back of the tables instead of the front, and seemed more than a little anxious.

"I gave them permission." Apparently Ekaterina had noticed my glance. "And the Inn will, of course, be picking up the tab for that portion of the meal consumed by the staff."

"Don't be silly," I said. "Grandfather will insist on treating them. Between the weather and the murder, they've all had to do much more than is in any of their job descriptions. And when are you having your dinner?"

"I will fill a plate and join you in a bit," she said with a smile. "As soon as I check on one or two more things. And I'm going to take a plate up to Mrs. Ackley. It's not her fault her husband turned out to be a homicidal maniac."

Her tone somehow suggested that she had had extensive experience comforting unfortunate women to whom this had happened.

"How is she taking it—do you know?"

"Not well," she admitted. Then her face darkened. "But she can't not eat." With that she slipped into the kitchen.

I saw the chief and Horace sitting nearby, deep in conversation. I stopped by to see them.

"This dinner almost makes up for the walk here." Horace hoisted a forkful of mashed potatoes as if giving a toast.

"Horace and I were just discussing the fact that Mr. Ackley was probably responsible for the attack on you," the chief said. "We found two key cards on him, one of which appears to have the same kind of access as the one that was taken from you. We'll figure out for sure when Ekaterina has time to do some digging in her card system."

"I should have told you that I'd found Ackley wandering around in the basement Saturday afternoon," I said. "He claimed he'd gotten there through a propped-open door and then got lost in the maze, and it sounded perfectly plausible to me. He even pointed out the doorstop he claimed had been used to prop open the door he used to get into the staff-only parts of the hotel. He played me."

"Even if you had told us, I'm not sure we would have found it suspicious," the chief said. "Since we were unaware that he had any connection to Dr. Frogmore."

"And we knew whoever stole Serafina's key card had accessed the freight elevator," Horace said. "We just didn't know why."

"Do we now?"

"We have an idea," the chief said. "Apparently his original plan was to burn down the Inn with as many ornithologists as possible trapped inside."

"Please tell me you're kidding."

"No." The chief shook his head.

"For someone who supposedly wants to exercise his right to remain silent until he gets a lawyer, he's sure been pretty verbose," Horace said through a mouthful of burrito. "His original plan was to check out, put his wife on a plane for home, telling her he had a business meeting somewhere, come back here and set the Inn on fire, and then shoot anyone who tried to escape. He used Serafina's stolen key card to scout out the staff-only parts of the hotel for a likely place to set his fire. And then to plant evidence in Dr. Lindquist's and Dr. Blake's rooms."

"What evidence?"

"Matchbooks from some restaurant or other," the chief said. "That would be identical to the matchbook he was going to leave at the scene of the crime. At least that's what he's claiming now."

"Do many restaurants still give out matchbooks?" I asked.

"Evidently," the chief said. "But since we found no matchbooks of any kind in either room, we're not sure whether to believe him."

"It's a little worrisome," Horace said. "What if he actually planted something else? Something more dangerous."

"Something directly related to the poisoning," the chief added.

"If Mr. Ackley planted matches in their rooms, the housekeeping staff would have confiscated them," I said. "Ekaterina's orders. She's a little paranoid about guests setting the hotel on fire. She'd have kept the matchbooks, of course, so she could give them back at checkout if their owners cared enough to complain."

"That would explain it," the chief said.

"I'll go and ask her." Horace stood.

"Finish your dinner," the chief said. "It will keep. At any rate, he'd already planted the matchbooks before the snowstorm came along to derail his arson scheme."

"So when he realized burning down the hotel would incinerate him and his wife along with the rest of us, he changed his plan and decided to kill Frogmore instead?" I asked.

"He's not talking about that," the chief said. "And we

can't interrogate him until we get a lawyer here for him. I expect he assumes it's perfectly safe to talk about the arson plan, since it never came off, but he's wary of getting into the things he actually did, like attacking you and killing Frogmore."

"My theory is that he didn't necessarily target Frogmore at all," Horace said. "He used his illicit access to the staff-only areas to poison something he knew was headed for the banquet, and it was pure luck that he got one of his biggest enemies."

"Doesn't sound all that plausible to me." The chief shook his head. "Too big a coincidence. At the very least, I think we'll find he put the poison in something that had a good chance of getting to Frogmore."

"We'll know more once we get him back to town and hook him up with a lawyer," Horace said.

The chief nodded.

"So are you going to get Randall to take you back to town?" I asked him. "Or did Ekaterina find you a room for the night?"

"Actually, your grandfather offered me the study in his cottage," the chief said. "He assures me that the Inn's Murphy beds are actually quite luxurious."

I was relieved. Not that I'd have hesitated to offer the chief space in our cottage, but things were already a little chaotic with Horace and the boys in residence.

"Let me know if you need me for anything," I said.

The chief nodded, and they went back to police talk.

Chapter 31

I decided to go back for . . . thirds? Fourths? I'd lost count. On my way to the buffet, I stopped by Grandfather's table to speak to Dr. Lindquist, who was now happily eating his way through a plate piled high with various tentacled delights from the Japanese section.

"Glad you were able to make it," I said.

"Yeah, I could be eating bread and water in solitary," he said.

"Now, now," I said. "The meals at the Caerphilly jail are catered by Muriel's Diner, and the only complaint we've ever heard is that the portions are so large it gives the prisoners indigestion."

"Okay, that almost makes me sorry I didn't get to eat there," he said. "Still, I guess I owe a debt of thanks to this Ackley guy."

"For what?" I asked. "Terrorizing the whole conference and threatening to shoot Grandfather?"

"Well, no." He grimaced. "That must have been pretty awful, no question. But you have to admit, things were looking pretty grim for me until he had his meltdown. Incriminating evidence found in my room, my own confession about borrowing the housekeeper's key card, plus your police chief found out about the time Frogmore claimed I'd tried to strangle him at a conference last year."

"Tried to strangle him?"

"Actually, I only threatened, but for some reason Frogmore managed to convince people I'd actually tried it.

So if Ackley had decided that having killed Frogmore he could declare victory and go home, I'd still be up the creek."

He had a point.

"I'm surprised no one recognized Ackley," I said. "If he was a major figure on the lumber industry side of the whole spotted owl thing."

"You mean why didn't *I* recognize him, right?" He chuckled at the idea. "Frankly, I never heard of him, so maybe he wasn't all that major a figure. Or maybe he was, but before I got involved. The whole controversy started thirty or thirty-five years ago, remember. I may look like an old fogey, but the spotted owl thing, as you call it, was already well underway by the time I hit grad school. And I've done some reading about how it all started, but the name Ackley never showed up."

"Or Ackwood Lumber?"

"Nope." He shook his head. "Although frankly, even if he was still involved in some way—most of us on the conservation side of the issue don't meet the high muckety-mucks of the timber industry. Just their lawyers. And another thing—it's a Pacific Northwest battle, remember. Only four of us here are from that part of the world—Frogmore, Czerny, Green, and me. And Green and Czerny are younger than I am."

"Which leaves Frogmore"

"Yeah. Frogmore." He popped another small tentacle in his mouth, chewed thoughtfully, and swallowed before answering. "Okay, say Ackley was active on the lumber side twenty-five or thirty years ago—it only makes sense that Frogmore would have heard of him. Might even recognize him. But if he did, why didn't he out him to the rest of us? I mean, why wouldn't he?"

"No reason," I said. "Unless he and Frogmore were really on the same side."

"Bingo!" I tried not to look at the odd bit of seafood he waved to underscore his point. "And it would be very interesting to find out exactly why Ackley was here in the first place. No offense, because I really like Caerphilly—at least what I got to see of it before the snowstorm. I wouldn't mind having more of a chance to look around—and I'd definitely come back to the Inn in a heartbeat. But it's not all that well-known a tourist destination."

"Please don't let Mayor Shiffley hear you say that," I said.

"How about not nearly as well-known as it deserves to be?" he said, with a laugh. "So you've got to admit, it'd be a pretty odd coincidence if Ackley just happened to show up here the same weekend as the Owl Fest."

"You think he came to kill Frogmore?"

"Could be. Or maybe he came to meet with Frogmore, got mad at him, and knocked him off."

"And instead of just letting an innocent bystander take the fall, he stages a highly dramatic hostage situation?"

"He probably lost it." Lindquist shrugged. "He was unbalanced to start with. We may never know. Just as we may never know for sure whether Frogmore was in bed with the lumber industry."

"Don't despair," I said. "There's going to be a murder trial, remember? Which means that both the defense and the prosecution will be digging into the connection between Frogmore and Ackley."

"You think they'll find anything?"

"Ackley may have lost his lumber company, but I get the impression he's still got enough money to hire a good defense attorney," I said. "And Caerphilly may be a sleepy little town, but Chief Burke spent over a decade as a homicide detective with the Baltimore PD. If there's dirt, one side or the other will find it."

"I hadn't thought of that." He grabbed his wineglass. "Here's to the chief finding all the dirt!"

I clinked my glass with his, and left him to wallow in his tentacle feast.

I headed for the buffet again. Heavenly—they'd just brought out another batch of brisket. I took a little of that—okay, a decent portion—and added a Christmas tamale and a slice of country ham.

"Whose idea was this, anyway?" Grandfather appeared beside me, holding a half-filled plate. "Much as I'd like to claim credit for it, I know I didn't think this up."

"Ekaterina," I said.

"Smart lady." He speared a slice of the ham. "She's saving a couple of possible weekends for Owl Fest 2020. Weekends that are earlier in the year and don't conflict with anything she can think of. Talk to her, see which one you think works best, then book it and tell me what I should put on my calendar."

"I can do that," I said. "What—"

"Aha! That's good to see." He pointed back at his table where Dr. Craine and Melissa McKendrick were absorbed in a conversation. "Vera Craine would make an outstanding external advisor for Melissa's doctoral committee. And I think she'll agree to do it if she sees what a sharp cookie Melissa is."

He beamed at seeing the progress his academic matchmaking was having.

"And now I should go let Ben Green tell me about his new project. He's suggesting that we drive the barred owls out of the spotted owls' territory by setting up thousands of loudspeakers out in the woods to broadcast barred owl cries of pain and distress."

"Thereby convincing the barred owls that bad things will happen to them if they stay?" I asked. "Are they that gullible?"

"More important, are barred owl distress cries that different from spotted owl distress cries?" he said. "Because it's no use chasing out the barred owls if we freak out the spotted owls at the same time. Needs testing."

Grandfather ambled back to his table and soon he and Dr. Green were as deeply engrossed in conversation as Melissa and Dr. Craine.

Michael and the boys greeted me with delight when I returned to our table.

"So, are we having Christmas here or at home?" Josh asked.

"We don't know yet," I said. "It depends on when the snowplows get here."

"Well, we're ready for them," Jamie said. "We've shoveled the whole parking lot."

"And plowed the driveway," Josh added.

"With a little bit of help from the Inn staff," Michael said with a chuckle.

"Well, yeah, they did a lot," Jamie said. "Especially the plowing."

"Since some people think we're not old enough to drive a tractor." Josh sounded scornful of the entire idea.

"So once the plows come by, we go home?" Jamie asked.

"Maybe," I said. "We don't know how much longer Great will need our help here."

"And there's also the fact that we don't know how the road leading out to our house is," Michael added. "Mr. Beau and Mr. Osgood could still have a lot of plowing to do."

"We should get a snowmobile," Josh pronounced. "It would be very useful at times like these."

"Perhaps we should discuss it with Santa," Jamie said, with a look of utter innocence on his face.

We had all reached that phase of a meal that hobbits would call filling up the corners. Many of the conference attendees would have been content to loll around the ballroom filling up corners all night, but Mother had other ideas.

"It's time for the group caroling!" she called. "Everybody who's coming to the group caroling, follow me to the lobby."

A few Grinch-like souls might have stayed behind, but most of the crew obediently trooped out to the lobby, where Rose Noire handed around photocopied wads of carol lyrics and Sami turned down the canned carols.

I spotted Grandfather slipping out of the lobby toward the cottages.

"You feeling okay?" I asked. It had been a long day.

"I'm fine, and before you ask, there's nothing wrong with my Christmas spirit. Got something I want to do. Get it off my mind before I start enjoying the carols. I'll be back."

He looked okay, so I shoved any worry to the back of my mind and went back to the lobby.

Mother, as self-appointed musical director, was in her element. We began with "Good King Wenceslas," and continued with "Jingle Bells," and "Deck the Halls." We were just about to start on "The Twelve Days of Christmas" when Sami rushed to the front door and peered out.

"The snowplows are coming! The snowplows are coming!" he shouted.

A stampede followed, as nearly everyone in the lobby tried to rush outside to get a glimpse.

And it was Beau Shiffley's snowplow, which caused a lot of merriment for the out-of-towners who hadn't seen it before. He normally kept the antlers from a ten-point buck mounted on the front of his plow, but he upped the ante for the holiday season. Attached below the antlers was a life-size plush reindeer head with a blinking red nose, and a dozen or so strings of twinkling multicolored lights festooned the sides of the plow.

We all swarmed out into the parking lot, cheering and waving. Beau stepped out of the cab and acknowledged the cheers by raising both fists and shaking them, the way a winning boxer might in the ring.

Ekaterina strode out with a covered cup of coffee, and a thermos containing more for later, and Beau thanked her and took a few sips while we serenaded him with a full-throated rendition of "We Wish You a Merry Christmas."

"I guess he didn't have to do much here," Jamie said with considerable pride as he watched Beau's snowplow disappear down the drive again. "Just a little cleaning up around the edges."

"Let's go back in," Josh said. "It's freezing out here."

Back in the lobby, Ekaterina had set up a complimentary coffee, tea, and hot chocolate service right beside the front desk, and everyone stopped for a short hot beverage break before starting the singing again.

I looked around and realized that Grandfather hadn't reappeared. Not that this was necessarily a bad thing. He'd had a long day, and he might have just gone to bed. Still. He was no spring chicken.

"Next, let's do 'We Three Kings.' Page four of your carol sheet," Mother announced.

"I'm going to look in on Grandfather," I whispered to Michael while everyone was still shuffling their sheets. "Back in a little bit."

At the door that led out into the courtyard, I waited to hear the first few bars of the carol before slipping outside.

Where it was still bitter cold, but at least there was nothing falling from the sky. I hoped we'd eventually find out how much snow the storm had actually deposited on Caerphilly. No way to tell here in the courtyard, where the shoveled snow had been piled as high as six or seven feet on either side of the paths.

I knocked softly at the Jefferson Cottage door and then

used my master key to slip inside. As I walked down the small hallway, the first thing I saw of the living room was Percival's cage. Apparently, after his star turn at the conference, they'd brought him back here rather than return him to the dubious safety of the storage room. An excess of caution, if you asked me—Mr. Ackley was now locked up, and they'd confiscated the key card he'd stolen from me. And there was no sign Percival had ever been one of his targets. But as long as it was Grandfather who had to live with him, I wasn't going to argue.

Grandfather and the chief. Well, only for one night.

They'd had to move the sofas a bit to fit in the cage, and it almost completely blocked my view of the sliding glass doors leading out to the terrace. Or, under the present circumstances, out into the Jefferson Cottage branch of the boys' tunnel and cave system. The cages containing the mice and crickets destined to be the owl's future meals sat on the floor between his cage and the sliding glass doors. Were they going to be warm enough there? I made a mental note to check. After I figured what was up with Grandfather.

Percival opened an eye when he heard me and almost immediately closed it again, no doubt because he recognized me as an unlikely source of mice.

Grandfather was sitting on one of the sofas with a sheaf of eight-and-a-half-by-eleven papers in his hands. His reading glasses were perched on his nose. When he heard me he looked over them at me, then put his papers down and took a sip from the glass of bourbon on the coffee table.

"Feeling antisocial?" I sat down on the other couch.

"I had some stuff I needed to read," he said. "Remember what I told Ned Czerny earlier today? When I was trying to console him?"

"You mean when you told him to grow a backbone and

find a boss who wasn't as much of a jackass as Frogmore? At least that's what Dad told me he'd heard. Your notion of how to console people is so refreshingly different from most people's."

"Maybe your father missed that I also told him that if he needed some ideas about what to do with himself I'd be happy to talk to him about it."

"You're thinking you might help him—as you did for Dr. Craine when she was down?"

"That was different. Vera's brilliant. You could tell even back then that she had a bright future ahead of her if she could just get past the damage Frogmore had done. Czerny's no Vera Craine. Not exactly a first-class brain. I've never felt that a high-powered research-oriented institution like Buckthorn was a good fit for him anyway."

"What would be a good fit, then?" I asked. "Teaching high school biology?"

"Heavens, no." Grandfather looked amused. "The students would eat him alive. But surely there's someplace he'd fit in. I suggested he and I talk later, to see if we could figure out what he was interested in and suited for. I was figuring we'd do a phone call sometime in the next week or so. I was most definitely not expecting to have him scurry back carrying a copy of his curriculum vitae plus every single academic paper he's ever had published."

"You're thinking it was a little pushy?" I asked.

"Well, I did offer to help, but it's just kind of weird, if you ask me. I can't think of many reasons why someone would be carrying all that with him to a conference."

"I can only think of one—that he was already planning to do a little job hunting." Grandfather nodded as if he agreed with me. "Of course you realize that he didn't necessarily bring hard copies of all that." I went on. "He could have brought a flash drive with all the documents, and printed them out in the business center after you offered to read it."

"True. Still weird even if he had them all with him on a flash drive. And thank God he's not particularly prolific." He eyed two stacks of paper on the coffee table. Not a minuscule collection, but still, not impressive as a lifetime achievement, even for a relatively youthful professor like Czerny.

"Won't that count against him in the academic job market—not being prolific?"

"In some places, yes. And frankly, even before I started reading, I'd decided it made sense to steer him to someplace a good deal less competitive."

"So that's why you're looking a little down—you've promised to help someone who isn't going to be that easy to help?"

"You know why I didn't just shove Czerny's CV and his publications in a box to look at when I had more time? Did that once before, about fifteen years ago, and it didn't go well."

"Didn't go well how?"

"Long story." He leaned back, took off his glasses, and rubbed his temples. He looked tired. I should probably tell him to go to bed and tell me his story tomorrow. But my curiosity was aroused.

"I've got nothing planned," I said aloud. "What happened fifteen years ago that didn't go well?"

"A grad student came to me. Young woman named Julia Taylor. She was . . . frustrated. Her doctoral advisor really wasn't a good fit for the direction she wanted to take her research. To be blunt, his input was not just useless but downright counterproductive because he didn't know squat about her topic and had no interest in learning and tried to get her to do something that would be useful for his career."

"So she came to you instead?"

"And unfortunately I didn't know much more about her topic than her advisor did, but at least I was willing to admit it. And I said I'd see if I could think of anyone who could help. She gave me her draft and a bunch of file folders full of data, and I took it all with me on a long trip. I forget which one. Was it that bat rescue in Australia? Or maybe filming the *Return to Galapagos* special? Long trip, anyway. Six, eight weeks. When I came back she had disappeared. No one knew where she'd gone. Took me forever to track her down."

"Define forever."

"Couple of years."

"I'm impressed with your perseverance."

"She impressed me. But it didn't do any good. She'd given up. I tried to guilt-trip her, telling her the world needs more women scientists, but she gave me an earful. Told me to butt out of her life. That if she didn't want to deal with the all the nonsense anymore, that was her decision."

"Did she just say nonsense?" I asked. "Or was it sexist nonsense?"

"Probably sexist nonsense." He shook his head. "I don't remember. It's been fifteen years."

Fifteen years during which not a lot had changed for the Julia Taylors and Melissa McKendricks of the world.

"Maybe she'd have given up anyway," he went on. "World's full of ABDs—that's—"

"All but dissertations," I said. "I know. Ph.D. students who complete their course work but never finish their dissertations and so never get their degrees."

"I felt as if I'd failed her. Didn't help her at the moment when she really needed it. So when Czerny was moaning about his career being over. I figured, yeah, he probably is feeling pretty devastated right now, losing his mentor and all. I offered to help. I was kind of taken aback when he showed up with this whole stack of stuff, but I told myself 'Don't screw it up this time.' So I brought it all back here, ordered myself a Basil Hayden, and sat down to slog through it. And that's when things got really weird."

"Weird how?"

"Because I realized I'd seen it before."

"The situation with the distraught grad student whose advisor can't or won't help? That wouldn't apply to Czerny. Unless—"

"No, this paper." He lifted the top paper from the smaller of the two piles. "I think I've seen this specific paper before. It's her paper. Julia Taylor. The grad student who gave up before I got around to helping her."

Chapter 32

"Holy cow! Czerny stole this woman's dissertation? Are you sure? Fifteen years ago, you know."

"Can I be absolutely sure it's word-for-word the same paper?" Grandfather said. "Of course not. But it's the same topic, no doubt of it. Unusual topic. She had an interesting slant on some owl behavioral issues. I wasn't sure I agreed with her premise—in fact, since then, it's been studied and disproven. That didn't matter—I thought when she did her research she'd figure out herself that it wasn't valid, and maybe come up with something useful and even more interesting along the way. Because it was interesting. *She* was interesting. Different. Had an original mind. And she had a fairly distinctive writing style—light, almost breezy, very down-to-earth, but without sacrificing accuracy or scientific rigor. I remember thinking she'd be a natural for writing the sort of books or articles that make scientific material comprehensible and entertaining to the general public. Or teaching, if her oral style was a match for the written."

"Doesn't sound like Czerny's style."

"No." Grandfather glanced at the larger of the two stacks of papers and grimaced. "Most of his stuff is turgid, overwritten—you can see Frogmore's heavy editorial hand. They're crap. But his doctoral dissertation, and two of his early published papers—there's some interesting stuff there. But he didn't write them. Not the whole of them. She did. I'd stake my life on it."

"How come nobody ever noticed this before?" I asked.

"I doubt if many people outside of Czerny's doctoral committee ever read his dissertation," Grandfather said. "And Julia Taylor never finished hers, so the only other person in the world who could have spotted the resemblance would be her advisor—and he's been dead a decade now, poor sod. And as for the rest of Czerny's publications . . . well, I wouldn't have read them before. These places he's publishing them are not exactly the top academic journals in the field. Some aren't even reputable journals. They're scam operations that will publish any garbage you send to them if you pay their fee."

"Why would someone do that? I know professors have to publish or perish, but surely nobody's going to be fooled by the spurious publications."

"Some of the fake journals look legit. Some of them have names vaguely like those of legit publications. Look at this one." He held out a sheaf of papers. "He included a copy of their masthead, which lists me as a member of their advisory panel. Never heard of the crooks. When we get back to civilization, I'll be turning this over to my attorney. But not all institutions have a sufficiently rigorous tenure process. Evidently Buckthorn doesn't. If their committee just ticked off the number of his publications and settled for 'oh, yeah, that sounds vaguely familiar,' he'd get away with it."

"So Czerny's CV isn't likely to help him get a good job anywhere else."

"It's likely to get him fired from Buckthorn if I tell them what I know."

"It'll be your word against his," I pointed out.

"Not if I show them what that poor young woman sent me. Pretty sure I still have it all in the files—you know what a paper pack rat I am. I might even be able to find her to testify against him. I'll sic Trevor on it when he gets back from wherever it was he felt he had to go for the holiday."

"Bermuda. He has family there, remember?" I tried, once again, not to resent the fact that Grandfather's assistant was almost certainly sitting on a beach drinking a rum swizzle or a dark 'n' stormy instead of being here to do much of the work that had fallen on me in his absence. "And what will you tell Dr. Czerny?"

Grandfather blew out his breath in what I took for an expression of exasperation.

"No idea. I probably shouldn't say anything until I finish all of these." He waved his hand at the stack of paper.

"Oh, so you're jumping to a negative conclusion before you've reviewed all your data—how unprofessional." I smiled to show I was only teasing.

His answering smile was lukewarm.

"No, I think I have enough data to cast serious doubts on both his integrity and his academic credentials," he said. "But that's a good point. I don't just need to read all of these very closely—I need to do some more digging. On top of stealing someone else's topic, I think he may have faked his data."

"Yikes."

"So maybe the best thing to do would be to just avoid him for a while. Till I can do a full investigation of this whole thing. And till I get over the urge to punch his lights out for the cheating bastard I'm pretty sure he is."

"Sounds reasonable. Shall I put him at the top of the list when the airports open and Ekaterina and I start trying to help your attendees get home in time for Christmas?"

"Definitely." He took another sip of his bourbon and went back to gazing with a gloomy expression on his face at the two stacks of paper on the coffee table.

Percival opened one eye and peered at me. No, not

at me—over my shoulder. A few seconds later someone knocked at the door.

"Owls have good hearing, right?" I asked as I stood up.

"Oh, yes." Being asked an ornithological question seemed to cheer Grandfather up. "Nearly all of them have very highly developed auditory processing systems—helps them hunt at night, you know. And in many of them—barn owls, for example—the shape of the face acts as a sort of funnel to channel sounds more effectively to the ears."

I headed for the door to see who was visiting.

"And they have excellent directional hearing," Grandfather was saying behind me. "They compare the difference between when a sound hits their left and right ears—they're sensitive to a difference of as little as thirty millionths of a second. Then they swivel their heads until the sound hits both ears at the same time, and bingo! They know where to go to catch their prey."

I opened the door and wasn't thrilled to see Grandfather's visitor.

"Hello, Dr. Czerny," I said, loudly enough for Grandfather to hear.

"I came to see Dr. Blake," he said.

"It's really late, you know," I said. "Are you sure—"

"Let him in, Meg," Grandfather said.

"Are you sure?" I said. "You should be in bed."

"Never put off till tomorrow what you can get over with today."

"I'm not sure that's how the saying goes." I stood aside to let Dr. Czerny in.

Czerny scurried into the living room and sat on the sofa opposite Grandfather. Perched on the edge of it, really. With his stoop-shouldered, hunch-necked posture, he looked more than ever like a buzzard. I saw him glance at the stacks of papers and then back at Grandfather.

I came over and leaned on the arm of Grandfather's sofa.

"So?" Dr. Czerny gave a bright smile. "What do you think? Any suggestions about where I should apply?"

Grandfather was rubbing his temples again, eyes closed. Then he sighed and opened his eyes again. I could spot the precise moment he came to his decision.

"Tell me," he said. "Did Dr. Frogmore know when he hired you that you'd stolen your dissertation from Julia Taylor? Or did he find that out later?"

Czerny's mouth fell open, and all the color drained from his face.

"Or was it the falsified data in your subsequent publications that he found out about?" Grandfather went on. "Either way, he made you pay, didn't he? Turned you into his flunky. Kept you so busy doing his administrative scut work that you hardly had time to do any research. Although it was probably pretty easy to be philosophical about that, since he'd have stolen anything worthwhile you came up with anyway. So no, I haven't yet had any ideas about where you should apply. It's going to take a while to think of a place that'd be willing to hire a plagiarist. A plagiarist who might soon have his Ph.D. revoked."

"You're crazy." Czerny stared at Grandfather for a few moments, then looked up at me. "He's losing it. Dementia. I have no idea why he's saying this."

"Grandfather's brain is just fine. But he's missing the most important point, isn't he?" I asked. Both Grandfather and Czerny looked at me, puzzled. "The part about you killing off Dr. Frogmore."

"You're crazy, too," Czerny said.

"I thought that lunatic lumberjack killed Frogmore," Grandfather said.

"Lunatic lumber baron," I corrected. "And no, Dr. Czerny did. Didn't you?" I turned to Czerny. "We blew it. You had the same means and opportunity as any of the prime suspects. Better than most—you were sitting by him at dinner. But we all kept counting you out because we couldn't figure out a motive for you to kill him. Because we thought you had the strongest possible motive to keep him alive. You'd be killing the mentor who protected you, got you tenure, shielded you from being found out as incompetent. Killing the goose that was laying all those golden eggs for you. We couldn't imagine that you'd have any reason to kill Frogmore. But you did. He'd been blackmailing you. And you wanted out. Now that the chief is here at the hotel—"

"Now that the chief is here, I think I'll be making my exit," Czerny said. "As soon as I figure out where the hell he parked his snowmobile."

He took his hands out of his coat pockets. He was holding a gun. I have never liked having guns pointed at me or my family to begin with, and this was the second time tonight.

"Don't be an idiot, man," Grandfather said. "You can only go so far on a snowmobile. Just turn yourself in and tell them you have no recollection of poisoning Frogmore. They do it all the time on television."

"I don't think it's that easy." He turned to me. "You know where the snowmobile is, don't you?"

"No, I don't. No idea." I didn't want to tell him that the snowmobile had only dropped the chief off and headed back to town. He might do something crazy. Crazier than what he was already doing.

"I don't buy that," he said. "A busybody like you—you always have to know everything that's going on. Tell me where the snowmobile is or I'll shoot him."

He pointed the gun at Grandfather.

"Okay," I said. "It's— Wait. Just one question—how the Dickens did you manage to get the nitro spray on his food without anyone noticing?"

"I wasn't going to do it till after the banquet. Thought I'd slip it into an after-dinner drink. But when those idiots in owl costumes began doing their can-can dance, everyone in the place was watching them and laughing their eyes out. I pulled out the little bottle I was keeping it in and dumped it in his Scotch and water."

"Hell of a thing to do to your mentor," Grandfather growled.

"Mentor!" Czerny shrieked so loudly that both Percival and I startled. Grandfather didn't seem the least bit upset. "Frogmore was my jailer. Yeah, when the Taylor woman abandoned her research, I picked it up and carried it through. Why not? She wasn't going to use it. But I never should have let Frogmore find out. He made my life a living hell. I should have killed him years ago. I'd do it again. But I should have picked something that would work slower. I didn't realize he'd go that fast. I wanted him to suffer. And by the way, I know what you're doing, Blake, and I'm not falling for it."

"I'm not doing anything," Grandfather said.

"Flicking your eyes over at the door to the terrace," Czerny said. "I know damn well there's three, four feet of snow piled up out there. Nobody's going to come dashing in from the terrace to rescue you."

"I was looking at the damned owl," Grandfather said. "You seem to have startled him."

Grandfather was right. Percival was wide awake and staring out toward the terrace.

"He's already been shot once," Grandfather continued. "Try not to take him out too when you start blasting."

"Oh, very funny." After a brief glance at Percival, Czerny focused back on me. "I mean it. Where's the snowmobile?"

"I don't know, but maybe I can figure it out—let me think a sec." I frowned as if thinking hard enough to bring on a headache. "The chief came in the front door. He probably parked it right outside." I was trying very hard not to look over in the direction of the door to the terrace, because my peripheral vision told me it was slowly sliding open. What in the world could—no! It had to be the boys, coming in through their tunnels. Were they trying to sneak in to play a prank on their great-grandfather? Or were they attempting some kind of foolhardy rescue? In either case, I had to get Czerny out of the room before they came in.

"Yes, I'm pretty sure it's right outside the front door." I was having a hard time keeping my voice steady. And keeping my eyes away from the sliding glass door. The cold air was coming in through the opening. Any second now Czerny would notice. How could I get a message to the boys to stay safely outside—or, better yet, to run away and get help? I heard a slight metal snick—what were they doing?

"Maybe you and I should go out there and look for it, then," he said. "Let's go."

Suddenly a live mouse sailed over the top of the cage and landed on Czerny's head. He yelped, dropped the gun, and slapped at his head with both hands. I dived for the gun, and then shrieked as the mouse leaped off Czerny and onto my shoulders. Luckily I managed not to drop the gun in my surprise, and the mouse quickly scuttled away. I heard a squeaking noise and another mouse landed on Czerny. Followed by another.

And then Percival rose up. He uttered an unearthly screech and dived toward the latest airborne mouse—which had just landed on Czerny's head.

Czerny screamed and dived for the floor, which reduced the damage Percival's talons did when he seized the mouse. Percival landed on the mantel with the mouse in his talons, dislodging the evergreen garland draped over it and knocking several small breakable things to the floor in a tinkling crash. He leaned down to pluck the mouse from his talons, and it disappeared into his bill. Except for the tail, which dangled down for a few seconds until Percival took another gulp and sucked it in.

I stood up, still a little shaky, and pointed the gun at Czerny, who was still cowering on the floor.

"Freeze, you scum-sucking plagiarist." I hoped my voice didn't sound as shaky as I felt.

"Hey, Mom," Josh said. "Should I throw another mouse?"

"Stand by," I said. "Percival still has to catch two of the ones you've already thrown." At least I hoped the owl could manage it. I wasn't looking forward to breaking the news to Ekaterina if he didn't.

The cottage door slammed open. I kept my eyes on Czerny.

"Police! Freeze!" The chief. "Meg? Dr. Blake."

"We're both fine," I called over my shoulder. "And I have Dr. Czerny's gun and am pointing it at him so he doesn't try anything else stupid."

"Chief," Grandfather bellowed. "Give us a minute to secure the owl before you enter."

"Secure the owl?" the chief echoed. "Do I even want to know?"

"Jamie, we need to lure Percival back into the cage," Grandfather said. "Toss me a mouse."

"It's Josh. Jamie went to fetch the cops." But another mouse came flying over the cage. Grandfather caught it deftly.

I fixed my eyes on Czerny so I wouldn't have to watch. Although I deduced from their comments that between them, Josh and Grandfather used one of the mice to lure Percival back into his cage.

"All clear," Grandfather called. "Safe to come in now, Chief."

The chief and Horace raced in. The chief kept his gun trained on Dr. Czerny, who didn't put up any resistance when Horace secured his arms behind him. Then Horace scrambled to his feet, pulled a gold-embossed evidence bag out of one of his pockets, and held it open so I could drop in the gun.

"Let's hope we've got the real killer this time," I said. "Dealing with all these gun-waving loonies is really taking a toll on my Christmas spirit."

"These people attacked me!" Czerny shouted. "I came here to retrieve some papers I lent Dr. Blake, and they pointed a gun at me and sicced their vicious owl on me. They'll probably tell some wild story about me killing Dr. Frogmore—they're crazy."

He looked around with an expression that really did look like outraged innocence.

Grandfather held up his phone and pressed something. Czerny's recorded voice picked up in mid-sentence.

". . . life a living hell. I should have killed him years ago. I'd do it again. But I should have picked something that would work slower. I didn't realize he'd go that fast. I wanted him to suffer."

Grandfather clicked the phone off.

"Meg," he said. "When you get a chance, remind me to thank whoever set up that dictation software on my phone. Turned out to be pretty useful after all."

Chapter 33

"Careful! You almost knocked the head off one of the wise men!"

"Take it slowly, then. I can't see where I'm going, and there's a pointy little glass star that nearly puts my eye out whenever you stop suddenly like that."

I was standing on the Inn's front walk, sipping a cup of hot chocolate and watching as several tall, lanky workmen from the Shiffley Construction Company loaded our Christmas tree onto a flatbed truck. After extensive discussions about how long it would take to undecorate the tree Mother had set up in the Madison Cottage and return all the ornaments to our almost completely denuded tree at home, Randall Shiffley had offered to have the tree moved as is.

Moving a fully decorated twenty-foot fir tree is no small project. I wasn't the only person standing on the sidewalk watching.

"Amazing!" Lachlan Pearce was documenting the whole ordeal on video with his cell phone's camera. And would probably be sharing it with his friends and family, once the Wi-Fi was back. I rather enjoyed imagining a flock of swimsuit-clad, flip-flop-shod Australians, sitting on a beach somewhere, taking a break from prawns and cricket to watch how the crazy Americans celebrated Christmas.

A little farther down the sidewalk a burgundy-and-gold bus with "New Life Baptist Church Choir" painted along the sides was slowly filling up with departing scientists and their suitcases. Although flights were beginning to take off from Dulles Airport, long-distance shuttles and taxis were still hard to come by, so the Reverend Wilson had offered the use of the bus—and Deacon Petrie, its seasoned driver—to transport anyone determined to make the attempt to get home for Christmas.

The Vosses were among the bus passengers, so I enlisted Mrs. Voss to make sure Reverend Wilson's kindness didn't go unrewarded.

"Don't worry," she said. "I've already started taking up a collection. We'll tell Mr. Petrie that it's to cover gas, and if there's any left over he should use it for that lovely choir. And there will be plenty left over. Meanwhile, this is for you."

She handed me a long cylindrical package wrapped in what I recognized as one of the papers Mother had brought along for her package-wrapping nook.

"You shouldn't have," I said. "Should I open it now or save it for Christmas Day?"

"Open it now if you like," she said. "Or I can tell you what it is so if you don't like it you can regift it without having to rewrap it. It's my crewelwork owl. Remember, George drew Ned Czerny in the Secret Santa, but you can't expect us to go ahead and give him a present after he tried to shoot your grandfather."

"That's wonderful." I hope she realized I meant it. "I love crewelwork, and your owl's one of the most impressive examples of it I've ever seen."

"Enjoy it."

"Am I the only one who thinks it a little odd that Dr. Czerny even signed up for the Secret Santa?" I asked.

"George and I figure he was hoping he'd draw someone important so he could ingratiate himself." She laughed.

"And when we'd exchanged all the other presents, we figured out he'd drawn Jeff Whitmore. There was a bottle of wine wrapped up with poor Jeff's name on it. He turned it over to your cousin Horace for forensic testing. Didn't look as if it had been opened, but Jeff didn't want to take any chances. I'm going to get on board and stake out a good seat. Thanks for everything!"

She gave me a quick hug and trotted over to the bus.

In addition to the bus, there were eight or ten cars either parked in the long loading zone or double-parked beside it, as people who'd driven to the conference prepared to make their trek home. The lobby was crowded with people watching the Weather Channel on the Inn's TV, listening to various radios, and taking turns using the available satellite phones to call relatives and friends to ask about road conditions along their routes. Ekaterina had set up a huge map of the eastern half of the country behind a sheet of glass, and Sami was kept busy with his dry-erase markers, updating the map as reports came in about conditions along various major routes.

And Ekaterina had waived the usual checkout times so guests wouldn't have to worry about that when making their decisions about whether to go or stay.

"It's not as if we expect a great many people to arrive today," she said, in a philosophical tone. "And if some of the departing guests encounter difficulties and turn back, we will take care of them."

Although I sensed she wouldn't be unduly distressed if none of them boomeranged back and she was left with only the fifty or so guests who'd either chosen to stay on or resigned themselves to the fact that travel to their ultimate destinations was impossible. She and the entire Inn staff could use a little relative peace and quiet.

From what I could learn, the roads in Caerphilly were in pretty good shape compared with most places east of the Mississippi. Our governor had declared a state of emergency, and in some parts of Virginia the National Guard was hauling first responders around in Humvees and trucks, and dispatching debris-reduction teams with chainsaws to clear away the thousands of fallen trees that would otherwise interfere with the snowplows. But Caerphilly probably boasted more chainsaws per capita than your typical county, and since a great many of those chainsaws belonged to members of the Shiffley clan, who would turn out in force when Randall gave the word, our recovery was proceeding with lightning speed.

"So there's no need for us to trouble the National Guard," Randall had said with more than a touch of pride when he dropped by early in the morning to run the chief back to town. "In fact, we'll probably be reaching out tomorrow to see what we can do for less fortunate neighboring counties."

I could tell the idea of playing Good Samaritan to neighboring counties really psyched him. I wondered if he was actually going to follow through with his idea of sending a couple of Shiffley cousins with chainsaws on the New Life Baptist bus, in case it ran into difficulties with downed trees in one of the less fortunate counties that lay along the route from Caerphilly to Dulles Airport.

I was distracted from that thought by the arrival of another vehicle—still a sufficiently rare occurrence that nearly everyone in the loading zone stopped to see what it was and a few people from the hotel came running outside to join in the gawking.

This time it was Chief Burke in his police cruiser. He parked as close as he could to the front door, and the cruiser had barely come to a stop before someone jumped out of the passenger seat and sprinted for the hotel. His grandson Adam.

"Hi, Ms. Langslow," he called in passing before disappearing into the Inn. No doubt he already knew where to find Josh and Jamie.

The chief followed at a more leisurely pace.

"The boys will be glad to see Adam," I said. "They've been dying to show off their tunnel system."

"And Adam convinced me that his life would be incomplete unless he saw it." The chief smiled as he glanced at the door through which his grandson had disappeared. "Any chance I can leave him with you for a while? No school today, of course, and Minerva's got a busy rehearsal schedule with the choir."

"The boys would never forgive me if I said no," I said. "They'll be looking for Adam's help on their new project."

"Do I even want to ask?"

"They were inconsolable about going home and leaving their tunnels behind until Michael pointed out that we have just as many feet of snow at home—snow in which they can build a whole new system of tunnels."

"Adam will be delighted," the chief said. "And I suspect Ms. Ekaterina will be pleased that I'm taking both prisoners back with me. Both prisoners and Dr. Frogmore's body. Ah, here they come."

The chief had evidently been the lead car in a small caravan. Vern Shiffley was parking his cruiser near the chief's, and a hearse from Morton's, the local funeral home, continued past the front door, heading around to the loading dock on the far side of the hotel.

"Your dad's going to get started on the autopsy as soon as he gets our victim to the hospital." The chief wore a look of profound satisfaction. "And we have defense attorneys on their way to the jail to meet our two prisoners. Did Horace take off yet?"

"Half an hour ago," I said. "With his entire trunk and most of the backseat taken up with the evidence bags."

"Evidence bags." The chief shook his head. "They're

going to laugh at those fancy gold-trimmed bags down at the Crime Lab."

"Maybe," I said. "But Ekaterina also packed several matching bags full of pastries and desserts for Horace to take with him. If they give him too much grief over the silly bags, they'll soon regret it."

"I wonder if it's too late to swap places with Horace," the chief said. "He did very well under difficult conditions this weekend—maybe I should take the evidence down to Richmond and let him interrogate the suspects."

"Somehow I think he'll be happier hanging out with his forensic buddies right now," I said. "He seemed to enjoy being the on-site point person, but I bet he's got a new appreciation for how hard it is. Here's hoping the interrogations go well."

"I'm optimistic," the chief said. "Given the extent of the video evidence against Mr. Ackley, I think his attorney's only option will be to go for an insanity plea. And frankly, if you ask me, the loony bin's the place for him, as long as they can find a way to keep him there a good long time. And as for Dr. Czerny . . . I must remember to thank your grandfather for his quick-wittedness in turning on his phone's dictation app. Although even without that, things would be looking a little bleak for him. Dr. Frogmore might not be very popular in ornithological circles, but he was a bigwig at Buckthorn College. We're getting excellent cooperation not only from the college administration but also from both the Buckthorn County sheriff's department and the Oregon State Police. Apparently Dr. Czerny made no provision for the possibility that he might come under suspicion. If you're doing an Internet search on ways to poison someone there are elementary precautions you should take."

"Like using a computer that can't easily be traced back to you," I said. "I always research my poisons at the library."

"So Ms. Ellie was telling me." He had a good poker face. "There's also not bookmarking your research sites on your home computer."

"Yikes! How clueless is he?"

"And we may already have determined where he got the nitro. Another professor in the Buckthorn biology department kicked up a fuss last month when the spray he kept around for his occasional angina attacks went missing."

"Hard to prove Czerny took it."

"We're tracing the batch number. We should be able to prove it was unlikely that anyone else did."

"So the bad guys won't get away with it."

"Let's not jinx it," he said. "Strange things can happen in a court of law. But I'm reasonably certain that we'll be able to give the county attorney a pretty solid case. Where's your grandfather taking that owl, anyway?"

Grandfather had appeared on the sidewalk, followed by a bellhop pushing a cart that held Percival's cage.

"Back to the raptor rehab unit at the zoo," I said. "You don't need the owl for evidence or anything, do you?"

"No, your testimony and Dr. Blake's should be sufficient."

"That's good," I said. "He'd make a rotten witness. Just imagine it—the prosecutor asks him, 'Do you know Dr. Edward Czerny?' and Perce would just say, 'Who?'"

"I don't know," the chief said. "He'd be better than some witnesses we've seen. At least he'd give a hoot."

The chief and I both laughed. Grandfather looked cross.

"Hmph. Suddenly everyone I talk to seems to be making bad owl puns."

"See you later," the chief said.

Another Shiffley Construction Company truck—this

one a panel truck—pulled up to the curb. Grandfather watched as two of Randall's workmen loaded Percival into the back.

"Have you got the black widow spider?" I asked.

He reached into his coat pocket, took out the jar with the perforated lid, and held it up for a few seconds before stuffing it back into his coat pocket and climbing into the truck's cab.

"See you back at the house," he said.

The chief and I waved as the truck pulled out.

"Well," the chief said. "Those prisoners aren't going to transport themselves."

"I bet they could if you let them," I said. "But probably not to any destination you'd want them going to."

He laughed and headed inside the Inn. On his way he passed Dr. Craine, who was dragging her suitcase behind her.

"Meg! There you are!" she said. "Your grandfather said you could give me a ride."

"Er. . . . okay," I said. "Where to?" Not, I hoped, someplace too far out of my way.

"Your house, actually." She frowned. "Did he not tell you he invited me to stay with you for a couple of days?"

I burst out laughing.

"Not in so many words," I said. "He told me he'd invited half a dozen people who couldn't get home and didn't want to spend the holiday in a hotel. I'm relieved to see that at least one of them is someone I'd have gladly invited myself if I'd known she was stranded."

"That's a relief," she said. "I might be able to get home today if I really work at it, but I could end up stranded halfway, and even if I succeeded I'd only be arriving to an empty house—my son's spending Christmas with his wife's family and I lost my husband a few years ago. So I figure I'll stand back and leave the plane seats to people who really want them. Actually, I suspect Monty's eager to have me stay so he can talk me into serving as Melissa's external advisor. Once I get settled in, I'll tell him that I already told her I'd do it."

"Better yet, wait a few days," I said. "He doesn't often have to butter up people to get favors. He could use the practice. And it might be amusing to watch."

"Okay." She chuckled at the prospect.

"Do you need help with your luggage?" I asked. "I could send the boys."

"This is all I've got." She gestured to the modest suitcase she'd rolled out behind her. Not quite a carry-on, but not much larger. I nodded approvingly.

I led her over to the Twinmobile, shoved her suitcase in the back, and assigned her the shotgun seat.

"My goodness, look at that." She pointed to the loading area. Melissa McKendrick had pulled up in front of the hotel in a battered old Honda Fit. Two bellhops were loading the car's trunk and backseat with luggage. She'd only had a backpack when we'd searched. Where had all that luggage come from?

Then I saw it. Ekaterina was supervising as Sami and one of the bellhops half escorted and half carried Mrs. Ackley down the Inn's front walk.

"I'll go see what's up," I said.

"You are, of course, welcome to stay on, Mrs. Ackley," Ekaterina was saying as I came within earshot. "But of course we understand why you might prefer to leave."

Sami and the bellhop succeeded in levering Mrs. Ackley into the Fit's front seat. She was, for once, silent. I hoped for Melissa's sake she stayed that way.

Everyone stared, and a few of us waved as the Fit drove off.

"Thank goodness," Ekaterina said. "You must help me think of something I can do to thank that young woman.

I have been trying for two hours to get a cab for Mrs. Ackley."

"Is she leaving town?" I liked to think if I were ever arrested for murder in some other state, Michael would at least stay around long enough to make sure I had a good defense attorney.

"Taking a room in one of the bed-and-breakfasts. Because there are too many unhappy memories here." Ekaterina sniffed slightly. "I suppose if I were married to a homicidal maniac, I would also be in a hurry to put a distance between myself and all the people he tried to kill. Aha! The bus prepares to leave."

The last few stragglers were climbing on board. I spotted Whitmore, Belasco, and Smith—the three lost lambs—in the queue. Two teenage Shiffleys were already on board, their chainsaws safely stowed in the luggage compartment. And Nils Lindquist was standing by the door, looking impatiently back at the hotel.

"Just one more minute," I heard him say. "He can't have gone far."

Ben Green came running out of the hotel, dragging his suitcase, followed by Sami, Chantal, and Serafina, all of whom appeared to be carrying items the absent-minded scientist had left behind.

"Oh, dear," Green said, when they caught up with him. "It's going to take some doing to fit all that in my suitcase."

"And we don't have time right now," Lindquist said. "Let me have that stuff. We'll deal with it when we get to the airport."

With his arms full of his friend's nearly forgotten items, Lindquist half coaxed, half shoved Green toward the bus. But Green resisted all his efforts until Rose Noire came running out of the hotel carrying something wrapped in blue and lavender. She handed it to Green, and he beamed as if she'd given him the moon.

"I'll be in touch," he shouted over his shoulder as Lindquist dragged him onto the bus.

No sooner had the door closed behind them than Deacon Petrie started the motor. We all lined the sidewalk to wave good-bye. Ben Green opened one of the windows and stuck half his body out, waving wildly.

Another window opened, and Lindquist's head popped out.

"Hey, Meg," he shouted. "Tell your grandfather it was a great conference. Is he really having it next year?"

"Yes," I shouted back.

"Great! Owl be back!"

A mixture of groans and laughter greeted this remark, along with a few calls for him to shut the window to keep the freezing air out. He popped back inside, pulled the window shut, and the bus began lumbering down the driveway.

As I waved at the departing bus, I felt a sudden surge of happiness. They were going home. Everyone was going home.

We were going home.

At the end of any trip, even the most enjoyable, I always looked forward to being home again. Sleeping in our own bed, sitting down to breakfast at our own table, relaxing in the evening in front of our own fireplace. Even the daily chores of taking care of our ever-growing menagerie— the llamas, ducks, chickens, sheep, cows, and dogs—took on a rosy hue when I'd been away from them for a while.

But it wasn't just home I was looking forward to—it was Christmas at home. We could have hung our stockings from the elegant fireplace of the Madison Cottage, but I preferred seeing them back on our own familiar hearth. Even with Melissa's improvements, the canned music at the Inn couldn't hold a candle to carols played on our own piano and sung by friends and family. Soon I'd be cooking the enormous turkey Michael had brought home from a local free-range poultry farm, and I could probably dragoon a few of the visiting relatives and ornithologists into helping out with the rest of the dinner. With luck, there would be enough snow on the roof to discourage Dad from his usual Christmas Eve ritual of climbing up on it to stomp around in heavy boots while shaking an armload of sleigh bells. The boys would make their usual mad dash downstairs on Christmas morning, and we'd have the usual hot chocolate and hot spiced cider while—

"Mom?"

I turned to find Josh, Jamie, and Adam all dragging suitcases. My twins had their own; Adam was bringing mine.

"Can we go now?" Jamie asked.

"We have a lot of work to do," Josh added.

They hurried over to the Twinmobile and began loading their suitcases.

Michael was following them, dragging his own suitcase.

"Why don't you take Vera and the boys over to the house?" he added, as he shoved it into the luggage compartment, where it only just fit.

"But we have—"

"At least another carload of stuff to pack and bring," he said. "Let me handle it. After running your grandfather's whole conference and foiling two killers, I think you deserve a break."

"And there's also all of Grandfather's stuff. It'll take you forever."

"Ekaterina's got a crew helping me pack," he said.

"Come on, Mom." The boys had scrambled into the Twinmobile.

"If you're sure." I decided not to argue with him. I was ready—well, not quite ready for a nap, but definitely ready to be home. So I got into the Twinmobile and started the engine, accompanied by enthusiastic cheers from the boys.

I set off, but stopped after a few feet and rolled the window down.

"If you need me to come back and help later—"

"Don't worry." He dropped to one knee and began singing "Owl Be Home for Christmas." At least a dozen of the assembled ornithologists joined in, and they serenaded us till we were out of sight.

Read on for an excerpt from

The Falcon Always Wings Twice

— the next Meg Langslow mystery
from Donna Andrews,
available now in hardcover
from Minotaur Books!

Chapter 1

"I think they're plotting to bump off Terence today," Michael said.

"Bump him off?" I echoed. "Not for real, I assume."

"Don't get your hopes up. Bump off his character. In the Game."

"I could live with them bumping him off for real," I said. "Just as long as they pick a time when we both have alibis."

Michael chuckled. No doubt he thought I was kidding. Of the two dozen actors, musicians, and acrobats my husband had recruited to perform at the Riverton Renaissance Faire, Terence was my least favorite by a mile. He was rude, selfish, greedy, lecherous, and just plain obnoxious. Unfortunately, he was also an integral part of what we'd come to call "the Game"—the ongoing semi-improvisational entertainment that had become so popular with visitors to the Faire.

"Most Renaissance fairs just replay the story of Henry the Eighth and one or another of his wives," Michael had said when he'd explained the idea to my grandmother Cordelia, the Riverton Faire's owner and organizer. "Or Queen Elizabeth beheading Essex. What I have in mind is something much more exciting. We have this fictitious kingdom, and all the actors belong to one or another of the factions fighting to control it, and they plot and scheme and duel and seduce and betray each other. And they do it loudly and publicly at regular intervals all day long, in period costume and elegant Shakespearean prose."

"Sounds like a cross between an old-fashioned soap opera and that *Game of Thrones* TV show," Cordelia had said. "I like it."

And thus was born the troubled kingdom of Albion.

The Renaissance Faire was Cordelia's latest entrepreneurial project. She'd started the Biscuit Mountain Craft Center a few years ago in a converted art pottery factory and it had grown from a summer-only venue to a year-round institution offering classes in a wide variety of arts and crafts. This summer, she'd decided to limit the classes to Monday through Thursday, and organize the Renaissance Faire Friday through Sunday.

Of course, her venture relied heavily on the talents of various family members—especially Michael, who took charge of the entertainment, and me, in the role of her second in command. I didn't know whether to hope the Faire succeeded or secretly root for a failure that would let us return to spending long, lazy, relaxing summers back at home in Caerphilly.

I glanced across the room to where Michael—aka Michael, Duke of Waterston—was preening in the mirror. Okay, maybe preening was a bit harsh. After all, he was getting ready to go onstage. He appeared to be performing minute adjustments to the billowing sleeves of his white linen shirt and the fit of his red-and-black leather doublet.

I could have used the mirror myself, just for a minute, to see if running a comb through my mane had tamed it sufficiently for me to go out in public or if I should just pull it back into a rough French braid. Probably wiser to opt for the braid in either case. I'd be doing blacksmithing demonstrations at 11:00, 3:00, and 6:00, and in between I'd be running around like crazy, taking care of the thousand and one problems that would crop up during the day.

Odds were at least a few of the problems would include Terence. Would be caused by Terence. Would bring me totally into sympathy with any reasonably nonviolent plot to get rid of Terence.

"What happens if they kill off Sir Terence in the Game?" I asked aloud. "Can Cordelia fire him? Or will you have to bring him back as a different character?" Much as I disliked Terence, I had to admit that he was good at whatever you called what Michael and his troupe were doing. He was among the best at improvising faux Elizabethan dialogue, threw himself with relish into his role as Albion's archvillain, and was sufficiently skilled at stage combat that he was permitted to draw his sword occasionally—though only in scenes with others of similar skill. Most of the actors—and for that matter, most of the costumed staff—were under strict orders not to draw their swords under any circumstances, for fear that they'd skewer themselves, each other, or the innocent paying bystanders.

"Dunno." Michael shook his head slowly. "The show would be a lot less lively without him."

"Yes, but everyone here would be a lot happier," I pointed out. "And—"

Someone knocked on our door.

"Who's there?" Michael called.

"Are you two coming to breakfast?" My grandmother Cordelia.

"Are we late?" Michael glanced at the wrist where his watch would be if he weren't in costume.

"No, breakfast isn't over for another half an hour," I told him after checking my bedside alarm clock. Then I raised my voice to call out. "Come in!"

Cordelia opened the door with a little more force than necessary and strode in.

"Good. There you are." Her tone seemed to suggest that she'd been searching for us long enough that the effort had made her cranky. Which was pretty silly—neither Michael nor I were early risers. What were the odds that we'd be anywhere but in our bedroom before break-fast? She, on the other hand, was a total lark, so I wasn't surprised to see her already decked out in the red-and-black brocade gown she wore for her role in the Game, as Good Queen Cordelia of Albion. Maybe that was part of the problem. I'd have been cranky too if I'd had to get up this early on an already warm July day and put on a corset—not to mention a farthingale, the Tudor version of a hooped skirt.

"Good morning to you, too," I said aloud. "Something wrong?"

"Can you come down to the Great Room and deal with your grandfather?"

"Grandfather?" I was surprised. "What's he doing here? I assume you weren't expecting him."

"Of course I wasn't expecting him. And yet there he is, filling up the Great Room with all his anachronistic gear and demanding that I find a quiet place where he can put his birds." She was toying with the slender jeweled stiletto in her wrist sheath—was she only doing it for ef-fect? Or had her annoyance with Grandfather already reached a level that had her subconsciously reaching for weapons?

"Birds?" Michael echoed.

"What's he bringing birds for?" I asked

"I have no idea. He hasn't deigned to explain them to me."

More likely she hadn't stayed around to hear his ex-planation. Not for the first time I wondered how she and Grandfather had managed to put up with each other long enough to produce Dad. And I mused that it was probably a good thing the teenage Cordelia's letters telling Grand-father she was pregnant had all gone astray. If they'd ever actually gotten married, one of them would undoubtedly have killed the other long ago. On their good days they managed an uneasy truce that allowed both of them to enjoy the company of their descendants. Evidently this wasn't a good day.

"He showed up with a cage full of wrens." She pursed her lips. "Well, only three wrens as far as I could see, but they're in a very small cage, and besides, I fail to see why he thinks we need any of his wretched birds."

"I'll talk to him."

"Remind him that we've got falcons hunting here," she added, as she turned to go. "So he should keep his charges in their cage if he doesn't want them becoming hors d'oeuvres. Of course, maybe he'd like that. You know his irrational fondness for predators."

"I'll talk to him," I repeated. "In the Great Room, you said?"

"Last I saw. While you're at it, explain to him that we don't have a spare room for him, and even if we did, I'm not sure I'd let him have it."

"No room at the inn. Check."

"Thank you." Her face relaxed a bit, and she gave me a rueful smile, as if to reassure me that she wasn't blaming me for Grandfather's shortcomings. "Sorry. Not fair to take it out on you."

With that she sailed out.

I sat down on the bed.

"I thought we were going down to deal with your grandfather," Michael said.

"And to have breakfast." I closed my eyes and took a deep breath. "I just want one more moment of peace and quiet before starting the day."

I opened my eyes again and looked around the room. It was a very nice room, simple and serene, furnished with vintage country oak furniture and decorated with some of the crafts produced by Biscuit Mountain students and instructors. A white-on-white quilted bedcover. Fresh peonies in a hand-thrown vase. An old-fashioned rag rug. Several watercolors of Appalachian wildflowers.

And one of the most comfortable beds I'd ever slept in. Or did it only seem that way because I wanted so badly to crawl back into it and sleep till noon?

"Okay." I stood and grabbed the authentic medieval-style brown linen foraging bag I used to hold all the things I need to haul around with me—my baggage usually exceeded what I could stow in a belt pouch. I patted the bag to make sure it held my notebook-that-tells-me-when-to-breathe, as I called my giant to-do list, now housed—at least on Ren Faire weekends—in a leather binder hand-tooled with dragons and unicorns. I made sure I had a couple of the fake quill pens I used to write in it.

Armed with my trusty notebook, I could feel my good mood returning.

"All ready," I said. "I suppose we should go deal with Grandfather before he spoils Cordelia's whole day."

Chapter 2

We exited our room and made sure it was locked, because we'd long ago figured out that no power on Earth could keep the tourists from sneaking into the main building and exploring anyplace unlocked. Cordelia didn't mind having them in the craft studios—she made sure the six on the ground floor each had an appropriately costumed crafter on duty at all times to give demonstrations and keep equipment and finished products from disappearing. A gratifying number of people got excited enough to sign up for future classes. But having random tourists snoop in our bedrooms was another story.

We hurried downstairs to the Great Hall, a huge double-height room that had once served as one of the Biscuit Mountain Art Pottery Factory's main work rooms. Cordelia hadn't completely redecorated in Renaissance style, but the existing Mission or Arts-and-Crafts furniture wasn't jarringly anachronistic, and the few decorative touches she'd added—faux tapestries, a suit of armor in one corner, a pair of crossed broadswords over the mantel—made the room a satisfactory Renaissance Faire setting for any but the most persnickety purists.

Especially when the room was thronged with costumed Faire workers—a smattering of Riverton residents eager for the weekend jobs, quite a few of my fellow craftspeople, and a horde of eager college students. And Michael's actors, of course, already hamming it up.

Out on the terrace, the three acrobats were somersaulting, cartwheeling, performing handstands and backflips—their warming up exercises. I wished, not for the first time, that they wouldn't do them quite so close to the railing that separated them from the twenty-foot drop onto the wooded hillside below. The juggler was rehearsing tricks at the far end of the Great Hall—not using Cordelia's best teacups this time, so I left him to it.

But Grandfather was nowhere to be seen.

"Probably in the Dining Hall by now." Cordelia had appeared at my elbow and seemed to be reading my thoughts. "Making his second or third trip through the buffet line."

She led the way and pointed to where Grandfather was sitting with Dad and my cousin Rose Noire. Dad was in the long black robe that he insisted a Renaissance-era doctor would wear. The wide-brimmed black physician's hat and the bird-like plague doctor's mask were on the table beside his plate, so he was ready to go on duty. His first aid tent was right beside the large booth where Rose Noire would be selling her organic herbs and teas, potpourris, hand-dyed wool, and dried-flower headpieces, which worked out nicely—he could roam the Faire as much as he liked, knowing that if anyone showed up in need of his medical services she could summon him in minutes.

Rose Noire's own outfit wasn't quite as rigorously authentic—in fact, it looked as if she was planning to audition for the role of Ophelia in some New Age–themed production of *Hamlet*. But it would pass muster under Cordelia's relatively relaxed scrutiny. Grandfather, on the other hand—

"And he's not in costume." Cordelia's scowl grew, if possible, even fiercer.

I'd have said Grandfather *was* in costume. He usually was by my standards—just not Renaissance costume. His entire outfit was calculated to telegraph "Bold scientific adventurer! Man of brains and action! Twenty-first-century pioneer!" As usual, he was wearing shades of brown, green, and khaki: a faded green Blake Foundation t-shirt, dark khaki cargo pants, and a sort of fisherman's vest in a lighter shade of khaki—or maybe the same shade but slightly more faded. His sturdy brown hiking boots were spackled with half a dozen colors and textures of dirt or mud.

And the numberless pockets covering both pants and vest were bulging with potentially useful items. At countless moments over the years I'd seen him patting half a dozen of the pockets before pulling out items as various as fishing line, duct tape, a tourniquet, an EpiPen, waterproof matches, a compass, a metal tinderbox, water purification tablets, Dramamine, Imodium, sunscreen, Band-Aids, a slide rule, Benadryl, tweezers, antibiotic ointment, eclipse-watching glasses, a pocket-sized flashlight, safety pins, waterproof pens, pencil stubs, a first aid kit, and random coins from six continents and countless countries.

Very picturesque. But yes, a walking anachronism. I suddenly had to suppress the urge to giggle, and put on my most solemn face.

"I'll talk to him," I said. "Cheer up. Michael and I will take care of it. Go back to enjoying the Faire."

She frowned at me for a moment. Then her face relaxed. She nodded and strode off, looking a little more cheerful.

I strolled over to Grandfather's table. He and Dad appeared to be discussing the relative merits of sausage and bacon, having heaped their plates high with an ample test supply of both—no doubt to Rose Noire's great dismay, since she was a committed vegetarian.

"Meg! Look who's here!" Dad sounded a little anxious. Perhaps he'd seen what Grandfather's arrival had done to Cordelia's mood. Rose Noire gave a little wave and dashed off.

"I need to set up my booth," she called over her shoulder.

Yes and she probably also wanted to get out of the way if my grandparents were going to have it out.

"So what are you doing here?" I asked Grandfather.

"Not very welcoming, are you?" Grandfather seemed to be enjoying himself, watching the various costumed staff members dashing about.

"Not entirely awake," I said. "And not all that happy to be playing referee between you and Cordelia before breakfast. Sorry if I sounded unwelcoming—let's try again."

I stood up straighter, arranged my features into the bright if slightly artificial smile I used for dealing with particularly annoying tourists, and pretended to spot him for the first time.

"Grandfather!" I exclaimed. "How nice to see you! I had no idea you were coming. And what are your plans for this beautiful day?"

"I think I liked you better surly," he said. "I thought maybe I'd see if your grandmother would like the benefit of some real expertise."

Real expertise? I'd be the first to admit that Grandfather was a man of many talents—biologist, environmentalist, even television personality, thanks to all his wildlife documentaries. But if he had any expertise in history it was news to me. Dad also looked puzzled but said nothing.

"And I brought the birds," he said, waving his hand vaguely at a small cage that sat on the floor near the end of the table. "*Troglodytes aedon* and *Thryothorus ludovicianus.*"

"Wrens," I said, remembering what Cordelia had told me.

"Oh, very good!" He sounded surprised—even impressed. "Yes, two house wrens and a Carolina wren. Finally getting serious about your bird identification, I see."

"I just don't get what you plan to do with them."

He fixed me with what was obviously intended to be a look of withering scorn. Long exposure had made me largely immune to his tricks.

"I thought perhaps you'd like some actual wrens at your Wren Festival," he said finally.

I couldn't help it—I burst out laughing as it dawned on me: he thought we were saying Wren Fest, and assumed we were talking about an ornithological event, similar to Owl Fest, the ornithological conference he'd held in Caerphilly over the holiday season.

"Ren Fest is short for Renaissance Festival," I explained. "More commonly called a Renaissance Faire. An historical reenactment. No birds involved."